SHAPE

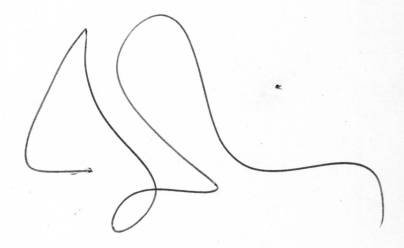

SHAPESTONE

Further translations from the original Gibberish by

James Bibby

VICTOR GOLLANCZ

LONDON

The right of James Bibby to be identified as the author
of this work has been asserted by him in accordance with
the Copyright, Designs and Patents Act 1988.

First published in Great Britain in 1999 by
Victor Gollancz
An imprint of the Orion Publishing Group
Orion House, 5 Upper St Martin's Lane,
London WC2H 9EA

To receive information on the Millennium list, e-mail us at:
smy@orionbooks.co.uk

A CIP catalogue record for this book
is available from the British Library

ISBN 0 575 06867 1

Typeset by SetSystems Ltd, Saffron Walden, Essex
Printed in Great Britain by
Clays Ltd, St Ives plc

For Ricko, Tim and Ade
(who did their best to kill me using the
Stuttgart beer festival as a weapon)

Acknowledgements

Thanks to Frank Murphy for computing expertise. Thanks also to Caroline Oakley, who edited the Ronan books and helped to make them what they are. Now you all know who to blame.

Oh, and R.I.P., Inspector Morse.
You will be sadly missed . . .

How wonderful is death! – Shelley

To die will be an awfully big adventure. – J. M. Barrie

Bollocks! It will be a pain in the arse . . . – Tarl of Welbug

PROLOGUE

Badal liked to tell people that archaeology was a family tradition and that his father had been completely immersed in the subject. This was, in a way, true. His father had been a grave-robber whose career had come to a sudden end when, much against his will, he had been included in the concrete foundations of a new pyramid by an irate monarch after being caught red-handed in the act of looting a royal tomb.

This hadn't deterred Badal from following in his father's footsteps, but he had gone about things in a much subtler way. Whereas his father had preferred breaking into some ancient vault in the dead of night and stuffing as many of the grave goods as he could carry into a large sack, Badal had gone to the University of Koumas and had taken a degree in archaeology.

As a member of the team that had spent three years excavating a series of royal tombs in the desert, south of the city of Chi Qentika, he had found plenty of chances to syphon off some of the uncovered wealth: a gold ring here, a jewelled mace there. It hadn't made him rich, but it had provided a nice little sideline. Now, at last, he had stumbled across something that would make him rich beyond his wildest fantasies.

For the past six months, the team of archaeologists had been excavating a tomb complex that dated from the First Age. It housed the mummified remains of Priapean the Fourth, the last ruler of the ancient realm of Qital. They had found incredible riches in the tomb, and now that the dig was drawing to a close, a detachment of soldiers had been sent out to accompany the train of wagons that would ferry their discoveries back to Koumas. Security was tight, and Badal had begun to fret that he might not be able to get away with as much as a single gold coin. But then, that very afternoon, he had made his discovery.

He had been on his own, attempting to decipher some hiero-glyphics in an underground corridor just inside an entrance on the northern side of the complex, when he had become aware that there was a faint current of air seeping through a tiny gap in the stone wall. Intrigued, he had inserted the point of a trowel and waggled it about, and all at once a segment of the wall about two feet square had swung back. Behind it, a musty passage stretched away into darkness.

His heart in his mouth, Badal had closed the secret door again. Despite an almost overwhelming urge to investigate, he had instinc-tively known that this was something best tackled in the dead of night, when no-one else was about. He'd learned from experience that the ancient tomb-builders didn't put secret doors in place to guard a few old bones in a coffin. Whatever was at the other end of the passage was probably pretty valuable.

However, with security as tight as it was, Badal had known that he wasn't going to be able to smuggle anything out of the camp, and so he had spent the next few hours gathering together some vital equipment: three days worth of supplies, a fast horse, and a nice big sack. It was time to try his father's tactics. Take the money and run.

Shortly after midnight, Badal crept back into the underground corridor and opened the secret door. Shadows flickered in the light of his torch. Wedging the door so that it wouldn't close behind him, he began to crawl along the dry, dusty passage. After some twenty yards it bent to the left, and then all at once it opened out onto a large chamber, maybe thirty feet square. As the torchlight fell upon the contents of the chamber, Badal stared transfixed and breathless. Then, drawing air into his lungs, he began to laugh.

In the centre of the chamber was a marble plinth upon which rested the body of an old man, almost perfectly preserved despite the several hundred years that must have passed since he had been laid there. Beside him rested a wooden staff and a silver orb, and the floor around the plinth was etched with an intricate design and painted with the runes of the ancient Qemmalian language. On the floor at the head of the plinth stood a solid gold coffer some three feet long, and it was the sight of this that took Badal's breath away.

The coffer was filled to the brim with gold coins, jewels and precious stones that flashed and twinkled in the torchlight as though lit from within. Badal was not prone to exaggeration, but he reckoned that the contents of this one chest were worth ten times as much as the sum total of treasures that the dig had so far discovered. For what seemed like an age he stared, and then he dropped to the floor and, with hands that shook with excitement, began to fill his sack.

He worked quickly, sifting through the contents of the coffer, ruthlessly discarding the weighty gold in favour of lighter, easy-to-carry jewels and gems. There was no sorrow in this, for he knew that with luck the entrance to this tomb might not be discovered for months, or even years, and he might get other chances to return and collect more of the hoard.

Eventually the sack was as heavy as he dared to carry and he turned to go. But then something caught his eye and he turned and stared at the corpse. On the thin, bony chest lay a golden amulet in the shape of a dragon's head, and at the corpse's side was a slender, wavy-bladed dagger with a jewelled pommel that was carved into the shape of a matching dragon-head. Somehow, they seemed to be calling to Badal, begging him to touch them, to pick them up and take them with him.

Hoisting the sack onto his back, Badal stepped forward to examine these artefacts, but as his feet trod upon the designs on the floor he stopped, for he thought that he had heard a noise like a sudden exhalation of breath, a faint sigh almost of relief, as though something long awaited had at last happened.

For several seconds he paused, his ears pricked, but he heard nothing more, and so he stepped forward to stand beside the frail, mummified corpse. Reaching out, he ripped the dragon-head from round the thin, leathery neck, and then he snatched up the dagger and left the chamber. And as he disappeared into the narrow cramped passageway, a dark shadow seemed to drift across the chamber to follow him.

The secret door was still ajar when he reached it. Badal placed his sack on the floor of the passage before turning to examine the workings of the door, for he wanted to ensure that he could close it securely so that it remained undiscovered until he returned.

As he did so, there was a movement in the passageway behind him. Badal stared back towards the chamber, and then his face contorted with horror and he scrambled out through the door, dragging it closed behind him. Then he backed away, his eyes staring wildly, his lips moving silently.

For a few moments nothing happened, but then a thin black shadow began to seep through the tiny hole between the stones, like a small jet of smoke. Gradually it began to solidify, coalescing into a shape so foul that Badal could not bear to look at it. He backed away, his eyes tight shut, retreating until he was pressed against the sand that blocked the passage and there was nowhere left to go. For an age he crouched there, his eyes squeezed shut, and then he felt the faintest of touches against the skin of his neck, and suddenly his nostrils were full of the stench of rotting, of something so foul and putrid that he nearly vomited.

Badal opened his eyes. And screamed.

The screaming woke the whole dig. Soldiers and archaeologists stumbled out of tents and blundered about the camp-site, trying to locate the source of the noise. Eventually they found Badal lying in the blocked passageway. He was alone, curled into a terrified ball, with his eyes screwed rigidly shut and his mouth stretched wide in the rictus of a scream. Clutched in his hands were two items that must have come from a tomb: an ancient amulet in the shape of a grinning orc's head and a slim, wavy-bladed dagger. He was stone cold dead.

At first, they thought that Badal must have interrupted a grave-robber, who had murdered him. But then they found his horse, saddled and provisioned for a long journey, and realised that he had been up to no good. But what had killed him was a mystery, for there wasn't a mark on him.

Marden, the commander of the soldiers, ordered the wide-eyed, jabbering archaeologists back to their beds and posted three guards at the entrance to the corridor. Then, when everyone else had gone, he crouched down beside Badal's corpse and gently pulled the orc-head amulet from his hands. It was an action he was to regret for the rest of his short life.

CHAPTER ONE

Darian's death came as a complete and total surprise to him. In fact, you could have knocked him down with a feather, although what the orcish berserker actually used was a heavy, razor-sharp hand-axe that sliced through Darian's helmet as though it was cardboard and carved into his skull, killing him instantly. One moment his body had been a smoothly-functioning unit that moved effortlessly through the familiar moves of combat, the next moment it was a useless pile of warm meat that slumped pathetically to the floor.

But then the whole battle had been just a little on the unexpected side. The Kuhbadorian army had marched out of Koumas that morning, expecting to deal with a few hundred roistering orc raiders from the Irridic Mountains. Instead, they had been confronted by an organised, confident orc army some two thousand strong.

Darian hovered uncertainly above his body and wondered what the hell was going on. He felt a bit of a fool, really. He had spent the whole of his adult life as a devout atheist, happily ridiculing those who professed any sort of belief in an after-life, and yet here he was, dead, and yet undead, as it were.

He stared at the shell of his body with a morbid fascination. He'd seen plenty of butchered corpses before and had become inured to the sight, but this was different. He'd never thought that one day he'd be looking down at his own. That axe had made one hell of a mess of his head . . .

Suddenly, he realised that the battle was still raging about him. He peered around, wondering what effect he would have on those still alive, but nobody seemed to be taking a blind bit of notice. He seemed to be invisible to the living, although he could see his own form, his spirit, like a tenuous, misty image of the lifeless body beneath him.

In fact, now that he came to think about it, he realised that he could see the spirits of those others slain in the battle, hovering above their own corpses. They too appeared to be staring uncertainly about them, but as he watched, one or two began to rise slowly, hesitantly upwards.

All of a sudden, thoughts of Valhalla entered Darian's mind, and he realised with something of a shock that there really was such a place and, what was more, that as a warrior slain in battle he had the equivalent of a lifetime membership. All around him, the spirits of his fallen comrades were streaming up towards the sky in an excited, jubilant, ghostly mob. But then Darian discovered that he had a bit of a problem. For some reason he couldn't follow the others.

Darian tried whatever the spiritual equivalent of straining every muscle in his body was, but to no avail. He couldn't move more than about thirty feet in any direction. It was as though he had been shackled to his corpse by a thirty-foot length of chain. He tried and tried but it was no good, and eventually he gave up, exhausted. If he had still been inside his body it would have been hot, sweating and breathless. Instead it was lying on the ground, cold, bleeding and lifeless, and appeared to be determined to spoil his chances of eternal bliss.

He stared moodily down at his corpse. He was feeling a little pissed off with it. It had always been quite a good body when it had been alive, but now it was dead it was a pain in the arse, quite frankly. Was this some sort of punishment for a lifetime of atheism?

No, it couldn't be! The spirit of Toran Blackshield had been one of the first to rocket skywards, and Toran had lived a life devoted to sacrilege and desecration, leaving a trail of burning monasteries, ravished nuns and buggered monks behind him. No, there had to be another reason.

Darian mulled it over for a while, but got nowhere. Then all of a sudden he realised that he was alone. The fighting was over and night had fallen. Living humans with flickering torches were moving amongst the corpses that littered the battlefield like so many fireflies, but all the other ghosts had vanished. Every now and then one would appear hovering above a body as another mortally-wounded soldier died, but they quickly went rocketing skywards in pursuit of their fellow spirits.

Selfish bastards, thought Darian. *You'd think one of them might stop and see if they could give me a hand.*

Time passed. The sun rose again. Darian watched morosely as human burial parties gathered up the mutilated bodies and healers searched for and tended the wounded, and every now and then he made another fruitless attempt to follow the others.

After a while he became aware of an individual who was moving amongst the bodies, briefly examining each one as though searching for something. It was a young woman, small, with long, dark hair and a pale, unsmiling face. Although she was dressed in plain brown leather trousers and jerkin, it was clear from the way the burial parties deferred to her that she was someone of importance.

Darian looked on disinterested as she moved from corpse to corpse, occasionally stooping to turn a head or uncover a face, but apparently without finding whatever it was that she sought. When she reached his corpse she muttered an exclamation and stopped. Then reaching down she jerked something loose from round his blood-stained neck. For a moment she examined it and then, slipping it into her pocket, she turned and strode purposefully away.

Unpleasant thoughts about the sort of punishment that should be meted out to small women who go round looting corpses chased fleetingly through Darian's mind. How dare she steal whatever it was that had been round his neck? But this was followed by a feeling of puzzlement. What on earth had she taken? He had never actually worn anything round his neck . . .

Or had he? For some reason, Darian was finding it very difficult to hold on to his memories. It was like peering at his life through a thick veil of fog. But then the fog lifted for a moment and a single memory came drifting into view.

Of course! It was that amulet that Lord Marden had given him on the eve of the battle, an ugly black metallic thing in the shape of an orc's head that Lord Marden had vowed would bring him luck. But Darian had been sure that there had been more to it than that. What else had Lord Marden said?

Before he could cudgel his reluctant memory into further revelations, Darian was yanked sideways like a dog on a leash and found himself being dragged unceremoniously away from his body. *What*

7

the . . . he thought to himself, but then found that he couldn't remember any of the swear-words that he would usually have used at this point. *What the, er, the something-or-other has happened to my memory?* he thought. *What the thingammy-jig is going on?*

He could see the slight figure of the woman weaving her way through the corpses, some forty feet in front of him, and he realised that he was being tugged along in her wake. She wasn't exactly hanging around now, and Darian had already been dragged quite a way. He looked back, but he could no longer distinguish his own corpse amongst all the others. With a pang of fear he realised that he might never see it again.

Oh, – hell! he thought, but he still couldn't remember the words. *Oh, how's-your-fathering, thingammy-jigging, what-do-you-call-iting hell!*

Then he realised that the woman had come to a horse that was tethered to a hedge at the side of a road. He watched apprehensively as she untied the reins and then, vaulting lightly into the saddle, swung the horse around and began to canter back eastwards towards Koumas.

– ! thought Darian, and the next moment the unseen chain snapped tight and he was pulled reluctantly after his unknowing captor like an insubstantial and very unhappy balloon on the end of a string.

As she stabled her horse in a yard behind the *Black Wand*, a quiet and rather run-down Koumas tavern, Macoby was a troubled and thoughtful young woman. As the only daughter of the Regent of Koumas, her life had been one of the privilege and ease. Everything that she could possibly desire had been provided, the very instant she desired it, by a swarm of polite and deferential servants or handmaids. Until recently, the biggest problem she had ever had to face was the succession of eager, spotty and unprepossessing young princes whom her father had lined up for her approval, in an attempt to get her suitably betrothed. But even that hadn't been a real problem. Macoby had no intention of getting hitched to some skinny adolescent with terminal acne and had put her foot down, knowing full well that she could twist her doting father around her little finger.

But then all of a sudden, six months ago, her world had collapsed into turmoil. She'd fallen in love for the first time, with her brother

Marden's best friend, Sarakkan. He was everything she wanted: handsome, intelligent and good company. Unfortunately, he was also everything her father didn't want; even though he was a captain in the Palace Guard, he was the son of a peasant and had less money than a bankrupt parrot. At the same time, Myal of Minas Lantan, the brooding and somewhat sinister eldest son of that city's latest ruler, had started taking an interest in her and had proposed marriage.

Macoby had wanted to turn Myal down like a bedspread, but to her disgust, her father had refused to let her and had kept harping on about the guy's good points, such as his money, his connections, his breeding, his money, and his power. Not forgetting his money. Despite this, Macoby had refused to bow to the pressure.

But then her father had fallen prey to a mysterious wasting disease, turning in a matter of weeks from a strong, forceful leader into a querulous old man. As he had weakened, he had begun to pressure her into agreeing to the proposed marriage, and she had found it harder and harder to refuse. At first, she had been able to count on the support of her brother. But then, a week ago, Marden had turned overnight from the happy, confident soul she had grown up with into a surly, withdrawn and uncommunicative man. Even Sarakkan had been unable to get through to him. It was then that he had taken to wearing the ugly amulet.

Then finally had come the last straw – the orc invasion. The initial word had been that a couple of hundred partying orcs from the Irridic Mountains had crossed the Alovaq river at Lampa Sanda and had taken the small town of Clinthill. Word had gone out to nearby cities, and as many soldiers and militiamen as could be quickly mustered had gathered at Koumas for what was regarded as the simple task of wiping the floor with the invaders. No-one had taken the orcs seriously. Some of Macoby's friends had even suggested taking a picnic and riding after the army to watch the rout from some suitable vantage-point.

But, that night, Marden had come to his sister's room in the castle and warned her that he feared their army was marching into a trap. He had also told her that, if he was right, hidden forces were at work and that she too was in considerable danger. Trust no-one but him, he had told her, but had refused to say more.

When next day the word had come back to Koumas that the army was facing an invading force ten times bigger than reported, Macoby had swapped her expensive clothing for plain, everyday riding-gear and had slipped out of the city. She had ridden hard through the night in pursuit of her brother but by the time she reached the battlefield, it was all over. The orcs had been put to flight, but at a massive cost.

She had searched for Marden amongst both the living and the dead, but she had been unable to find him. She had, however, found the strange amulet he had taken to wearing recently, but it had been around the neck of a soldier she didn't recognise. She had stooped to take it from the blood-soaked corpse, and the instant she touched it a strange chill had crept over her. All at once she had known that her brother was dead, and that as he had warned, she too was in danger. And so, on returning to Koumas, she had decided to lie low for a while and attempt to work out just what was going on.

Leaving her thoroughbred Brannian stallion sniffing suspiciously at a manger of hay that was older than he was, Macoby left the tumbledown stables and crossed the rubbish-strewn, cobbled yard. Pushing open the door of the tavern, she marched into the main bar-room and then stopped dead.

The smell that hit her nostrils would have stopped a rampaging stone-giant in its tracks. Macoby thought she could pick out the distinctive aromas of smoke, boiled cabbage and urine (or possibly smoked cabbage boiled in urine), but these were heavily masked by the stench of stale beer, which in turn was almost hidden by the overpowering body odour of the huge, hairy, bare-chested landlord who was leaning on the bar that stretched the length of the room and talking to the blowsy, overweight woman on the other side.

At the sound of the door closing, the landlord turned from flirting with the barmaid, angry at being disturbed. Then his eyes took in Macoby and his pock-marked face creased into a leer, exposing teeth like twin rows of decaying tombstones. It was like a graveyard unfolding.

Taking her courage in both hands, for it was threatening to do a runner, Macoby faced up to him.

'I'd like a room, please.'

The landlord smiled. Now his face looked like a graveyard that had just received very good news indeed.

10

'Excellent!' He leered. 'And who might you be?'

'Er . . . Lona.' Macoby thought that a little anonymity might be safest.

'Well, then, Lona. Follow me!'

The landlord turned and led the way through a door at the back of the room and up a twisting staircase. Macoby followed, trying not to inhale. At the top was a dark passage lined with shadowy wooden doors. It was lit only by a single guttering tallow candle in a sconce on the end wall, that was giving off wisps of black smoke which actually smelt worse than the landlord.

Macoby readied herself as the gross bear of a man stopped outside the farthest door and leered down at her.

'The rates are two silver *tablons* a night, breakfast included.' The leer grew closer, until Macoby was examining it from a range of about six inches. 'But, of course, we could always come to an alternative arrangement . . .'

'I think not.' Macoby was pleased that her voice was steady. She flicked her eyes downwards and the landlord followed her gaze. His face paled as he saw that she was holding a small but extremely sharp dagger half an inch away from his groin.

'And if you try it on again,' she continued, 'I promise you that when I leave this verminous hovel I will be wearing your testicles for earrings. Understand?'

The landlord nodded and backed slowly away, his eyes on the dagger. His face had gone the colour of a maggot. Trying not to grin, Macoby opened the door, stepped through and closed it behind her. Then, breathing a sigh of relief, she looked round at her temporary lodgings.

The room was sparsely furnished, but at least it seemed fairly clean. There was a wooden bed and a single wooden chair. The wooden boards of the floor were bare, and the wooden panelling of the walls was plain and undorned. Whoever had designed the decor had clearly been of the opinion that, when it came to bedrooms, you couldn't have too much wood.

Macoby crossed to the bed and tested the mattress with her hand. It was about as flexible as granite. She shivered. The room was cold, despite a small fire that burned in the fireplace.

Sitting in the chair, she took from her pocket the black metal amulet that had been her brother's. She stared at it and the sightless eye-holes of the ugly orc face stared back. It looked as though it had been beaten and battered into a horrid parody of a face, but then most real orcs had faces that looked as though they had been beaten and battered into a horrid parody, so it was remarkably accurate.

It's unlike Marden to wear something so foul, she thought. *I wish I had something more elegant to remember him by.*

And to her amazement, as she watched, the black amulet seemed to melt and flow, changing colour and form, until a slender golden pendant in the shape of a lion's head lay in her palm.

Macoby stared at the jewel, stunned. Then she became aware that something was easing itself slowly through the door. Something that looked unpleasantly like the dead body from round whose neck she had removed the amulet, even down to the horribly-crushed metal helm, but something that was nebulous and ghostly. In fact, something that was so nebulous and ghostly that it didn't need to open the door to enter the room but just crept through the solid wood like rain creeping through a very cheap coat.

Macoby shrank back into the chair as the ghost drifted across the floor and ended up hovering apologetically by the fireplace.

'What do you want?' she gasped.

The ghost studied her with a vaguely baffled air and shrugged his shoulders.

'Buggered if I know,' he said, but then he smiled happily. 'Well, how about that!' he continued. 'My memory is starting to come back.'

And to Macoby's surprise, he began reciting a list of obscenities that went on and on until she threw the chamberpot at him.

CHAPTER TWO

The Monastery of Magical Research in eastern Kuhbador was founded in 921 by Saint Cedric the Fey, a deeply pious monk with a natural, though untutored, ability with magic. Cedric intended the monastery to be both a religious centre and a place where magical spells and enchantments could be recorded and preserved for study. The official title that he gave the monastery was the Scriptorium for the Preservation of Arcane Material, and although the Cedrician monks soon discovered that being known as the SPAM meant that they weren't treated by the general public with quite the amount of reverence that they felt they deserved, they settled happily into the job of recording for posterity every item of magical knowledge that came their way.

Then one day, a young and rather precocious novice who was recording the Cydorian version of the incantation for a *Fireball* spell asked Brother Synahms, the monk in charge of novitiates, how the spell worked. Brother Synahms told him sharply to get on with his work, but the question stuck in his mind. So you muttered a few words, and if you were one of the fortunate people who had that innate ability known as The Power, a fireball was formed out of thin air. Well, it happened, all right, there was no question about that. But *how* did it happen? That was a very good question indeed.

That evening, Brother Synahms put the same question to Saint Cedric. There was a long pause whilst the monastery's founder and abbot thought about it.

'I haven't the faintest idea,' he told Brother Synahms. 'But I think maybe we should start trying to find out.'

The name of the monastery was immediaely changed to Saint Cedric's University of Magic, and a new regime of experimentation and research began. However, the monks soon found that the general populace had started poking fun at them again now that they had become SCUM, and so a deputation of brothers went to Saint Cedric's office and begged him to change the name.

'All right,' said the saint. 'I suppose it was a bit egotistical of me, anyway. We'll call ourselves the Sacred College for the Understanding of Magic.'

'But then we're still SCUM,' answered Brother Pedant, who wasn't one to let things like this get by him.

'Okay, okay!' replied Saint Cedric. 'If you're that concerned about a name, we'll try something a little more grandiose. How about calling ourselves the Sacred College for the Recording and Observation of Thaumaturgy and the Understanding of Magic?'

But when it was pointed out to him that this was SCROTUM, Saint Cedric lost his temper and threw an inkwell at the others, then locked himself in his room for two hours, sulking furiously. After this, no-one quite had the courage to bring up the subject of names again.

In 934 the fame of the monastery spread, after Saint Cedric had the misfortune to become Midworld's first magical martyr. In an attempt to convert the King of Qemmal, he had been trying to use magic to recreate the Miracle of the Burning Bush, a well-known event from the monks' Holy Book. Unfortunately, he got the incantation slightly wrong, and instead of causing a minor conflagration in a small piece of unimportant shrubbery, he set fire to the queen's private parts. Mere seconds later, his head was hacked off by the sword of a highly enraged (and remarkably good-looking) courtier, a precipitate reaction which made the king extremely and justifiably suspicious.

Over the years the monastery gradually grew bigger, changing from a small foundation of twenty brothers and novices into a much larger conglomeration. Then, in 986, it doubled in size. However, this was not over a period of several months through a sustained building programme, but instantly, as a direct result of some over-zealous research by Brother Lemmy into a recently acquired magical artefact. One moment the monk was puzzling over an ivory sceptre that had just come from a newly excavated First Age tomb, the next moment there was a blinding flash of flame in which every scrap of Brother Lemmy's body hair was instantly incinerated.

The other monks rushed him to the infirmary, where he was

sedated with a bottle of the best Cydorian brandy, and it was only after all the fuss had died down that they discovered that every single monastery building had been replicated in the field next door. They now had two churches, two refectories, two cloisters, two scriptoria and two infirmaries. Even more intriguingly, they found that the duplicates of each were somehow linked to the originals, so that if you walked in through the door of the new infirmary, turned round and walked out again, you sometimes came out of the door of the old infirmary. Items left in a cell in one dormitory often disappeared, turning up in the corresponding cell in the second, and monks who went to sleep in their own cots in the old building sometimes awoke to find that they had mysteriously transferred to another monk's bed in the new building. Or, at least, that's what they told the Abbot . . .

These duplicated buildings did much to enhance the reputation of the monastery as a seat of magical knowledge, and from then on, its reputation grew until it became known throughout Midworld quite simply as the Monastery of Magical Research or, more irreverently, the Abbey-cadabra. Much previously-lost arcane knowledge was gleaned there over the years, and the Cedrician monks became renowned for their ability with spells and charms.

Eventually, it became customary for those brothers who had good ability with magic to travel in the outside world, using their powers to aid those who needed help in return for just their food and drink. Throughout the east, the blue of the Cedrician habit grew to be welcomed both in town and village. And it was not unknown for those who had too many mouths to feed, or who wished their children to have the security and education that they were too poor to provide, to send a young boy to be raised as a novice, dedicating his life to the order. Few of these novices ventured out into the world again, preferring to stay close to their brethren. But one was destined for greater things, although none would have guessed, for the one thing at which he excelled was causing trouble . . .

Abbot Tellow was relaxing in his cell one evening when there was an excited knocking on the door. Sighing, he laid down his copy of *Anthrax the Wizard – Mighty Magician or Sad Young Perv?* by the Sage of Welbug and then cleared his throat.

'Enter!' he called.

The door opened and Brother Behidormus came in. He was one of the older monks and was normally a quiet, placid man, but now he seemed unusually agitated. He was shifting from foot to foot and wringing his hands, and his eyes blazed with an excited, almost fervent, light.

'What can I do for you, brother?' asked the abbot.

'I'm sorry to disturb your meditations, Father Abbot,' the monk began, 'but I've found something in my work that I think you should see! It's . . . well . . .'

He stumbled to a halt as words failed him and stood there, his mouth working, his hands twisting ceaselessly about each other in his agitation. Tellow watched him for a moment, wondering what could have caused such a calm and phlegmatic man to become so flustered. He knew that Brother Benidormus was merely a translator, currently assigned to the deciphering of documents and scrolls that had been recently found during the excavation of a series of First Age tombs near the ancient city of Chi Qentika, on the Qemmal border.

'Perhaps you had better show me?' he suggested gently.

'Of course, Father Abbot!' said Benidormus with relief, and turning, he led the way out of the cell.

Tellow followed him down the cold stone corridor and out along the short covered walkway that led to the Old Scriptorium. The hinges of the heavy oak door creaked as they pushed it open, and then they were inside once more, striding down the dark silent hall, past the dozens of small wooden doors that sealed off the tiny, cramped workrooms. At last Benidormus opened one, peered in, and gave the sigh of relief that told the abbot that they were still in the correct Scriptorium.

Tellow followed the other monk in and shut the door behind them, then seated himself at one of the two plain, wooden chairs in front of the single desk that half-filled the room.

'Right then, Benidormus,' he said, using the unadorned name to show that they could now talk informally. 'What exactly is it that has got you so stirred up?'

Benidormus plonked himself down in the other chair and drew a scroll towards him with a hand that shook slightly. In front of him was a large pad of scribbled notes, and he consulted this briefly before opening out the scroll. The light from the single candle-stub gave the ancient parchment a golden tint, lending it an almost mystical quality.

'Bear with me, Ankos,' he said. He was one of the few monks who were allowed to address the abbot by his first name in such informal moments, for they had both joined the monastery at the same time, as callow youths, and they had always been friends.

'This document comes from the tomb of Priapean the Fourth,' he continued. 'It is one of a batch that arrived here two days ago. It gives details of the many grave goods that were buried with him. It also mentions two adjacent tombs and names their occupants.'

He paused.

'One of them is Adomo. The dark mage himself.'

Tellow nodded his understanding. Anyone who had studied magic would have heard of this legendary wizard, the court magician to King Priapean, who had used his vast ability to feed and to satisfy his wicked master's every whim or desire. His name was synonymous with evil and even now, hundreds of years after his death, people spoke of him in hushed and fearful tones.

Benidormus gently rolled up the scroll and placed it to one side, then leant forward and took up a small book that was resting on the desk beside the candlestick. It looked brand new, and the black leather that bound it shone dimly in the yellow light. He opened it and began to turn the pages. They too seemed to glow in the light, and Abbot Tellow could see that they were covered in a thin stream of finely-drawn hieroglyphics that flowed across the pages like a gently undulating sea.

'This book was found in Priapean's tomb alongside the scroll,' Benidormus continued, and the abbot threw him a sharp look. 'Yes, I know. That makes it more than six hundred years old. And yet it looks as though it was written yesterday.' He paused. 'Watch.'

Without warning, he leant forwards and blew out the candle. The room darkened instantly, but Abbot Tellow realised that he could still see, for a dim radiance was shining from the pages of the book.

'I'm beginning to understand why you came to me,' he said.

Benidormus snorted. 'I haven't even started yet!' he muttered. For a few moments he busied himself with relighting the candle, and then he picked up the book again.

'I've translated about half of this,' he went on. 'It appears to have been written by Jaip, who as you probably know was the court magician to Alfar the Pure, Priapean's successor. Legend has it that by the time Priapean died, Adomo had completely lost his marbles and was several charms short of an enchantment. Couldn't tell his dark arts from his elbow. However, it seems that he made a series of interesting predictions before he died, and Jaip recorded them for his king. This is that record.'

He paused again, licking his lips nervously, and Abbot Tellow suddenly realised that the other monk wasn't nervous or excited, but was quite simply scared. In fact, to judge by the way his hand shook as he began to thumb the pages of the book, he was very scared indeed.

'In a nutshell,' Benidormus continued, his voice quavering slightly, 'some of these predictions are frighteningly accurate. I can't vouch for the veracity of *all* of them, because there is a lot of stuff that is a little, well, shall we say inane. For example, I doubt if we'll ever know whether King Prohn of Cydor did lose his temper with the window-cleaner in 824, or whether 917 was a bad year for the stoats. But there isn't a single prediction that I can say was definitely wrong, and an awful lot that are spot on. And I mean *exact*.'

He stopped at a page halfway through the book and held it out for the abbot to see, jabbing at it with an excited finger.

'I mean, look at this stuff about the orc raids of 785. Not only does he get the year right, but he accurately names their leader, Gaz the Tall, and he goes on to list the cities that were sacked. And this was written more than three hundred years before the events took place!'

Tellow took the book and peered at the neat, distinctive handwriting. It had been a while since he had worked as a translator, but the descriptive hieroglyphics of the ancient Qitalian language still seemed comfortingly familiar, and the words that they represented came slowly but obediently to mind.

'In the year of 944,' he read hesitantly, 'there will be a . . . um . . . dearth, yes, that's it, a dearth of carrots throughout the northern lands. And other, um . . . base vegetables, is that? No, root vegetables, of course! Dear me! Still, it's been a while. And other root vegetables too shall become difficult to find. And those who seek out, um, parsnips, shall find them not . . .'

18

Tellow stopped reading. Lifting his gaze he stared at Brother Benidormus with one eyebrow raised quizzically.

'So he predicted the world-famous carrot shortage of 944, did he?' he murmured.

Benidormus looked embarrassed.

'Well, I told you he was several beads short of a rosary,' he muttered. 'As I said, some of his predictions are a little inane . . .'

'A little!'

'Okay, extremely inane. But ignore those. It's the others that concern me. When it comes to major, world-shattering events he's been accurate time and time again. Right up to the Shikara Wars and that business with the Orcbane Sword Corporation last year. What I'm trying to say is that if this book says something was going to happen, then you can bet your life it happened.'

'Hmm.' The abbot closed the book and stroked its supple leather cover thoughtfully, then handed it back to Benidormus. 'Then it is most probably a fake.'

'The archaeology guys swear it can't be. No-one had been in that tomb from the day it was first sealed until they opened it.'

'Has the book been carbon-dated?'[1]

'Yes, to 462 in the First Age. The date fits exactly.'

'Well, then,' the abbot mused, 'perhaps it is genuine. If so, it is certainly a remarkable find. But I don't see anything particularly worrying about it.'

'That's because you haven't read it. To go through this book from cover to cover is almost like reading a history of Midworld – apart from the fact that it's probably more accurate than most history books. But it's the last chapter that fills me with dread, for that is not strictly history. Not yet, at any rate.'

Benidormus paused and took a deep breath, as though seeking control of a voice that had grown shaky. He was gripping the book so tightly that his fingers were white.

'Go on,' urged the abbot.

'It predicts that Adomo's magical powers will rise again to threaten the whole of Midworld. Then it describes the exact events that will follow.'

[1] For information on carbon-dating and other Midworld oddities, see Appendix.

'And they are . . . ?'

'Oh, you know. War, death, torture, famine, disease. The triumph of evil, enslavement of the poor, the massacre of the righteous. Fire and brimstone, floods, and the burning and pillaging of every land between the mountains and the sea. And dismemberment. He seems very big on dismemberment.'

'And you believe that this will happen?'

Benidormus nodded unhappily. The candle had burned down quite low, and in the slightly dimmer light the skin of his face seemed taut and stretched, like parchment over a bare skull.

'Does the book say when?'

'Yes. Exactly five and one half lunar months after the third annular solar eclipse of the Millennium, as viewed from the city of Chi Qentika.'

'Come again?'

'Last Tuesday.'

A sudden yawning pit seemed to open up in the abbot's stomach, and he told himself not to be so gullible. Surely there must be some more rational explanation . . .

'Come, Benidormus,' he said, forcing a smile onto his face. 'Fetch some wine and replace the candle with a new one. You and I shall go through this book together, until I have read every word for myself.'

And so, as the night wore on and the fire burned low in the tiny hearth, the two of them worked through the hand-written record together. Deciphering the tiny pictorial script was slow and painstaking work, but the more he read, the more the abbot was forced to admit that the accuracy of the predictions was uncanny. But even more frightening than this was the description of what would befall the world after Adomo's power was again unleashed, and Tellow found himself sharing his colleague's conviction that they were facing a terrible danger.

However, the book offered them a single glimmer of hope. The final paragraphs spoke of a young but virtuous man who alone could prevent these events. It described his background as a novice in an eastern monastery, and with a thrill the abbot realised that it was their very monastery that was described.

20

With feverish haste he urged Brother Benidormus to help him through the translation of the final page, eager to find out who this youth could be. Eight separate steps for his selection were detailed and so, after fetching the Register of Novitiates from his office, the two of them went through each step, eliminating those who did not comply. Gradually, the realisation crept over Tellow that the chosen one must be Rudolfo, his favourite, an erudite and pious novice from Minas Orgun whom he was grooming to take over his position.

After the seventh step the abbot was certain. It was only when the very final step eliminated Rudolfo that doubt entered his mind.

'Are you sure?'

'I'm afraid it's definite, Ankos,' muttered Benidormus, rechecking his translation. 'That is, without doubt, the hieroglyphic for *west of*. Then, of the next three, the first stands for *Irri*, the one at the very end represents a mountain, and that graphically obscene one in the middle is a . . .'

'Yes, yes, I can see what that is.'

'Well, we've only got four novices from west of the Irridic Mountains. Three of them have already been eliminated.'

'So who is left? Who is the Chosen One?'

There was a pause. Tellow realised that Benidormus was all of a sudden unable to look him in the eye and was gazing shiftily at the floor, like someone who has just called to tell you that they've accidentally run over your dog with their chariot.

'Come on, who is it?'

Benidormus swallowed painfully.

'Glart,' he said.

The sound of the abbot's pencil snapping echoed through the room. He stared at Benidormus as though the man had slapped him in the face with a soiled codpiece, then buried his head in his hands. There was another pause.

'Glart?' The abbot's voice was muffled by his fingers.

'Glart.'

There was a third, much longer, pause, and then the abbot emerged from behind his hands.

'Well, you'd better find him and send him to me in my office,' he muttered. 'I'll brief him as best I can. And then . . .'

'And then what, Father Abbot?'

The abbot sighed deeply and contemplated a future that suddenly seemed a little bleak.

'And then I rather think I'll get pissed.'

When Glart had been born twenty years previously, his peasant parents had planned on calling him Kaledor, an elven name meaning 'beautiful gift'. Unfortunately, when he had arrived he hadn't quite matched up to this ideal. In fact, he'd been quite probably the ugliest baby in the whole town. The midwife had advised his parents that if it was looks they were after, they should keep the placenta and dispose of the baby, but they were determined folk, and they had vowed to love their little boy no matter what.

However, it hadn't been easy for them. Every smiling visitor who had leant over his crib to compliment him had ended up by saying, 'Oh, what a beautiful . . .' long pause '. . . blanket!' before recoiling in shock and demanding a stiff drink. Despite this, his parents had decided to press ahead with Kaledor, their chosen name, but then fate had taken a hand. The priest at his naming ceremony had swallowed a fly at the vital moment, and the child had officially become Glart.

For the next few years, as the ugly baby had turned into an even uglier toddler, his parents had closed their ears to the comments of their neighbours and had loved him as only they could, but the years of whispered jokes and stifled laughter had taken their toll. Realising that they could only offer him a life of poverty, and worried by the careless cruelty of the outside world, they had taken the heart-breaking decision to send him to a monastery as a child oblate.

And so, at the age of three-and-a-half, Glart had bidden a tearful and bemused farewell to his family and had entered the enclosed world of the religious order, becoming a Cedrician novice. Even here, his ugliness had caused some comment, but the Abbot had taken care to ensure that any teasing of the new novice had been kept to an absolute minimum and Glart had gone through childhood unaware that he had a face which could have stopped a clock dead in its tracks.

By the time he reached puberty, however, things had started to change. It was as though nature had suffered an attack of conscience about playing such a shitty trick on a child and had decided to do something about it. As he grew to adulthood his features had grad-ually altered until, by the time he was twenty, Glart was a different prospect altogether. The large, bent nose no longer seemed comical now that the rest of his face had caught it up. The dense, bushy eyebrows added character rather than a simian quality. The twist to the thickly-lipped mouth appeared to indicate a wry humour instead of some congenital defect. And while the overall effect could by no stretch of the imagination be called handsome, there was an individu-ality and a rugged charm to his features that made them interesting almost to the point of being downright attractive. *In fact*, the abbot thought, as he settled behind the large, wooden desk in his office, *I've a feeling that a lot of women are going to find Glart almost hypnotically fascinating.*

Of course, none of this would have mattered if Glart had been destined to spend the rest of his life behind the walls of the monas-tery. Nor would it have mattered if he had been a quiet, austere character, like most of the other young monks. But he had developed a couple of other character traits that, had, over the years, driven his abbot right up the wall and halfway across the ceiling.

The first of these two traits was a boundless enthusiasm for everything he did, a lust for life that caused him to throw himself whole-heartedly into whatever he was doing and take it to ridiculous extremes. For example, he had once spent several months working in the monastery brew-house, helping to produce the beer that was the monks' usual companion to their evening meal. The resulting concoction had been so strong that the first and only time it had been generally used, the dinner had degenerated into a raucous sing-song that had ended in a mass brawl.

The second trait was one that had begun with the onset of puberty and had become worryingly frequent in the past year. Glart had a tendency to Visions – and not simple, holy Visions either, but intense, vibrant and deeply disturbing ones. Visions that were like windows into other people's lives. Visions which he would describe in the minutest detail to those around him. Visions which didn't half cause a stir amongst the other monks.

All this had caused no end of trouble in the sheltered environment of the monastery. In fact, Glart had probably caused more disruption than anything since the visit by a delegation from the Sisters of

Perpetual Arousal, a few years before. Abbot Tellow had on several occasions considered recommending that this problematical young monk should transfer to a more suitable order such as the Seventh Day Hedonists or the Brothers of Mortality, and might well have done so had it not been for the fact that the youth had a natural talent for magic.

The abbot was just thinking that God alone knew what would happen when Glart was set loose in the outside world, when there was a knock on the office door and the novice himself was ushered in by Brother Benidormus.

Glart appeared to have tempered his usual exuberance a little and had the apologetic bounciness of a high-spirited puppy that thinks it might have done something wrong but isn't too worried because it knows that you love it anyway. He took the proffered stool without managing to knock anything over and sat facing the abbot on the other side of the desk, a look of enquiry on his face. Tellow motioned Benidormus to stand beside him, and then launched into a description of everything that the two of them had discovered.

'Of course, this may all be a complete coincidence,' he finished. 'There is probably no danger to Midworld at all. But I feel that we should take no chances. Adomo's predictions need to be taken into account. You, Glart, would seem to be the chosen one, and thus . . .'

The abbot let his voice trail away. Glart's face, which until then had been encouragingly attentive, had suddenly assumed the distant, unfocused expression that indicated another vision was under way.

'I see a woman . . .' began Glart.

The abbot froze. Glart's last vision of women, which had occurred while he was reading the lesson during mass, had been so intimate and so intensely described that most of the younger monks had needed to be herded into the cold showers and kept there for several hours before the frenzy eventually died down.

'She is in danger . . . in the city of Koumas,' continued Glart. 'Someone wants to kill her. He is close to her, even now. She is hiding, but he seeks her. She is alone in her room. I see her lying in her bed, her long, dark hair spread across the pillow, her lips slightly parted, her breasts rising and falling as she sleeps . . .'

'All right! That's quite enough of that!' snapped the abbot. Glart's eyes pinged open and focused on him in surprise, and Tellow realised

24

that he'd spoken rather more sharply than he had meant to. He shook his head, annoyed with himself. After a lifetime of celibacy, these disturbingly vivid descriptions were beginning to have a strange effect on him, and he knew that his next sleep would probably once again be filled with exotic, lustful dreams. *The sad thing is,* he thought tiredly, *I'm beginning to look forward to them* . . .

Manfully resisting the temptation of the bottle of Glart-manufactured maximum strength communion wine that was hidden in the bottom drawer of his desk, he dragged his thoughts back to the here and now.

'You must travel to Chi Qentika,' he continued. 'It is plain that whatever may be about to happen is based around those ancient tombs. I do not know what you can do, but I suggest that several of our more experienced brothers go with you, so that . . .'

'No!' interjected Glart.

The abbot stared at him in surprise, unused to being interrupted.

'This woman is the key,' continued the novice, 'and she is in Koumas. I must go there. And I must go alone.'

For the next ten minutes the abbot did his best to change Glart's mind, but despite all his arguments, threats, warnings and pleadings, Glart remained stubborn, and eventually the abbot gave in. One thing he had learned about this baffling novice was that any predictions he made had an unnerving habit of coming true.

'If these prophecies are wrong, then we have nothing to fear,' he mused. 'If they are right, then you are the only one who can find a way to prevent these terrible events. Therefore we must all put our trust in you. If, for reasons that you may not understand, you feel that you must go alone, then I must accept that.'

Glart merely nodded, and said nothing. Which was just as well, really. For it wasn't that he didn't understand his reasons. No, he understood them very well indeed. But he also knew that if he had told his abbot that the only reason he wanted to go alone was because he knew it was the only way he would be able to have any fun during his brief sojourn in the outside world, Tellow would probably have strapped a chastity belt onto him with his own hands and would have provided an enforced escort of the most fervently fun-hating, puritanical brothers available. And then Glart would have had a thoroughly miserable time. As would the rest of Midworld, for many a long age . . .

25

CHAPTER THREE

The door to the bar-room flew open, Macoby stormed through it and swept across to the bar like a small and extremely irate tornado. With a guilty start the landlord removed his hand from inside the barmaid's blouse and then stood shifting uncomfortably from foot to foot as Macoby stared angrily up at him.

'Is something wrong?' he muttered.

'Yes. My room, that's what's wrong!'

The landlord blinked. Customers who swore, shouted, fought, vomited or pawed at the bar staff he was used to, but he had never before experienced a customer who had dared to complain to his face, particularly in such a well-bred accent.

'Wot's wrong wiv it?' he asked.

'For starters, the bed. I'd like one, instead of a slab of wood with a hay-stuffed sack on top of it. And I'd like a real fire, with logs, instead of a few burning twigs that would make a candle look like a towering inferno. I would also like a comfortable chair, some wine and some food.'

Macoby paused. Out of the corner of her eye she could see that the foul-mouthed phantom from her bedroom was drifting slowly through the wall beside a stuffed bear's head.

'What I do *not* want, however, is *that* thing pestering me,' she added, gesturing with a dramatic arm at the ghost.

The landlord and the barmaid looked across the room.

'The bear's head has been pestering you?' asked the landlord.

'No, not that. *That.*'

Macoby stabbed an accusing finger at Darian's ghost, which was hovering near the wall and looking extremely embarrassed.

'The wall? You're bothered by the wall? Wot do you expect me to do, get rid of it? I need the walls to keep the top floors up!'

'I do not mean the wall!' yelled Macoby. 'I mean that flaming ghost over there! Can't you see it?'

But no sooner had the words left her mouth than she realised from the bemused expressions on their faces that they obviously couldn't. Neither the landlord nor the barmaid had the faintest idea what she was talking about.

'Oh, right!' said the landlord, in the ever-so-friendly voice of somebody who has realised that they are dealing with a lunatic who might turn nasty at any moment. 'Yeah! The ghost! Well, don't you worry about that. I'll chase him away for you. Er . . . that ghost, right?' he added hopefully, pointing at a spot six feet to the right of where Darian's ghost was now skulking in the corner.

'Forget it. I'll find another tavern.'

Macoby stomped across the floor and out of the door. The landlord watched her go, then breathed a sigh of relief and bolted the door behind her.

'We'll open up again in half an hour,' he told the barmaid. 'Just got time for a quick one first. Come here!'

The barmaid smiled and began to unbutton her blouse.

From his position in the corner, Darian's ghost watched the ensuing proceedings with a mounting interest. *Maybe there are one or two advantages to being a ghost after all,* he thought. *I mean those two wouldn't be going at it like that if they knew they were being watched. Especially in that position. Oh, now what's she going to do? Surely not!*

But then all of a sudden he was yanked sideways again and pulled steadily towards the door. *Oh, no!* he thought. *Not now! It's just getting interesting!* But there was nothing he could do. Once again he was being hauled away against his will, until with a muttered curse he disappeared through the wall, leaving the landlord and the barmaid in the privacy which they'd thought they already had.

Twenty minutes later, in a bedroom on the first floor of a tavern called the *Weyr Inn*, Macoby had just sat down in a slightly more comfortable chair to study her brother's amulet (which was showing an unnerving ability to change shape at will, and had currently adopted the form of an ivory cameo brooch) when she realised that once again a now-familiar shape was oozing apologetically through the locked wooden door.

27

'You again!' she muttered through clenched teeth, and jamming the amulet back in her pocket she looked round for something to throw.

'No, please!' The ghost's voice was audible but muffled, as though he was speaking from inside a roll of carpet. He winced as another chamberpot whizzed through his nebulous head and smashed against the door. 'I'm not doing this on purpose, honestly! I can't help it! I'm just . . . drawn here!'

Macoby scowled at him. She had quite enough on her mind, what with the things Marden had said, his disappearance, and the mysterious jewel that he'd left behind. The last thing she needed was to be stalked from crap tavern to crap tavern by a morose phantom.

'Fine,' she told him. 'Then stay here. But I need to think, and I'm finding it very difficult to do so when you keep popping through walls all the time. I'm going out. Do *not* follow me!'

With that she was gone, slamming the door behind her, and Darian's ghost was left hovering in the middle of the room. He too was finding it difficult to think. Doubts and thoughts were eddying about in his brain like tenuous, insubstantial vapours, impossible to grasp. This whole after-death thing was going to take some getting used to . . .

From his point of view, the real world now seemed dreamlike. Walls and doors were as insubstantial as a wall of water, and taking hold of solid objects was like trying to grasp smoke, although if he concentrated hard, he was finding that he could manipulate things just a little. With the exception of Macoby, humans appeared to be unaware of his presence. Animals, however, were able to sense him, particularly dogs and horses.

But strangest of all was the oddly familiar jewel that Macoby had shoved into her pocket. Darian's ghost could clearly see it through the material. It glowed as though on fire, and was by far the brightest thing in the strange netherworld that he now inhabited. But why was it familiar? Darian cudgelled his memory, but it still refused to work properly.

And then once again he was yanked unceremoniously towards the wall by the unseen force that was, quite frankly, beginning to get right up his nose. *Oh, shit!* he thought. *Here we go again*. Desperately he tried to stay where he was by grabbing hold of a bedpost, but his spectral fingers slipped through it, and with a last despairing curse he disappeared through yet another wall.

To clear her mind (and to escape from a ghost that was beginning to irritate her enormously), Macoby left the *Weyr Inn*, and wandered down Pox Street and into the old market. This was the roughest area of town, but even so she felt comparatively safe. If Marden was right and she was in danger, no-one would look for her here. Nor would word get back to any enemy; the simple clothes she was wearing were enough to ensure that no casual passer-by would recognise her as the daughter of the city's ruler.

She strolled down an alley past stalls laden with spices and fruits, cheap jewelry, glass ornaments and bales of cloth. The smell of the spices hung in the air and prickled at her nose, but it couldn't quite overpower the rich aroma of roasting coffee beans that was emanating from a small shop at the far end of the alley. Macoby sat herself down at an outside table and spent several frustrating minutes trying to attract the attention of the owner before eventually managing to order a tiny cup of the strong, bitter-tasting Qitalian coffee and a couple of small, sweet *bayeklad* pastries. Then she leant back in her chair and began to think.

What the hell had made her run off to that flea-ridden, ghost-infested tavern when she could be back home in the palace with access to every mod con known to man? What was she doing sitting here in this dodgy, run-down coffee shop when she could be sat in the dining room at home surrounded by hot and cold running waiters? She'd acted a little precipitately, considering that all she had to go on was her brother's fears.

But then, as she sipped her coffee, other little doubts began to surface. What had happened to Marden's body? Why was someone else wearing his pendant? Why had the orcs invaded? That hadn't been a typical undisciplined orc army. And why, if the orcs were winning the battle (as the soldiers she'd talked to afterwards had suggested), had they suddenly retreated?

By the gods! If only Marden hadn't been so secretive about his fears! That was completely unlike him. Normally he told her

29

everything, so what had prevented him this time? He must have suspected somebody close to them, somebody whom he couldn't name to her unless he was absolutely sure of their guilt. But who?

'Macoby!' yelled a voice nearby, and she nearly leapt through the red and white striped awning that shaded the tables. Jumping up, dagger in hand, she was about to dash off down the alley when she recognised the tall, muscular figure that was striding towards her, arms outstretched.

'Sarakkan!'

Sighing with relief, she sheathed her dagger and ran to meet the man she loved. He was grinning with happiness at finding her, and as she threw herself into his arms he gasped with pleasure at this display of affection.

'What's got into you all of a sudden?' he asked, and then he held her at arm's length and studied her. 'And more to the point, where the hell have you been for the past two days? We've all been worried sick! I've searched everywhere for you, absolutely everywhere!'

His eyes were shining, but now that his initial pleasure at finding her had ebbed, she could see that he was nervous and worried. Something was on his mind.

'If you've come to tell me about Marden, I already know.'

Sarakkan looked surprised.

'What have you heard?' he asked.

'Heard? Nothing. But I know in my heart he is dead.'

'True, some say they saw him fall in the battle,' Sarakkan told her sadly, 'yet his body has not been found. But that is not the news I bear.'

He shook his head and looked away, then ran his hand through his cropped brown hair.

'No, it's your father,' he said slowly, unable to meet her gaze. 'He's decided that . . . well, there's no easy way of telling you this, Macoby.'

He took her hands and looked straight into her eyes, his expression suddenly serious. Macoby could see that, despite the easy smile with which he had greeted her, he was a deeply worried man.

'Myal of Minas Lantan was the leader of our forces in the battle against the orcs yesterday,' he told her. 'He's ridden back here at the head of our army, a hero. Your father has said that this is the perfect time to announce that you and Myal are to be wed . . . aah!'

He gasped in sudden pain, and Macoby realised that she had squeezed his hand so hard her nails had dug into his skin.

'No!' she snapped. 'How can he say that? I have already told him I won't marry that . . . that cold, unsmiling lizard!'

Sarakkan smiled sadly. Lifting one hand, he stroked her hair gently.

'Love,' he said, 'I do not think your father will accept that. He too believes that Marden is dead, and that you are now his heir. He is determined to unite the two cities in this marriage, and he has said that if you will not be there to accept Myal's proposal, then he will accept it for you himself. He wants to make the formal announcement at tomorrow night's banquet in Myal's honour. I do not think that he will be easily gainsaid.'

'I will not marry that man, not while I have you! I cannot hurt you so!'

'Macoby, I do not count in all these affairs of state! I am nobody! If it benefits our city for you to wed Myal, then I must stand aside.'

'But I don't want to marry him!' Macoby wailed. 'Please, Sarakkan, help me!'

Her cry of near-despair caused Sarakkan to look sharply at her.

'Listen,' she said, taking Sarakkan by the hand again and drawing him to a chair by the coffee-shop table. 'Something's wrong. Marden warned me. He was convinced that someone was plotting against us.'

'I know.'

'You do?' Macoby was surprised.

Sarakkan nodded.

'He told me a week ago that he thought someone was out to kill him. And you. At first I just dismissed what he said. But I've been thinking about it. There are a lot of things that just don't add up . . .'

He trailed off into silence, staring down at the table top, and Macoby studied his face. He looked drawn and tired, and the muscles of his neck and jaw were clenched with stress. His skin was smeared with dust and dirt, and a cut across his forehead was encrusted with dried blood.

'The battle yesterday . . .' he continued, in a strained, faraway voice. 'It all went very wrong. There were far too many orcs, and we found we were outnumbered. And then Myal made some strange decisions. I was with Colonel De Wenchas and his cavalry. He was second in command. He reckoned that Myal got it so badly wrong

31

that he nearly lost us the battle. He wondered whether someone had put an enchantment on him.'

Macoby felt as though a cold, clutching hand had taken hold of her stomach. She knew that Myal had a wonderful record in battle and was renowned as a leader. Was he under some foul spell? What the *klat* was going on?

All of a sudden, the vague, fragmented doubts that had been hovering half-seen at the back of her mind coalesced into a frightening whole, and Macoby's mind went racing after the implications. She clutched at Sarakkan's hand in her excitement. He winced, and she realised that he had another recent cut across the back of his hand.

'You're wounded!'

'It's only a scratch. Look, we have to get back to the palace. Even if your answer is to be no, you must give it to your father before he commits you to this marriage. And you must see Myal and tell him yourself. The man's a stickler for convention and we don't want to end up at war with Minas Lantan just because the ruler's son thinks he's been insulted.'

'No. I can't go back yet . . . I need some time on my own, to think.'

'But we haven't got time,' Sarakkan began. 'Your father has promised Myal an answer to his proposal this very afternoon. Decisions have to be made, and Myal expects to . . .'

'Listen!' Macoby cut in. 'Did Marden ever show you this?' She shoved her hand into her pocket and took hold of the amulet, but then something in the corner of her eye caught her attention. An almost uncontrollable rage washed through her as she realised that the same pain-in-the-arse ghost had followed her again and was hovering half in, half out of the wall of the coffee shop, trying to pretend that it wasn't there.

'Why can't you leave me alone?' she yelled furiously, to Sarakkan's surprise. He stared at her with a hurt expression.

'How can I think with you following me round like a malignant shadow?' she added. 'By the Gods, I wish I was miles from here!'

Instantly there was a blinding flash, and Macoby found that she was sitting in a field of cabbages, all alone save for a few very surprised caterpillars. The sounds of the city had vanished, to be replaced by birdsong and the lowing of distant cattle.

'There you are,' said a voice. 'Sorted.'

She looked down and found that she was holding the amulet. It was now a grinning pig's head made of pewter, with eyes that glowed like rubies in firelight.

'That was you, wasn't it?' she said accusingly. 'I'm being screwed around by a cheap neck ornament!'

'Cheap? What do you mean, cheap?' said the amulet, crossly. 'Anyway, I only did what you asked,' it added sulkily. 'I heard you distinctly. I wish I was miles from here, you said. So now you are.' It paused. '*Some* people would be grateful,' it added, in martyred tones.

Macoby contemplated throwing it at a small mound of compost which was piled at the edge of the field, but then her curiosity got the better of her.

'So how did we get here? Magic?'

'I'm not at liberty to say,' the amulet replied, primly. 'However, I don't suppose it requires a giant intellect to work it out. Or even the intellect of a giant, which is pretty damn small. So yes, I think you can safely assume that it was magic. A *Transference* spell, to be exact. And now, if you don't mind, I'd like to rest.'

Macoby raised her eyes heavenwards, then looked around. Although the sun was low in the sky and it was beginning to get dark, she recognised the field as a place where she had picnicked one idyllically-hot day the previous summer. It was at least five miles from Koumas. Still, at least she was alone and could do a bit of thinking.

But then, with a faint and ever so weary *plop*, Darian's ghost materialised next to her. For a moment there was a stunned silence, and then Macoby exploded. And if there were any further rude words that the ghost had forgotten and wanted to recall, he was certainly in the right place now.

CHAPTER FOUR

Ever since he was a small child, Detective Inspector Heighway had wanted to do his bit in the fight against crime. While all the other children in the crowded Minas Orgun street where he lived had played at being gangs of orc raiders pillaging cities or dwarf treasure-hunters stealing dragon-hoards, he had run around after them shouting indignantly and trying to arrest them all. This hadn't endeared him to the other kids, or to his parents, who had had to clean the resulting blood off his clothes. But Heighway hadn't cared. He had known he was doing the right thing.

Then, on his eighth birthday, something had happened which had turned his vocation into an obsession. His parents had taken him to the local tavern for a celebration meal. But on arriving home afterwards, they had found that someone had broken in to their small terraced house and had stolen just about everything they owned. And that included all of young Heighway's birthday presents. From that moment on, the boy was determined to devote the rest of his life to catching and punishing criminals. It had become a personal crusade.

On the very day he left school Heighway joined the Minas Orgun branch of the Urban National Troopers (slogan: be a MOUNT and rise up in the world!), otherwise known as the city's police force. He had honestly believed that he was joining a band of tough but fair men who were dedicated to the pursuit of justice and who believed in solving crimes by tracking down the perpetrators and locking them up.

Unfortunately, it didn't take him long to realise that his colleagues had their own way of solving crimes, which was to arrest the nearest innocent bystander, find him guilty (no matter what the evidence suggested), and then lock him up or, if the prisons were getting a bit crowded, execute him. It was unjust, but Heighway was forced to admit that it was also quick, cheap and (from a percentage-of-crimes-solved point of view) highly efficient.

Despite this, Heighway had stuck to his principles. After eight years as a uniformed officer he had joined the Serious Crime Squad, and within a couple more years he had managed to carve out a little niche for himself as a detective who used the power of his intellect to solve crimes, rather than using the conventional methods of legwork, interviewing, and beating up anyone handy until they confessed.

He became quite proud of his reputation as a detective who refused to do things by the book, especially as the book most of his colleagues did things by was Rogash the Impaler's *Classic Techniques of Torture*. Not everyone favoured this book: the women officers in the squad tended to prefer Colin the Sinister's study of female torturers, *The Daughters of Pain*, whilst Fats Planket, the longest-serving officer, once took Heighway aside and recommended the two massive volumes of The Scribe of Welbug's *Human, Dwarvish and Elven Anatomy*. Fats particularly recommended slamming them together with the prisoner's testicles in between. He called it his painless persuader.

'Painless?' the naive Heighway had asked. 'But surely that must hurt?'

'Only if you get your thumbs caught in the middle,' had come the reply.

Eventually, the sheer unpleasantness of all this had begun to take its toll. Fed up with the limited opportunities to utilise his talents that his career had given him, Heighway had come to realise that unless he wanted to become as unthinkingly brutal as his colleagues he needed to move on. And so he had applied for a move to the city of Koumas.

Admittedly there were drawbacks to becoming an Urban National Trooper. The city's recruiting slogan sounded nowhere near as appealing, for starters. But the city had a reputation for honour and fairness, and he felt sure that it was a place where justice would prevail, and a police officer who had a talent for tracking down the real perpetrators of crime would be welcome.

Unfortunately, the city was so honourable and fair a place that in his first four years there, Heighway was only called upon to solve three murders. And as in each case the murderer had given himself

35

up within hours of the crime and had pleaded guilty in court, there was little need for him to exercise the formidable intellect which he was dying to unleash against some underworld mastermind. But then, just as he was beginning to think that if he wanted to exercise this intellect he was going to have to take up crime himself, all of a sudden he got his chance.

He was sitting in his office one afternoon, pulling rogue hairs out of his nose and wondering why they had started sprouting thickly there when the ones on his head were becoming sparser and sparser, when the door crashed open and Sergeant Raasay, his assistant, came lumbering into the room. This in itself was nothing unusual; they had so little work to do that Raasay had recently developed the habit of spending his lunchtimes in the *Boot and Scrotum*, the pub next door. He would usually come crashing back to the office at about three o'clock, and would then habitually fall asleep under his desk for a couple of hours.

Heighway looked up. Raasay was standing there, his lopsided face suffused, his mouth working as he sought to say something. Again, this was nothing unusual. Raasay liked to drink Ratbane's Special Brew, a beer noted for its strength and its vicious side effects, and after several pints he often completely lost the power of speech. Uninterested, Heighway returned to his study of nasal hair, and was just wondering why your eyes watered so much when you pulled out those little hairs right at the front of your nostril when Raasay suddenly found the words he was seeking.

'Inspector! We've got a case! Over at the army barracks in Neero Square! The chief says we've got to get over there right away!'

'Really?' Heighway studied his misshapen assistant languidly. *Pissed again*, he thought. *Can't really blame him. God knows, I'm in the pub often enough myself, and I'm good at my job. The poor sod would be much better off looking after the bells in some vast, Gothic cathedral. He's about as well-suited to police work as a troll is to ballet . . .*

'And what pressing problem have they got this time, eh?' he asked. 'One of the generals had his pencil stolen, like last time? Or is it something really important, like the one that we had to solve for them two months ago? The case of The Missing Chair Cushion?'

Raasay shook his head so violently that a little snowstorm of dandruff briefly obscured his features.

'No, sir! It's the real thing this time. One of the cavalry commanders has been murdered! Blood everywhere, they say!'

Heighway was so surprised that he nearly fell off his chair. A murder! He could feel the excitement flooding through him. At last! A chance to show what he was capable of! But then his natural caution reasserted itself. Better not get too excited until he'd checked out the crime scene. The army liked nothing better than to think that they were surrounded by enemies. It made them feel that they had some sort of purpose in life. As a result, they did tend to rather over-dramatise things. This might be nothing more than a suicide, an accident, or even a practical joke. But then again, it might not . . .

'Okay, Raasay,' he ordered, springing to his feet. 'I'm going to have a quick word with the chief. Bring the horses round to the front. We'd better get moving on this before the bloody army trample every single clue underfoot. Have we got anyone on the scene yet?'

'Detective Constable Kratavan, sir.'

'Kratavan, eh? Good, he knows what he's doing. He should be able to keep them under control for a bit. Right, let's move.'

When Heighway and Raasay arrived at the barracks, army officers were milling around like ants outside a nest that has had a good prodding with a stick. They parted to let the two police officers through, and a bewildered and bewhiskered old colonel led them up a flight of stairs to an oak-panelled corridor that was guarded by two extremely large policemen.

'Kratavan still here?' asked Heighway.

'Yes, sir,' replied one. 'Last door on the right. And the police pathomancer has just arrived, as well.'

'Oh great!' muttered Heighway. 'That's all I need. Which one have they sent me?'

'Madam Min, sir.'

Heighway sighed heavily and walked on down the corridor shaking his head. He wasn't a great fan of the magical arts, having no such talent himself, and he was convinced that there had to be a better, more scientific method of finding out exactly when and how a body had died than by the occult tomfoolery practised by Madam Min and her colleagues.

'Keep her out of my hair if you can, eh, sergeant?' he asked. Beside him Raasay nodded doubtfully. He had the simple man's respect and awe for anything magical and didn't share Heighway's cynicism.

Coming to the last door on the right they strode into the room and stopped dead. The air was thick with the sweet, cloying smell of recently-spilt blood. But then that wasn't surprising, because there was blood all over the expensive wooden desk in the centre of the room, blood all over the papers that covered it, blood on the thick woollen carpet, and blood on the ornate tapestries that covered the wall behind the desk. There was even blood on the ceiling. But most of all there was blood down the front of the cavalry officer's uniform that was being worn by the corpse that slumped in a chair behind the desk.

'Hurp!' said Sergeant Raasay, who had gone very pale.

'Not in here, sergeant!' ordered Heighway, and Raasay turned and scurried back out into the corridor.

Heighway turned back to study the scene. In front of the desk, the stout, black-draped figure of Madam Min was engaged in one of her arcane rituals. A lighted candle was perched on some papers near the corpse's outstretched left hand, and incense was burning in a small blackstone crucible beside it, giving off an acrid scent that made Heighway want to sneeze. Meanwhile Min was muttering some garbled incantation and making strange stabbing motions with her right hand. Nearby, Kratavan was lounging against the wall with a huge smile on his face, reading a copy of the *Koumas Gazette*.

'I'm glad you think it's funny,' snapped Heighway. Kratavan straightened up, looking abashed.

'Sorry, inspector,' he said. 'But I wasn't laughing. Have you seen this?'

He held out the newspaper and Heighway took it and scanned the page. It was open at the crime news, which was edited by Colin the Sinister, a crime-writer and journalist from Orcs Ford who was now resident in Koumas. *DC Kratavan nicks three!* screamed the main headline, and Heighway realised that the man had been grinning from sheer pleasure in seeing his successful arrest of three forgers splashed across the paper.

'I wonder what he's going to say about this case,' ventured Kratavan, and Heighway scowled. Colin the Sinister's column was never slow in criticising the police when they failed to get quick results.

'What have we got so far?' he asked, turning to look at the body.

Kratavan folded up his paper and began to tick items off on his fingers.

'Well, firstly, the stiff over there used to be a cavalry officer called De Wenchas. He was second in command during the defeat of the orcs yesterday. Secondly, someone has bashed him over the head with a wooden bowling ball and then sliced his throat open so viciously that his head has almost come off. Cut right through the . . .'

'Yeah, okay. That's enough detail!' Heighway looked across at the corpse with distaste.

'Thirdly, he doesn't seem to have had any enemies. Apart from orcs, that is. Everyone liked him.'

'Somebody certainly didn't!'

'And fourthly, three of his troopers saw him alive at nine this morning. Then no-one seems to have seen him until a servant brought his lunch up at one o'clock.'

Heighway peered at a small pile of regurgitated food near the door.

'I'm not surprised he brought his lunch up,' he murmured. 'I nearly brought mine up, too.' He looked across to where Madam Min seemed to have come to the end of her incantation. *Ah, well*, he thought. *Better find out what the old bag has come up with . . .*

'So, what can you give me, Min?' he asked. 'Any ideas on the murder weapon?'

The wrinkled pathomancer blew out the candle and then began to pack her accoutrements away in a large black case.

'The spirits have spoken,' she told him over her shoulder. 'The weapon is slim and very sharp.'

Unlike you, thought Heighway.

'So he hasn't had his throat sliced open with a banana, then?' he said out loud.

'No. A dagger. And a very old one, at that.'

'Yeah? How old?'

'I can't be precise . . .'

'No. You never can, Min.'

'. . . but I'd guess it's been around for roughly seven hundred years.'

So you do *have something in common with the murder weapon*, Heighway thought. Behind him, Kratavan whistled with amazement.

Madam Min picked up her case and hobbled to the door. Then she stopped and leered across at the inspector.

'Is there something else?' he asked her, curtly.

'Yes!' she cackled. 'The spirits have spoken once more. He will kill again. More people will die soon. More blood will flow. More living flesh will be ripped apart . . . What was that?'

She paused for a moment, her brow furrowed, as though she was trying to hear some whispered message. Then her brow cleared.

'Ah, bollocks!' she added. 'Apparently my dinner will be burnt by the time I get home!'

Then she was gone. Seconds later, Sergeant Raasay shuffled into the room. He stood looking miserable, trying to ignore the blood-soaked body. Heighway took pity on him.

'Raasay, get out of here before someone mistakes you for the corpse and buries you,' he ordered. 'Talk to Kratavan, then get back to the station and bring the chief up to date on what we've found.'

'Okay, sir.' The sergeant turned and shuffled out through the door, with Kratavan following. Seconds later, his head popped back in.

'Sir?'

'What is it, sergeant?'

'What shall I tell the chief you're doing, sir?'

'Tell him I'm looking for evidence.'

Raasay nodded and disappeared once more. Heighway sighed long-sufferingly, wondering whether every other detective inspector in Midworld was blessed with a sergeant whose mental processes would make a snail look like a bolt of lightning, or whether it was just him. Then, crossing to the desk, he turned his attention to the corpse.

So this was the famous Colonel De Wenchas. A tall, powerful man with curling black hair worn long in the way that was currently fashionable amongst the cavalry, he'd had the reputation of being one of the best tacticians that Koumas had ever produced.

Heighway crouched down beside him and picked up the heavy wooden bowling ball that lay on the floor beside the desk. It was obviously the colonel's, for its partner was still in a bag beside the wall. Heighway studied the wood for a moment and then held it next to the colonel's head. There was a small concave indentation in the back of his skull that exactly matched the curve of the wood. So Kratavan was right! Someone had obviously knocked him uncon-scious with his own bowling ball before slicing his throat open.

Placing the bowl carefully back into the bag, Heighway stood up, then leaned over the desk and tried to make sense of the papers that covered it, but it was almost impossible. They were soaked in blood, and the colonel's head was lying right across them. Heighway didn't dare to try and move it; the gaping slit across the throat was so wide that the whole head might have come off in his hands.

Then he noticed that a sheet of paper near the sprawling right hand was almost blood-free, but had a faint smear across it. In fact, now he looked closely, there was a rectangular blood-free area that could only have been caused by a sheet of paper being removed. The fact that, as it was removed, it had drawn a faint line of still-wet blood across the sheet beneath was intriguing. It must have been taken shortly after the murder, and the only person who would have done that was the murderer himself.

Heighway walked round to the other side of the desk and studied the position of the colonel's hand, then pulled the quill pen out of the ink-pot, dried the ink off on the colonel's hair, and inspected the nib. Eureka! It was covered in blood, even on the part that had been submerged in ink. Someone had replaced it in the pot after the murder. The only reason to do that must have been to disguise the fact that De Wenchas had been writing, which in turn meant he had been writing something which the killer wanted to remain unread.

Crossing to the door, Heighway turned and tried to imagine the scene. De Wenchas must have known whoever had killed him, for with the desk in that position there was no way anyone could have crept up behind him. He had been writing something that would have given a clue to his killer's identity, and had been taken by surprise, for there were no signs of a struggle. Therefore, it had been someone he knew and trusted.

Heighway grinned to himself, opened a small marble box on the desk and helped himself to one of the colonel's expensive hand-rolled cheroots. Lighting it, he breathed a cloud of aromatic smoke towards the colonel's body and grinned a second time. Things were beginning to come together. Somehow he just *knew* that this case was going to be the one to get him on the front page of the *Koumas Gazette*.

Strangely enough, he was dead right.

CHAPTER FIVE

As the massive wooden gate of the monastery thumped shut behind him, Glart resisted the urge to look back and kept his eyes steadfastly on the road ahead. This was the first time he had been beyond the confines of the monastery for seventeen years, and he found that he was filled with a huge, bubbling elation which almost overwhelmed him. He was tempted to burst into song or do a few little dance steps but he ignored the temptation, conscious that he was probably being watched from the gatehouse. Now that he was on the verge of a few precious weeks of freedom, the last thing he wanted was for some of Abbot Tellow's henchmen to come running after him and haul him bodily back into the claustrophobic confines of the abbey.

Instead, he concentrated on the dusty road that wound westwards between fields and orchards towards the low hills of central Kuhbador. All his senses seemed heightened; he could feel the warmth of the morning sun on his back, could hear each individual bird amidst the wealth of birdsong, could smell the scent of the wildflowers that lined the roadside. He wanted to laugh from the sheer joy of it all. At last! He was free to experience the outside world, if only for a while! He might be on a serious mission entrusted to him by the abbot himself, but as far as he was concerned, that didn't mean he couldn't have a little fun along the way.

It wasn't that Glart disliked his cloistered way of life. On the contrary, he had always enjoyed it, for he had known no other. It was just that he relished new experiences, new tastes and new sights, and these were severely limited inside the monastery. Now he would be able to sample so many things that his head spun at the thought. And he would probably have to deal with women!

Compared to the other novices, Glart had quite a steady, levelheaded attitude to the opposite sex. Thanks to his visions, he at least knew what they looked like, so they didn't hold quite so much mystery for him. But even he had been affected that one time a few years before when two nuns from another order, the Sisters of Perpetual Arousal, had stayed overnight in the monastery's guest-lodge. Abbot Tellow had kept them well away from the novices, but Glart had been on gatehouse duty when they arrived, and there had been something about their heavy-lidded stare, their full lips and their undulating walk that had got right inside his libido and had stirred it up with a stick.

But all that would come later. For the moment he was enjoying the simple experience of walking along a road, free of all his usual responsibilities and able to enjoy each moment as it happened.

After a while, the road began to wind its way up into the hills. The countryside had changed now, and the fields had given way to vineyards. The sun was higher in the sky, and Glart was beginning to feel thirsty. He took a drink from his water bottle, then turned and leant on his staff while he surveyed the view back towards the east.

The land stretched away before him for mile upon mile until, in the far distance, the Telluric Mountains could just be made out. Although the monastery was much nearer than the mountains he could no longer see it, and his spirits soared like a Frundorian lark as he realised that no-one would be stopping him now. He really was free!

Grinning, he sat down on a boulder and opened the small pack of food that he had been given. Inside was a tiny loaf of bread, a piece of cheese and an apple. They were barely enough for a single meal, but the Cedricians were a mendicant order. Glart was expected to find his own food and lodgings, performing whatever acts of minor magic he could manage in return. All he carried with him was his Cedrician staff, presented to him in a ceremony the previous night by the abbot himself, his water bottle, a bedroll, and a small leather scrip containing his own personal *Minutiae Carmenorum*, in which were written all the spells and blessings that he was qualified to use.

After wolfing down the food, Glart stood up again and sniffed the air. The sun was still shining, but he had a feeling that a change of weather was on the way. *It'll be raining by this evening*, he thought. *I'd better find a proper lodging for tonight.* And so, after giving one last look back in the direction of the monastery, he set off again towards the west.

By late afternoon he had travelled a long way. The road had meandered gently through the hills from valley to valley, past vineyards and olive groves and through the occasional small copse of trees. Yet, though the countryside was neat and well-tended, Glart had not met a soul to speak to nor passed a house or cottage at which he could stop to ask for water and to pass the time of day.

On he plodded, footsore and weary now, and wondering whether he was going to spend a cold, uncomfortable night in the open. But then at last, just as dark and ominous clouds were beginning to mass in the western sky ahead of him, obscuring the sun, he came across human habitation.

The road had been gradually wending its way uphill for perhaps a mile, to snake through a low pass between two dark and brooding hills. The countryside was moorland here, with little growing save for tough, wiry heather. Then, all at once, the road fell away before him to slope gently downwards, and he found he had breasted the pass and was standing looking out over the vast west Kuhbador plain. Much of it was hidden by the encroaching gloom, but below him, just a couple of miles away, he could see that the road ran straight to a small cluster of buildings that marked a village. With a sigh of relief, Glart plodded onwards.

It was nearly dark by the time he reached the village and the rain was beginning to fall in those first large, ponderous drops that signify the onset of a downpour. The road led between a double row of drab stone cottages with their small, shuttered windows and gnarled wooden doors closed tight against the night. Beyond them, it looped over an arched stone bridge across a stream, on the other side of which was a large, sprawling inn with a thatched roof. Ramshackle outbuildings clung to it like shy children clinging to their mother's skirts, and a warm and welcoming light shone forth from the windows. Above the door hung an inn sign which Glart initially thought depicted a couple of heavy bowling balls in a hessian sack. But then he saw the inn's name – the *Troll's Bollocks* – and realised his mistake.

Walking up to the inn as quickly as his aching limbs would allow, he paused in the shelter of the porch. This was the first time that he

44

had ever had open contact with people in the outside world, and he was feeling extremely nervous. Gripping his staff tightly, he told himself not to worry. *It's just a normal, everyday tavern*, he thought. *So let's just walk in and socialise with the other customers. There's nothing to it. Just pretend that they're other novice monks back home in the monastery, and don't let them faze you. And remember, you're a Cedrician, a magic monk. Abbot Tellow said that many folk are overawed by us, so be confident!*

This bit of positive thinking did the trick. Glart drew himself up to his full height and then opened the door and strode confidently into the tavern. But at the sight which met his eyes he stopped dead, completely and totally dumbfounded. His jaw dropped so far it only just missed his knees, and he could feel his confidence draining completely away.

For what must have been a full minute he stood there, staring round, and then he took a deep breath and staggered towards the bar. It wasn't the customers that had dumbfounded him, for there only appeared to be two of them, an elf and a cave-troll, who were sitting drinking together in one corner. Nor was it the landlady, who was busy behind the bar. No, it was the pub itself. Or, more accurately, it was the pub's decor.

Like many inns and taverns in Midworld, the whole place had been decorated around a theme. Only here, the theme wasn't famous actors, or gladiators, or hunting. No, the theme in the *Troll's Bollocks* was sex. And it wasn't a quiet, restrained theme either. The phrase 'in your face' sprang instantly to mind. Whichever way he looked, Glart found that he was staring at some blatant depiction or celebration of sexual shenanigans. The place was a shrine to shagging.

Glart felt his cheeks turning pink as he tried not to stare at the framed prints which adorned the walls – prints of couples at it with a vengeance in all varieties of costumes, places and positions. He felt the pink turning to red as his eyes fell upon a row of shelves covered with statues of impossibly-endowed orcs, erect elves and priapic gods, all of whom appeared to be pointing unpleasantly in his direction. And he felt the red shading towards crimson as he tried not to think of the uses for the vast range of other leather, metal and wooden objects and mechanisms that adorned the walls and hung from the smoke-stained wooden beams of the ceiling.

With his eyes averted he reached the bar and rested his hands on the cool wood. Then he looked up to meet the eyes of the landlady. Immediately his cheeks began to burn hotly and he knew that the crimson must be edging towards vermilion. He wouldn't have been surprised if jets of steam were hissing out of his ears. It wasn't her lazy smile, or her deep green eyes, or the low-cut blouse that showed off her voluptuous figure. It was the way her hand was caressing one of the beer pumps, which was carved into the shape of a large and extremely realistic phallus. In fact, he realised, all the other beer pumps were carved into the same shape. There was a whole row of ten or more of them, standing rigidly to attention. They reminded Glart of the last time he'd described one of his visions to the other novices in the shower.

'Hello, brother!' said the landlady, in tones which were so warmly welcoming that Glart thought his ears were going to melt. 'What do you fancy?'

Glart dragged his eyes away from her hand and fixed them on a point somewhere above her head, and immediately regretted it. He was focusing on a shelf above the bar which held a row of what appeared to be plaster casts of erect penises.

'I see you're admiring my collection,' breathed the landlady, and Glart swallowed so loudly that he could have sworn the windows rattled. The landlady smiled and made a noise that sounded like a cat purring on a distant mountainside.

'You look rather hot,' she said. 'Perhaps you'd like some nice, fresh lemon juice?'

She reached under the bar and then leaned towards him and held out her hand. He realised that she was holding a large lemon.

'Would you like me to . . . squeeze it for you?' she asked.

Glart's vision began to blur.

'You look like you could do with a . . . stiff one,' she continued. 'Do you touch . . . hard liquor?'

For a moment the room seemed to be spinning and Glart found that he was having difficulty in breathing. Then all at once everything clicked into place in his brain. Of course! This was simply an example of something Abbot Tellow had described as 'innuendo', and was apparently just a normal part of everyday socialising. Glart's vision cleared and the room stood still; the panic attack was over. He knew what to do.

Smiling confidently, he stared straight into the landlady's eyes.

'The harder the better,' he said, and then paused for an instant. 'Mine's a large one,' he added.

The landlady smiled back. It was as though Glart had passed some sort of test.

'I'd think a flagon of ale would be more in your line, brother,' she said, and now her tone was purely conversational.

'I'd love one,' Glart told her, doubtfully, 'but I'm afraid that . . . well, as a Cedrician, I don't have any money . . .'

'Oh, don't worry about that. We've had one or two of you magic monks in here before. You can eat and drink your fill, and later I'll find a couple of small jobs you can sort out with your magic, okay?'

Glart nodded. This was how he had been told it would be in the outside world, but he was relieved to find that the system actually worked. He'd just have to hope that his magic was up to whatever she required, but he'd been told that inns and taverns usually made simple requests, such as asking for a *Spell of Excellence* to be cast on their beer, and even for a novice that was straightforward, first level stuff.

As the landlady took hold of one of the obscene pumps and began to pour his ale, Glart dragged his eyes away, unwilling to watch. Instead, he buried his head in a menu that was standing on the bar. To his surprise, he found that it was a price-list of cocktails. He read down the list and wished he hadn't, for some of the names were even more blatant than the tavern's statue collection. *Ye Gods!* he thought. *Surely dwarves can't do that! And even if they can, who'd want to name a drink after it?*

The landlady put his beer in front of him.

'There you go,' she said. 'There's a pot of chicken stew bubbling on the fire in the kitchen. I'll bring you some through. I'm afraid it's a bit of a quiet night tonight and there's not much in the way of company here, but I'm sure those two over there wouldn't mind if you joined them.'

Glart turned to look at the elf and the cave-troll. Both appeared to have had quite a bit to drink, and their table was littered with empty glasses.

'Perhaps later,' he said. 'For the moment I need some rest and some quiet contemplation.'

He took his beer across to a table near the fire and sat staring into the flames for a while, thinking about his mission. Despite his determination to make the most of his time outside the confines of the abbey and to enjoy himself, Glart was at heart a dedicated and honest man, and he had already vowed to himself that he would do his best to accomplish his task. The trouble was that, as tasks go, it was pretty vague.

Apparently, from what the abbot had told him, he was supposed to stop some long-dead evil wizard's power from rising again and screwing up the world, and all he had to go on was a vision he'd had of a beautiful girl and a conviction that she was the key. He thought about this for a good while, turning it around in his mind and examining things from every angle, until he came to a single unescapable conclusion.

I must be out of my tiny mind, he decided.

When the landlady brought his food over he chatted to her for a while and discovered that her name was Malenda. No further customers had come into the tavern, and so after accepting another flagon of beer, Glart rose and made his way across to sit with the elf and the cave-troll. As he had thought, they were both very drunk, but they seemed happy for him to join them.

The elf, Legless, was a slim, wiry guy with the usual elven good looks, pointed ears, and flint-like green eyes that were currently having difficulty in focusing. The cave-troll was called Ugman, and appeared to be completely unlike most others of his species. Glart had heard that cave-trolls were a ferociously violent race who tended to hit first and ask questions afterwards (something they picked up from their teachers at nursery school), but Ugman was a complete pussy-cat. Despite being nearly seven feet high and built like a brick outhouse, he appeared to be very gentle. He also had a quick wit and a ready intelligence, whereas most cave-trolls had difficulty in counting as far as three without getting a really bad headache.

Their conversation was entertaining, if slurred, and tended to go round in ever-decreasing circles. Glart discovered that they were students at Koumas University. Ugman had just been to visit his family under the Telluric Mountains, and Legless had gone with him. They were travelling back to Koumas to continue their studies. After a few more beers they suggested that Glart might like to travel with them next day. Then they ordered another few more beers, after which they *insisted* he travel with them. Several more beers later, Glart agreed.

It was well after eleven o'clock by the time he made his unsteady way up the stairs to his room. He washed his face and was just about to get into bed when there was a gentle knock on the door. Wondering what anyone could want at this time of the night, he opened the door, and Malenda the landlady pushed past him and undulated into his room, carrying something on a tray under a white towel.

'You did say that you'd be kind enough to do a small job for me,' she reminded him.

'Well, yes,' Glart began. 'What is it that you want me . . .'

But then his voice ran down, because Malenda had removed the towel and he'd seen what was on the tray. There was a bowl of water, a jar of aromatic massage oil, two glasses of sparkling wine and a dish of what looked suspiciously like freshly-mixed, ready-to-use plaster of Paris.

Malenda sat down on the bed and looked at him steadily. She was wearing only a white shirt that reached halfway down her thighs. Her skin glowed and her green eyes sparkled and danced in the candle-light.

'I want to add you to my collection,' she said.

Glart tried to think, but his brain seemed to have jammed. He stared at the landlady like a hungry hobbit staring at a plateful of cream cakes. For a twenty-year-old who had never even touched a woman this was like a dream come true, but Cedrician monks were supposed to live life according to their vow of chastity. *Mind you*, he thought, *I'm still a novice. I haven't actually taken any vows yet . . .*

Then, once again, Glart thought back to the words of Abbot Tellow, and everything was suddenly crystal clear in his mind. He had been told that he had responsibilities which he was obliged to live up to. There were certain things that a Cedrician monk was pledged to do, and he must follow this rule. It had been made clear to him in his training that, in the outside world, once he had taken food, drink or lodging from some charitable person, he had a binding obligation to repay them in any way that he could.

I've drunk her beer and eaten her food, he thought. *I have a responsibility to do what she requires. Ah, well, I guess I can live with that . . .*

49

'Okay,' he said, smiling despite the fact that a whole swarm of butterflies had suddenly become airborne inside his stomach. Malenda grinned back at him.

'Good boy,' she said, and slid the shirt off her tanned shoulders.

It was a very quiet and contemplative threesome that set off from the *Troll's Bollocks* the next morning. Legless was quiet because he had a barnstorming hangover that was so bad he had sworn off alcohol for ever. Ugman was quiet because he had joined his friend in swearing off alcohol and was regretting it already. And Glart was quiet, partly out of respect for his new companions' mood, partly because he needed to plan ahead and decide what the hell he was going to do when he arrived in Koumas, but mainly because he was feeling so incredibly pleased with life that he didn't trust himself to open his mouth without either bursting into song or giggling like a maniac.

The going was easy, for the road was straight, and the land on either side was flat, fertile farmland. It was another sunny day, warm without being uncomfortable, and after the overnight rain, the countryside smelt wonderfully fresh. As they walked along, their spirits (and Legless' hangover) gradually lifted until at last they began to enjoy the journey.

By evening they had covered more than half the distance to Koumas, despite stopping to pass the time of day with several other folk. Glart was eager to find a comfortable tavern with an attractive landlady, and the other two had to explain to him that bed and breakfast didn't usually entail the little extras that he had enjoyed the previous night. As it was a warm evening with little prospect of rain, they suggested sleeping out under the stars, and the crestfallen Glart agreed.

It wasn't long before they had found a sheltered little woodland dell. Legless built a small fire, and Ugman boiled the eggs that Glart had been given by a grateful farmer, in return for a spell of *Cure Lameness* he had cast on the man's horse. They ate them with the bread that he had been given in return for a *Banish* spell cast on the rats that infested a small bakery, and then Glart broached the winesack that he had been given by Malenda as a memento of an interesting night. Legless decided to share the wine, on the grounds that it might help cure the remnants of his hangover, and Ugman joined in as well, on the grounds that he would be letting his friends down if he didn't.

As they sat round the fire, with the stars glinting in the pitch black sky, passing the wine back and forth and swapping stories, Glart thought of all the other novices back at the monastery. At this time of the evening they would be eating some plain, boring meal in the draughty refectory before trooping off to their hard, lonely beds. Suddenly, the prospect of returning there filled him with fear.

A while later, Glart wandered out of the dell to relieve himself. When he returned, Legless and Ugman were smoking a thick, hand-rolled cigarette which they were passing back and forth. Glart had tried smoking the previous night and had enjoyed it, and so when they offered the new cigarette to him, he accepted.

'It's really good shit, man,' Legless assured him. Glart was both revolted and surprised that they would make cigarettes from something so foul, but he had to admit that it tasted a lot better than he expected, and so he joined in with a will and tried not to think where it had originated.

That night, sleeping the sleep of the highly pissed and totally stoned, Glart had the most vivid vision he had ever experienced. He saw the woman with the long, dark hair again, and he saw himself meeting her in a small Koumas tavern. He saw the name of the tavern on the inn sign that hung above the door: it was the *Wyvern*. He saw that the woman was both worried and frightened. Then, to his embarrassment, he saw her in bed, lying in the arms of a man. There was something familiar about this man, but it was only when he turned in his sleep that Glart realised it was him.

But then he saw something that wrenched him from his vision and from sleep, jerking him bolt upright, wide awake, sober and sweating with fear in the darkness. He saw the woman again. She was dressed in leather riding-gear and was wet from the rain, and yet somehow he knew she was about to be married. She was walking into a chapel to meet her husband-to-be, happy and beautiful, but alone. And he saw the face of the man who was hiding in the shadows nearby. The man who was waiting to kill her.

CHAPTER SIX

Macoby was having one of the most embarrassing conversations of her life. She was sitting at a table in the *Weyr Inn*, sipping a mug of something that was supposed to be coffee but which tasted as though it had been made by boiling up dead tom-cats, and was arguing with Darian's ghost and with the amulet. Unfortunately, the tavern was quite full, even though it was only mid-morning, and no-one else could see the ghost. As a result, it looked as though she was having a heated conversation with a small pewter pig's head, and one or two of the other customers had already made pointed comments about loony madwomen who shouldn't be allowed out without their minders.

She would have gone back upstairs to her room, but she had hardly eaten for twenty-four hours and she was determined to have some breakfast. Nor did she want to wait until later for the conversation, because an awful lot of questions that needed answering had popped into her mind while she had slept, and she had a strange feeling that her two unusual companions might disappear at any moment.

The questions had begun mounting up the previous evening while she was sitting in that field in the encroaching dusk, miles from anywhere. When she had eventually finished verbally abusing the ghost (who had gone so pale that he was virtually ultra-white), there had been a long silence during which the ghost had sulked, the amulet had fallen asleep making a slight snoring sound, and Macoby had taken her anger out on a couple of passing caterpillars belting them flat with a handy rock. Then she had felt guilty about this, which had made her even crosser, and so she had spent some time staring at the ground and vowing to herself that whoever was behind all this was going to suffer.

When she had eventually looked up, the ghost had still been hovering apologetically nearby, and had looked close to tears.

'I'm really, really sorry,' he had muttered, 'but I honestly can't help it. Something is dragging me around after you!'

Macoby had given this a moment's thought, and the obvious solution had struck her.

'Come with me,' she'd ordered the ghost, and putting the snoring amulet down on top of a cabbage, she'd walked quietly away from it with the ghost following reluctantly. They'd gone about forty feet when the ghost had suddenly stopped.

'I'm stuck!' he'd said, mournfully.

'That's it!' Macoby had cried, clapping her hands. 'You're not tied to me at all, you're tied to that *klatting* amulet.'

For a few seconds she had contemplated just walking off and leaving ghost and jewel to the pleasure of each other's company, but then wiser councils had prevailed. Both of her newly-acquired companions appeared to be closely entwined with whatever was going on, and she needed to find out what they knew.

Returning to the amulet, she had picked it up and shaken it awake. After a lot of indignant spluttering, it had told her that, yes, it could do another *Transference* spell. Seconds later, she had found herself back in her bedroom at the *Weyr Inn*. Tired out, she had gone straight to bed.

After a fragmented night's sleep in which dreams of happy, childhood days with Marden had been interwoven with nightmares of hidden, nameless monsters, she had found herself awake (just), alert (almost), and hungry for food and for information. However, after hurrying down to the tavern and ordering coffee, her first question to the pig's head amulet (what exactly are you?) had been met with a reply that was unfathomable, unending, and verbose in the extreme. The only thing she could tell from it was that the thing really enjoyed the sound of its own voice.

Eventually, after it had told her that a chemical analysis would reveal it currently to be seventy-nine point four per cent tin, nineteen point six per cent lead, nought point nine per cent antimony, with a few trace elements making up the rest, and was just moving on to a brief lecture on atomic theory (whatever that was), Macoby realised that she'd had enough.

'Shut up,' she told it.

The pig's head looked hurt.

'I was only answering the . . .'

'Shut up! The landlord's coming over!'

The amulet lapsed into hurt silence and Macoby looped it round her neck by its chain and dropped it down the front of her jerkin. Then she watched as the landlord shambled across to her table. This particular landlord was short, thin and wiry, with scabrous, ugly skin and wart-ridden features. His lank, oily hair and his fang-like teeth gave the impression that he probably had quite a lot of orc blood in him, and Macoby thought she could tell where it had got in.

He walked round the table, through the ghost, who looked rather startled at this, and stood leering down at her. Macoby flinched. The guy's breath could have stripped wallpaper from ten feet away.

'The barmaid said you've asked for breakfast,' he snarled.

'That's right,' Macoby answered. 'I'd like scrambled eggs with salmon and chives, please. Not too heavy on the pepper. And some wheat bread, lightly toasted, with butter. And a small pot of apricot jam, if you could.'

The landlord looked down at her and raised a condescending eyebrow. He looked like a landlord who has just been asked for a unicorn burger with gryphon eggs.

'Oh, and could you replace the coffee, please,' carried on Macoby. 'This batch tastes like mud.'

'It should do,' came the reply. 'It was ground this morning.'

There was a short pause while the landlord rocked with mirth at his own little joke and Macoby looked at him as though she had just stepped in him.

'Very funny,' she told him. 'Now, about my breakfast . . .'

'Listen, miss,' he interrupted, and Macoby got the distinct impression from the way he said it, *miss* was Orcish for *pain in the arse*. 'We do a set breakfast here. I fries it meself. It's good, plain fare, none of yer poncified, la-di-da cookery. Now, do you want one or not?'

Macoby had already seen several customers eating the breakfasts. There appeared to be four choices: eggs fried in lard, steak fried in lard, steak and eggs fried in lard, and steak and eggs fried in lard with extra lard poured over the top. None of them were the most attractive prospects that she'd ever faced.

'I wish you knew how to cook a decent breakfast,' she told the landlord.

There was an ever-so-faint flash of light, so brief that at first she thought she'd imagined it. For the same brief instant, the landlord's sludge-brown eyes appeared to glow with a sudden inner fire. Then there was a long pause. He seemed to be thinking something over.

'I'll tell you what, he said, after a while. 'I could do you scrambled eggs and smoked salmon with a couple of freshly baked brioches. Or, if you fancy a change, what about a nice poached-turbot kedgeree with melba toast? No? Oh well, scrambled eggs is it, then.'

Macoby watched him disappear into the kitchen with amazement, then hauled out the amulet and stared at it. It was looking insufferably smug.

'That was you, wasn't it?' she demanded.

'Just a little *Enlightenment* spell,' it replied, trying to sound modest and missing by several miles. 'Nothing special. Your wish is my command, as they say. Oops!'

If a pewter pig's head could look embarrassed, all of a sudden this one was doing so.

'Ah-ha!' said Macoby, catching on. 'So not only can you do spells, but you also have to grant my wishes, right?'

'Look, there's no need to go jumping to conclusions, just because I've let my mouth run away with me a little.'

'I wish you to tell me whether you have to grant my wishes.'

'Oh, bugger!' The amulet looked as though it was trying to find a way round this one. After a few seconds it gave up. 'Oh, all right. Yes. As long as the magical spell exists to grant them, that is.'

Macoby shoved it back down her jerkin, then sat back and thought about this. It was pretty powerful magic, more powerful by far than anything she had yet encountered. So where on earth had her brother found this jewel?

She looked across at Darian's ghost, who had lowered himself into the chair opposite and was practising sitting in it, without much success. He would manage to stay on the seat for a few seconds, but would then start sinking through it towards the floor before hoisting himself back up with an exclamation of annoyance.

'Hey, ghost,' she said.

Darian's ghost gazed worriedly at her.

'Ghost,' he murmured, surprised. 'Yes, I suppose that's what I am. Heavy.' He thought about it. 'What a bummer,' he added, philosophically.

Ye Gods! thought Macoby. *Talk about the death and soul of the party . . .*

'Look, er . . .' She stopped, wondering what the convention was in polite society for addressing the spirits of the departed. 'Do you have a name?'

'Darian.'

'Well, Darian . . .' Again she stopped. 'My brother Marden knew a Darian. He was a soldier, I think.'

The ghost stared at her.

'The Lord Marden was your brother?' he asked. 'Then you must be the princess . . . um . . . oh, lord, my memory . . .'

'Macoby.'

'Macoby, yes.' The ghost lapsed into thought, concentrating so hard that he forgot about the chair and began to slide through it again.

'Lord Marden mentioned you a lot on that last evening, my lady,' he said, after a while. 'He seemed very concerned about you. He was talking of you when he gave me the amulet to look after.'

Suddenly Macoby was very still.

'Which amulet?' she asked. 'What did it look like?'

'It's difficult to remember . . .' Darian's ghost waved his disembodied arms in front of his face as though trying to clear away the mists that enveloped his memory. 'It was an ugly metal thing, an orc's face . . .'

Macoby hauled the amulet out from her jerkin. The pig's face was grinning unpleasantly.

'It's nice and warm down there,' it leered, 'nestling in between your . . .'

'Shut up! I wish for you to change back into the form you were in when I first found you.'

'Do I have to?'

'Just do it.'

The pendant gave a long-suffering sigh. Then it seemed to melt in her hand, flowing and darkening until once again it was the ugly, battered orc face she had first seen.

'Is this the one he gave you?' she asked the ghost.

'Yes,' he nodded. 'He asked me to keep it safe. But there was more. He charged me with something else, but I cannot seem to recall . . .'

Once again Darian's ghost drifted off into the netherworld of his memory. Macoby dropped the amulet down the front of her jerkin, then hastily fished it out again.

'I wish for you to keep your eyes closed the entire time you're in there,' she told it. 'Okay?'

The orc face frowned.

'Spoilsport!' it muttered as she dropped it back down her jerkin, and she could hear it grumbling to itself beneath the leather.

Macoby turned her attention back to Darian's ghost, who had got so distracted by trying to remember things that he had forgotten about his problems with the chair. As a result, he was now sitting on the floor, with his head and shoulders projecting above the seat.

'And you kept the amulet, as Darian requested?' she asked.

'Yes.'

'Then that must have been your body on the battlefield!'

The ghost nodded, and Macoby stared at him with a mixture of pity and horror.

'Many of us died,' the ghost told her, 'but all the others went on up. I couldn't. It must be because that thing is keeping me here. But I don't now why or how it is doing so.'

'Then we'll ask it,' she said, but at that moment the landlord reappeared with her breakfast.

'Later,' she added in a whisper to the ghost, then she fixed a hopeful smile on her face as the landlord crossed the room with a tray.

To her surprise, the battered wooden plate which he placed in front of her held a generous and beautifully-cooked portion of scrambled eggs with smoked salmon and chives. There was a rack of perfect toast, and a pot of butter.

'I'm sorry, we ain't got no jam,' he apologised. 'I'll make sure we've got some for tomorrer.'

'Thank you,' replied Macoby, a bit taken aback by this new example of the amulet's powers.

The landlord bowed and withdrew, and a few minutes later a serving-lad scuttled across with a fresh pot of coffee that was a vast improvement on the first one. Macoby sat and enjoyed the food, which was cooked to perfection, while her brain ticked over. Then, when she had finished and had enjoyed a second cup of coffee, she turned back to the ghost.

'Come on,' she ordered. 'We'll talk in my room.'

As she crossed to the door leading to the stairs, Macoby noticed that several perplexed customers were looking askance at their breakfasts. At the bar, two hulking great soldiers were complaining bitterly to the landlord about the exquisitely-served but insubstantial portions of eggs Benedict that they had been given.

That poor man is going to be forced rapidly up-market, she thought, grinning to herself. *That is, if one of those soldiers doesn't force something else rapidly up him first . . .*

Back upstairs in her room, she sat herself down in a chair beside her window, overlooking the busy street, and waited. A few seconds later, Darian's ghost drifted through the wall.

'You wouldn't believe what they're up to in the next bedroom,' he began. 'There's four of them, a bloke and three women, and . . .'

But then he saw the expression on Macoby's face and decided that to continue might be a serious mistake.

'If you're *quite* finished,' said Macoby, in a voice like ice cracking. There was a short, embarrassed silence.

'Right,' she continued, fishing out the amulet again. 'I think it's time we found out exactly what sort of a hold over you this cruddy jewel has.'

But the amulet couldn't, or wouldn't, give them a complete answer. It admitted that a *Soul Shackle* spell was holding Darian, but no matter how they tried, it refused to tell them who had placed it or how it could be countermanded.

'Look, there's nothing I can do!' it shouted heatedly, after Macoby had threatened to have it melted down and turned into a nose-stud. 'I can no more break the rules that govern me than you could lay an egg!'

And with that it lapsed into a sulky silence.

Macoby sat and thought for a bit, turning the amulet around in her hands. As the daughter of the Regent of Koumas, she had worn a lot of jewelry, but she'd never heard of anything that was as powerful or as chatty as this particular piece. Or as downright ugly.

'Could you change into something that's not quite so unpleasant?' she asked it, after a while.

The amulet sniffed.

'Good grief!' it muttered. 'Picky, picky, picky!'

'Please?'

'Oh, all right. What do you suggest?'

'Something a bit more feminine.'

The amulet shuddered, but then once again it melted and flowed, this time ending up as a pendant in the shape of a slender silver unicorn with tiny emerald eyes.

'Happy now?' the unicorn asked.

Macoby nodded, and turned her attention to Darian's ghost, who had got fed up with hanging around and had drifted across to the wall and shoved his head through to watch the goings-on on the other side.

'Darian,' she snapped. The ghost jumped and, dragging his head back into the room, he turned and looked at her guiltily.

'It's not fair,' he complained. 'I never had a go with three women when I was alive. I mean, *three* women! That's just plain greedy!'

'Tough,' she told him. 'Now, listen. You said Marden gave you the amulet to keep it safe?'

The ghost nodded.

'But why did he give it to you? Why didn't he keep it himself?'

'I think he knew that someone else was after it, and that he was in danger. I didn't know him well, although he trusted me. No-one would have expected me to have it.'

'Can you remember anything else he told you?'

Darian's ghost shook his head slowly.

'There was more, but . . . it won't come.'

Macoby remembered the questions that Sarakkan had raised, and his doubts about the battle.

'I want you to think back to the battle. Concentrate.'

The ghost took up a serious pose, one hand holding his chin, as though desperately trying to convince her that he was indeed concentrating.

'Was there anything . . . odd about it?'

'There were too many orcs. Their army was just a few hundred strong, we were told, but there were ten times that many. And they were beating us . . . we must have had reinforcements after I died, or we would have lost. They were too strong for us, far too strong . . .'

The ghost's voice began to quiver, and his eerie face shook. Macoby suddenly realised that he was crying unseen, formless tears.

'Look, I'm sorry,' she began, but the ghost just flapped a spectral hand at her.

'Don't worry,' he told her. 'It's a bit difficult to come to terms with, is dying. I'll get used to it.'

'Get a life!' muttered the amulet, and Macoby shushed it and quickly shoved it back inside her jerkin again.

'That's the spirit,' she told the ghost, then could have bitten her tongue, but he didn't seem to notice the unintended joke. She sat back in her chair and massaged her temples, bemused, then stared out of the window at the bustling crowds in the street below.

What the hell was going on? It seemed that every answer she found just raised a load more questions. Was this pendant the reason that Marden had died? And if her brother was dead, what had happened to his body? Was it his doing that Darian's ghost was trapped?

And then there were the questions that Sarakkan had posed. Who had reported that only a few hundred orcs had invaded when in fact there were two thousand? Why did they invade in the first place? Why was Colonel De Wenchas dissatisfied with Myal's actions? And, if Darian's memory of the battle was correct, why had the orc army retreated when they appeared to be winning the battle hands down?

After a bit of thought, Macoby came to the conclusion that she had two options. Firstly, she could ignore all the warnings and doubts, go back to the palace and start throwing her weight about until she got some answers. Or secondly, she could lie low and do a little bit of investigation of her own.

All at once she was convinced she was making a complete prat of herself. What the hell was she doing, hiding in some rundown, godforsaken tavern just because her brother had got a bit worried and had then disappeared? How could she be in danger in the palace, surrounded by guards and by friends? And she should be with her father . . . he was very ill, possibly dying. Sarakkan was right. She had to go home!

But then, just as her mind was made up, she saw a group of

soldiers making their way along the street, occasionally pausing to question local traders and passers-by. They wore helms with the distinctive red cockade of Minas Lantan, and she knew them instantly for members of Myal's personal guard. She wondered what on earth they were doing in this part of town, but then one of the stall-holders pointed to the *Weyr Inn*, and she recognised him as one of those who had been laughing at her in the tavern before breakfast.

The leader of the soldiers nodded to the trader, then shouted an order at his troops. Immediately, they began to push their way hurriedly through the crowds towards Macoby's refuge. Somehow, she had a feeling that they weren't on their way to sample the wonderful new breakfasts. No, there was only one thing inside this tavern that they could be seeking. Her.

Ducking back from the window, a hand to her mouth, Macoby wondered what Sarakkan had told her father. Was she now engaged to Myal against her will? Had he sent his soldiers out to bring his reluctant bride back to the palace by force? And then she remembered Sarakkan's doubts. Could Myal really be under an enchantment, or was there something even more sinister going on? What if someone *did* want to harm her, and that person was him? But why? What possible reason could he have? No – there was no time to think of that now. She had to decide what to do.

Quickly she ran through the alternatives open to her. She could hide – but if that stall-holder had told them she was here, they would look until they found her. She could face the soldiers down and refuse to leave with them. But what if they were under orders to kill? These soldiers were fiercely loyal to Myal and would do whatever he had commanded . . .

By the gods, she had to escape! She'd wasted too much time, and now she'd be seen if she went down the stairs. It would have to be , the window!

Macoby leapt up and peered out. The last of the soldiers was just entering the front door of the tavern. She grabbed the window-sash and heaved, but the *klatting* thing was stuck fast and refused to open. Macoby seized the chamberpot from under the bed and was just about to hurl it through the glass when the obvious escape route hit her.

Yanking the amulet out from her jerkin, she yelled at it.

'Get me out of here!'

'Where to?' asked the unicorn.

'Anywhere! No, urm . . . Colonel De Wenchas's office!'

'I'm afraid I can't do that.'

Close to panic, Macoby stared at the objectionable little jewel. Was it all part of the plot? Was the amulet conpsiring against her as well?

'Why not?' she gasped.

'Because you've never been there before. I can only take you to places where you've already been. That's how I see to transport you, by using the scenes in your memory.'

There was a heavy hammering on the door.

'Take me to wherever Sarakkan is!'

'Sorry, can't do that, either.'

'Well, transport me to Neero Square,' she hissed. '*Klatting* quick!'

'Tut, tut!' said the pendant. 'Language!'

There was a loud *crash!* and the door flew open, but then every-thing was instantaneously blanked out by a blinding flash, and all of a sudden Macoby found she was standing beside one of the massive linden trees surrounding the vast square, still clutching the chamber-pot. She sagged against the cool bark of the tree, weak with relief.

'You cut that a bit close,' she muttered under her breath, but the amulet didn't deign to reply.

Then there was another one of those faint, apologetic *pops* that she was beginning to get used to, and Darian's ghost was once again hovering beside her. As usual, no-one else seemed to be aware of his presence, but there was a small pack of pi-dogs rooting around near some bins, and they sent up a furious racket of howling, barking and snarling. Macoby realised that everyone in the square was turning to see what the source of the commotion was. For someone who was trying to keep a low profile, she seemed to be attracting an awful lot of attention.

'Let's move it!' she snapped, forgetting that wherever she went, the amulet and the ghost were forced to follow.

'Where are we going?' asked the ghost.

'To the army barracks,' she told him as she crossed the square. 'I've heard a few interesting rumours that Colonel De Wenchas wasn't too impressed with our army's tactics at the battle yesterday. I want to find out more.'

'How are you going to do that?'

'Well, it's a bit of an outlandish idea, but I thought I might try asking Colonel De Wenchas. I mean, call me optimistic, but he might just be able to help.'

Darian's ghost mulled this over.

'You're being sarcastic, aren't you?' he said, in injured tones.

'Got it in one,' she replied.

They came to the end of the row of linden trees. Ahead, on her left, Macoby could see the high sandstone wall that shut off the army barracks from the outside world. As she strode across the worn-down cobbles towards the gateway, she was suddenly seized by a conviction that she was being watched, but when she looked around, no-one appeared to be paying her the slightest bit of attention. In fact, the only people in sight were an old flower-seller on the other side of the square and three drunken winos who were arguing in slurred voices near the entrance to an alleyway.

Shaking her head and telling herself to get a grip, Macoby strode through the gate, then stopped dead and stared at the scene ahead of her. The barracks building was set back from the square, with a large courtyard in front of it that was usually full of soldiers involved in marching, drilling, and all those other pointless wastes of time beloved of army officers. But today, the courtyard was all but deserted, and the main building was sealed off by temporary red and white striped barriers. A few uniformed officers were clustered on the near side of these barriers like chicks that had lost their mother, staring forlornly at the offices from which they had for some reason been excluded. On guard in front of the main entrance were a couple of very bulky policemen, and two more were on duty at the barrier.

Macoby realised that a change of plan was required. Something out of the ordinary was obviously going on, and if high-ranking officers were being kept out of their own barracks, the policemen on duty obviously weren't going to allow some unknown chit of a girl into the place. She would have to pull rank.

Reaching into the small, secret pocket inside her jerkin, she pulled out her signet ring and slipped her index finger through it. Then she marched openly into the courtyard and up to the barrier.

The two policemen looked down at her with the undisguised

contempt that their species reserves for anyone who is, firstly, female and, secondly, not another policeman.

'I've come to see Colonel De Wenchas,' Macoby said.

'This ain't a *klatting* side-show, darling,' sneered the larger of the two. 'Now, why don't you run along home and cook the lunch.'

Macoby smiled sweetly at him and held out her hand. Her ring glinted in the morning sunshine. The policeman glanced at it and then did a rapid double-take as he recognised the royal arms of Koumas etched into the design.

'The daughter of the Regent of Koumas does not cook lunch,' she told him, regally. 'She has a large staff of cooks, chefs and scullery-maids to do it for her. And she has numerous pot-boys to do the washing-up, several of whom are policemen who have been demoted from the National Troopers for making just the sort of serious mistake you're currently making . . .'

The policemen had gone the sort of dirty, off-white colour of very old underwear.

'Your highness,' he gasped. 'I didn't recognise you! Er . . . of course you can see the colonel!'

'He is here, then?'

'Yes, he's still here.'

He turned and signalled to one of his comrades by the entrance to the building, and a minute later, Macoby was following this second man along a twisting corridor that led towards the rear of the barracks.

As they came to the end of the corridor, the officer took a wooden torch from a rack in the wall and lit it, then led her through a door and down some stone steps to the basement. Macoby followed doubtfully. Where the hell was he taking her? Surely such an important commander wouldn't have an office down here in the bowels of the building?

They began to walk along a cold, stone-flagged corridor that was unlit save for their torch. The walls were bare, undecorated plaster, and spider-webs hung from the ceiling. Nervously, Macoby loosened the small but lethally sharp dagger she kept hidden in a sheath on her lower arm, ready to defend herself should this turn out to be a trap. But when the policeman ushered her into a cold, marble-lined mortuary and she saw the blood-stained body lying on a stark stone slab, she understood. The colonel was dead!

'I need to be alone to pay my respects,' she told the policeman. 'Leave me the light.'

'Er . . . right then, ma'am.' He nodded doubtfully and handed her the torch. 'I'll be outside if you need me.'

As the door closed Macoby crossed to stand beside the colonel's corpse and lifted the torch to examine him. It wasn't too difficult to work out how he'd died. Whoever had smashed his skull open and slit his throat had done a thorough job.

'This was not done during the battle,' said the ghost. He was floating on the other side of the slab and was looking down at the colonel with an expression of sadness.

Macoby refrained from saying that if it had been done during the battle, the guy would have found it very difficult to express his doubts to Sarakkan afterwards.

'How do you know?'

'Because that was the day before yesterday. He was killed exactly twenty-five hours ago.'

'Are you sure?'

'Yes. It seems to be a talent that ghosts have. I can look at someone's corpse and tell exactly when they died.'

'Can you tell who did it?'

'No.'

'Great!' Macoby thought for a moment. 'What about you?' she asked the amulet, which was still nestling next to her skin. 'Can you help?'

'What?' came a muffled reply from inside her jerkin. 'Help what? Where?'

'Aren't you paying attention?'

'Look, you ordered me to keep my eyes shut!' There was an air of self-righteousness about the amulet's voice that set Macoby's teeth on edge. 'How am I supposed to know what's going on?'

'I wanted to ask Colonel De Wenchas here a few questions, but someone has murdered him. Can you help?'

'Er . . . well, I suppose we could try a *Regenerate the Dead* spell.'

'What? You mean you could bring him back to life?'

65

'No, not exactly. He'd still be dead, but he'd be a zombie, able to talk, and to totter round, and to carry out a few basic tasks, although they're very slow, are zombies. Apparently, the spell is quite popular with unscrupulous employers as a method of finding cheap labour. You get quite a lot of them working behind Post Office counters.'

'Would it help us?'

'Probably not. You tend to find that the dead don't have very accurate memories of what happened to them when they were the living.'

'You're telling me!' muttered Macoby, with a sidelong glance at the ghost.

At that moment the door swung open and another policeman advanced into the room. He was a detective constable, smaller and slimmer than the others, but with a sharpness and an air of intelligence about him.

'Can I help you, my lady?' he asked, in the voice of one who would like to say 'What the *klat* do you think you're doing?' but is prevented by royal protocol.

'No, thank you,' Macoby replied gracefully. 'I've finished paying my respects to the colonel.'

'Then I shall see you to the door, my lady.'

It was a polite but firm request for her to leave, and Macoby could tell that the officer suspected her reasons for being there.

'That would be most kind of you, constable . . . ?'

'Kratavan, my lady. DC Kratavan.'

Macoby nodded, and allowed herself to be ushered through the door.

'Do you have any idea who did this?' she asked him.

'We're following up a number of leads.'

'In other words, no.' Macoby couldn't keep the anger out of her voice. 'The colonel has been dead for twenty-five hours, and you haven't discovered a single . . .'

'How do you know that?' interrupted Kratavan.

'What?'

'How do you know how long he's been dead?'

'I overheard one of your officers talking,' lied Macoby, furious with herself for making such a stupid mistake. Kratavan nodded, but she could see that he was not entirely convinced. *I'd better get out of here before I get arrested for murder*, she thought. Putting on speed, she fairly shot along the corridor to the stairs, and Kratavan almost had to run to keep up with her.

As they reached the front door she turned to thank him and was shocked to see the suspicion etched plainly on his face.

. 'Well . . .' she began.

'I think the inspector would appreciate a word with you, my lady,' Kratavan cut in.

'Tell him to contact me for an audience at the palace,' she ordered loftily, and strode out of the door. As she had expected, Kratavan didn't dare stop her, and she fairly flew across the courtyard and out into the square.

Walking quickly across the cobbled pavement, she dived down the first side-alley she came to, half-expecting to hear sounds of pursuit, but no-one was following her. *This is ridiculous*, she told herself. *You're likely to be the next Regent of this city, and yet you're diving in side-alleys like some petty sneak-thief! Pull yourself together, girl!*

She looked around, wondering where the ghost had got to, but there was no sign of him. The only other occupants of the alley were the three winos who were slumped against the wall, dead to the world. She turned away from them and hauled the amulet out into view.

'Okay,' she told it, 'I want some answers.'

'Right then,' it replied. 'Forty-two. To get to the other side. Three point one four one five nine. Chicken tikka.'

'What the hell are you going on about?'

'I'm giving you some answers,' the amulet replied, primly. 'If they're not the answers you want, then maybe you could do me the favour of telling me which question you have in mind.'

'I wish that you'd tell me what's going on,' Macoby snarled.

'Coo, the easy ones first, eh? Well, you're about to be assassinated, for a start.'

Macoby stared at the detestable thing in horror. Then she heard the merest scrape of a boot on cobblestones from behind her and she swung round to find that the amulet was right, and death was mere seconds away.

The three winos were creeping silently towards her with drawn daggers in their hands, awake, alert and most definitely stone-cold sober. They were just a few feet from her, and beneath their outermost rags she could now see the distinctive garb of the Guild of Assassins. With horror she realised that she had walked straight into the jaws of a trap.

As she opened her mouth to scream for help, they sprang at her. In an instant, her dagger was in her hand, and more by luck than by skill she just managed to divert the first slash, gasping with fear as the lethal blade missed her neck by no more than an inch. Instinctively she riposted, and her blade slammed home into the chest of the nearest assassin. At the same time she saw the other two blades lunging towards her unprotected body.

'Save me!' she screamed, and there was an instantaneous and distinctly soggy explosion. The two remaining assailants simply burst apart, and she and the whole alleyway was showered by flying gobbets of flesh, blood and tissue.

As the pattering of fragments died away, Macoby slumped weakly back against the wall and stared at the mess in front of her. One assassin was lying on the ground, her dagger lodged between his ribs. The other two had just disintegrated, and for twenty feet in either direction the walls and the paving-stones were pebbledashed with their fragmented remains.

Trying not to retch, Macoby looked at the amulet.

'What the *klat* did you do to them?' she whispered.

'Hit them with a *Fireball*,' it told her proudly. 'I didn't have much time, so I did it from the inside. Effective, huh?'

It paused, and Macoby had the distinct feeling that it was surveying its handiwork.

'You don't think I overdid it a bit, do you?' it added.

'No,' she told it, in a voice that trembled almost as much as her body was doing. 'You did just fine. Now get me out of here.'

'Okey-doke, skip. Where do you want to go?'

Macoby tried to think of somewhere in Koumas where she might be safe, somewhere where she wouldn't be known, and where noone would think of looking for her. For some reason, her mind flew back to when she and Marden had been children. Their nanny had been engaged to marry a soldier, and she had occasionally taken the two of them with her to meet him outside the small tavern in which he had lodged.

'A tavern near the south gate. I think it was called the *Wyvern*. Can you take me there?'

The amulet thought for a moment.

'Those are old memories,' it told her, 'but they should be enough. If the place hasn't changed, we can go there.'

'Wait a moment,' Macoby said, before reaching down to tug her dagger free from the corpse. And then, to the amazement of the old flower-seller who was peering fearfully round the corner, she just vanished into thin air, leaving the alleyway to the hordes of flies that were homing in from all over town on what looked like being the feast of their lives.

CHAPTER SEVEN

Inspector Heighway was sitting in the snug of a bar called *Lush Pastures*, nursing a pint of Old Organs bitter and reading the *Koumas Gazette*. It was open at the crime page, and the inspector was studying Colin the Sinister's reports on a drugs cartel that had been masquerading as a milk products importer (*The Cheddar Dairy Co.* screamed the headline) and on an illegal sword-fight that had lasted a whole morning (*The Duel that was Hours*). To Heighway's relief, there was still nothing about the murder of Colonel De Wenchas.

Good! That meant he had more time before Superintendent Weird started issuing threats and orders about clearing the case up quickly. Heighway drained his glass contentedly and was just wondering whether he had time for another one when Sergeant Raasay came rushing in, seething with excitement and bouncing up and down like a small boy on the morning of his birthday.

'Inspector!' he yelled. 'There's been another one! Only it's not one, its three!'

'Three what, Raasay? Be precise, man!'

'Murders, sir! And Kratavan saw the person who did it, and he says this is far to big for him and he wants you to quickly get down there, sir.'

'You've just split an infinitive, Raasay.'

'Sorry, sir,' said the sergeant, peering down at his trousers and wondering which bit an infinitive was and whether he'd be able to darn it.

Resisting the urge to buy a bottle of beer and hit Raasay with it, Heighway stood up and headed for the door, with his sergeant trailing behind.

'You know, you really should do something about your grammar,' he said. Raasay nodded eagerly.

'You don't have to tell me, sir! She's unbearable now. She just sits in her chair all day, swearing, and if you go near her she throws food at you. My Dad says we're going to have to put her out to grass.'

'Raasay?'

'Yes, sir?'

'Shut the *klat* up.'

Kratavan was waiting for Heighway in *Sodden Ridiculous*, a quiet, friendly bar just off Neero Square. He was cradling a whisky, and kept staring about him as though expecting that, any minute now, something extremely unpleasant was about to creep up on him. Heighway got the impression that the detective constable was a badly frightened man.

Nodding a greeting, the inspector walked past him to the bar and ordered a bottle of Badmutha, an orcish wheat beer. He was beginning to feel a bit guilty about his subordinates' drinking habits. They all seemed to respect him and wanted to be like him, and the fact that he did most of his best thinking with a beer or two in front of him had not been lost on them. There were times when it was almost impossible to get a report written in their office because everyone was just too pissed.

Resolving, not for the first time, to drink a bit less, Heighway sauntered across to Kratavan's table and sat down opposite him.

'Sergeant Raasay tells me that you've got some news,' he began. Kratavan nodded, then knocked half of his whisky back in one go.

'Three more murders, sir, in an alley just round the corner from here. We think the victims were all members of the Guild of Assassins, although it's impossible to be sure with two of them. They look more like an explosion in a giant hamburger factory.'

Kratavan paused to finish his drink and then signalled to the barman to bring across another one.

'Any suspects?' Heighway asked.

'One. A woman. Dark hair, slimly built, five-feet high, about twenty years old.'

Heighway sighed and buried his face in his hands for a moment. Kratavan had obviously had several whiskies too many.

'Sergeant,' he said long-sufferingly, 'one five-foot high woman killing three members of the Assassins Guild is not murder. It's more like self-defence. That is, if it isn't a miracle. Any idea who the woman was?'

'Yes, sir. The Lady Macoby.'

'*What!* The Regent's daughter? Are you sure?'

'Yes, sir. I saw her myself, just before it happened. She'd come to the barracks, throwing her weight around and demanding to see the colonel. One of the constables on duty here came and got me. I found her in the mortuary with the colonel's body. She was acting suspiciously. What's more, she knew exactly what time he died.'

'Did she, now!'

'Yes, sir. She said she overheard the guards talking, but they swore blind she couldn't have done. And anyway, they don't know the time of day, let alone the time of the colonel's death.'

Kratavan paused as the barman brought a couple more drinks across, then at Heighway's urging he went through the whole story in detail while the inspector sipped at his beer and grew more and more excited.

'Are you sure the woman in the alley was the same one?' he asked, as Kratavan finished his story.

'Positive, sir. The guards watched her walk out into the square, and an old flower-seller saw everything else.'

Heighway sat back in his chair and sniffed contentedly at the delicate, slightly sweet aroma of the cloudy wheat beer.

This was very good news indeed, as far as he was concerned. It all sounded rather like corruption in high places. Wonderful! He'd been looking for such a case for the whole of his life. This would be the making of him! But it needed to be carefully handled. Kratavan was right to be scared, for if the very rulers of the city were involved in murder, then everyone who came close to unveiling their role would be in severe danger.

'Okay, Kratavan,' he said. 'Sergeant Raasay is outside, trying to work out what the word "surveillance" means. Go and explain it to him, and tell him I want him to organise a watch on the colonel's body. Then you can show me the new victims.'

Kratavan stood up.

'Where will you be, sir?'

'I'll be here, finishing my beer in peace.'

*

Twenty minutes later, Heighway stood in the alley trying to ignore the flies and the rising tide of nausea, both of which threatened to engulf him. He was used to dealing with corpses that had met a violent end, but he'd never seen one that had been killed quite so thoroughly, let alone two. The whole alleyway seemed to be decorated with tiny bits of moist human.

In the entrance to the alley, Raasay was bent double, noisily getting rid of another lunch. Heighway shook his head in sympathy, then stepped gingerly through the scattered fragments of flesh and knelt down beside the one comparatively unscathed body.

The man had been a member of the Assassins' Guild, all right. Beneath his disguise of rags he wore the distinctive black and gold robes, and near his outstretched hand was the ceremonial assassin's dagger. He had died from a single stab wound to the chest. Maybe it had been delivered in self defence, but even so, there was something distinctly strange going on. How on earth had a girl like the Lady Macoby managed to best three members of the Guild of Assassins?

Heighway wafted away a few flies that seemed intent on crawling up his nose and stood up. He looked round at the mess of human tissue that coated the surroundings and frowned.

'Are you sure there were two of them?'

'Positive, sir,' answered Kratavan, who had just finished interviewing the flower-seller.

'Hm. Not much left for the funeral. Madam Min seen them yet?'

'Yes, sir.'

'And?'

'She got very excited. Said that the other two were killed by a spell, and a very powerful one at that.'

'What type of spell?'

'*Fireball*, she reckoned.'

'Anything else for us?'

'Well, I did ask her if she had any thoughts on who might have cast the spell.' Kratavan paused and scratched his head doubtfully. 'She said it wasn't a who, it was a what.'

'A what?'

'That's what she said.'

'You know what that means, don't you, Kratavan?'

'No, sir,' said Kratavan, eagerly.

73

'It means that the daft old biddy has lost the plot completely.'

Heighway bent down to brush a gobbet of congealing human intestine off the knee of his trousers and looked at his flesh-encrusted shoes with fastidious distaste. Then he straightened and clapped Kratavan on the back.

'Right then, my friend,' he told him. 'You and I and Sergeant Raasay are going to go and change our footwear. Then we'll go back to the station, write up our reports, and prepare a press release. And *then* we're going to interview the main suspect. I expect we'll find her up at the palace.'

Kratavan stared at him in astonishment.

'But we . . . I mean, she's . . . I mean, we can't just march into the palace and . . .'

'Oh yes we can. Anyway, she said we should contact her at the palace for an interview.'

'Yes, but . . . the Lady Macoby, sir!'

'Listen, Kratavan, I don't care whether the colonel was murdered by some old tramp or by the Regent's daughter herself. Whoever did it committed a serious crime, and we're going to arrest them. If it's the Lady Macoby, then yes, you're right to be worried. All hell may well be let loose about us.'

'So what do we do, sir?'

'We do our job.'

'But someone will stop us, sir! We're getting in too deep!'

Someone may well *try* to stop us, Kratavan. We could be opening Pandora's box. There may be an attempt to hush this up. Someone might try to buy us off. And if so, do you know what we do?'

'Take the money?'

'No, Kratavan. We open the box.'

CHAPTER EIGHT

He strode backwards and forwards along the balcony outside his guest room, occasionally pausing to stare towards the army barracks as though he might see some sign of what had occurred there. But even though he was high up on one of the palace's main towers, there were too many buildings in the way, and anyhow, the deed would have been done by now.

He turned away, cursing his rash nature. He knew he had acted too precipitate. So what if Macoby had disappeared? That didn't mean that she suspected him. For years, he had planned and schemed, calmly carrying out the various strands of a complex plot that would culminate in him becoming the absolute ruler of the whole of the country of Kuhbador. Marriage to Macoby was an integral part of this plot, and yet he had panicked and arranged her death, purely because she had disappeared and he was worried that she might suspect him.

The man knew that her brother had suspected him as well, but he was sure that Marden would have said nothing definite to his sister. He had been too honourable, that one, and he would not have accused another man unless he was one hundred per cent sure. But he had been getting too close to the truth and he had possessed the amulet, and so he had died. Anyway, it was a vital part of the plot that he should die, and it was so much neater that it should be during battle, so much easier!

He paused and rested his hands on the stone ledge of the balcony. That had been where he had made his first mistake. He should have ensured he was present before Marden died, and then he could have discovered what he had done with the *klatting* jewel. He had it the evening before battle, and so he must have passed it to someone. But who?

There was a gentle knock on the door, and the man turned and went back inside the dark, luxurious room in which he was quartered. *I must start again*, he thought as he strode across the deep, soft carpet. *I must find some other way of getting control of this city.*

He opened the door a fraction and peered out, then opened it wider to allow the shadowy figure of a soldier to slip past into the room. The soldier bowed, the red cockade on his helmet almost black in the shadows of the room, then handed him a small scroll of paper.

'News from the Guild, my liege!' the soldier whispered.

The man sighed and took the scroll.

'So the deed is done,' he said heavily.

'No, my liege. They have failed! The Lady Macoby escaped, three assassins are dead, and the Guild cannot find her.'

He stared at the soldier, a renewed hope springing up.

'Are you sure, man?'

'Yes, sire! I have seen their remains myself!'

'Then cancel the contract at once! She must live . . . for now.'

The soldier nodded and turned to go, but the man caught him by the sleeve.

'Are you sure no-one connects this contract with me?'

'No, my lord. The Guild suspect another. There is no trail to lead back to you.'

The man nodded, and the soldier slipped silently from the room. Then, turning, the man crossed to the window and walked out onto the balcony again.

I must hold my nerve, this time, he thought. *I must find Macoby and wed her. Then, and only then, will it be time for her to join her brother in death . . .*

And he stared out across the myriad roofs of the city that one day would be his alone to rule.

CHAPTER NINE

Glart fell in love with the city of Koumas the moment he first saw it in the distance. The early afternoon sunshine was bouncing off the tall, slender towers and making them glitter and gleam like a fairy-tale palace. The place seemed impossibly romantic, especially to someone who had grown up inside the dark, brooding buildings of the monastery.

As he and his two companions drew nearer, Glart began to get some idea of the sheer size of the city. He had expected it to be bigger than the villages that were the only centres of habitation he'd so far seen, but the vastness of Koumas took him by surprise. The city walls stretched for miles, and behind them nestled a host of buildings, a stone-built warren that housed unimaginable numbers of people, a hive of bustling humanity.

Glart slowed as they neared the East Gate and then stopped and stared up at the towering battlements nervously. For a country boy from a monastic background, the place was daunting. Ugman noticed the worried look on his face, and clapped him on the shoulder with a vast, scaly hand.

'First time in the big city, huh?' the cave-troll asked. 'Don't let it get to you. I felt the same the first time I came here, too. And I had to get over the fear factor, as well.'

'What fear factor?'

'You *have* led a sheltered life, haven't you?' answered Ugman. 'The fact is, people tend to be afraid of cave-trolls. Not surprising, really. Most of us tend to hit people as soon as look at them.'

'And if you've been hit by a cave-troll, you stay hit,' interjected Legless.

'So people gave me a wide berth,' Ugman continued. 'Now life in a troll community hadn't exactly prepared me for the task of going out and making friends. Cave-trolls aren't noted conversationalists.'

'You can say that again,' added Legless. 'An average troll conversation tends to be along the lines of *Ug. Ug. Grunt? Ug. Ug? Grunt.*
And that might take half an hour.'

'I used to sit in the university bar waiting for people to come up
and talk to me, while all the other people in the bar were waiting for
me to go away. But then, after a while, people began to realise that I
was no threat.'

'It was when he started growing his hair,' said the elf. 'People
cottoned on to the fact that a hippy cave-troll might not be quite as
fierce as the rest.'

Ugman grinned and slapped the elf on the back, knocking him
forward by some six feet.

'It was Legless here who was the first one to buy me a drink and
then sit and talk with me,' he said.

'And that was *klatting* hard work,' the elf told Glart, as he picked
himself up. 'He hadn't come out of his shell much. All he contributed
to the conversation at first was the occasional *ug*. Then after his hair
had got really long and he'd been hanging out with students for a
few weeks, that changed to *ug, man* . . . which is how he got his
nickname.'

'So what's your real name?' asked Glart, intrigued.

'Bonecruncher,' said Ugman.

'Ah. Nice,' said Glart, paling slightly.

'It's a good, old-fashioned troll name, is Bonecruncher,' said its
owner, indignantly. 'Trouble is, humans don't like troll names very
much. You get talking to some bloke in a pub and you tell him that
you're called Fleshripper or Brainmuncher or some other traditional
troll name, all of a sudden they remember that there's this really
important engagement which they've forgotten about, and they go
rushing off without even buying their round.'

'Personally, I'd love a name like that,' said Legless, a little sadly.

Ugman grinned and gently nudged Glart in the ribs, winding him
quite badly.

'You know why that is, don't you?' he said.

'No,' wheezed Glart, checking his ribs with one hand to see if they
were still in one piece.

'Ask him what his real name is,' continued the troll. 'Go on, ask
him!'

78

Glart looked enquiringly at the elf, who all of a sudden was finding the crenellations of the city walls extremely fascinating.

'Well?' enquired Glart.

Legless glowered at him.

'It just so happens,' he said with dignity, 'that my parents followed an old elven tradition of naming their children after the strength and beauty of the natural world. For example, my sister is called Sunrise and my brothers are named Cedar and Rainstorm.'

With that he turned and marched purposefully towards the East Gate, where a group of five gate guards were leaning against the wall, casually inspecting all the incoming travellers. The other two followed him.

'I think they're rather beautiful names, actually,' the elf added, over his shoulder.

'I agree,' Glart told him. 'What's yours?'

There was a pause that lasted for several seconds.

'Primrose,' muttered the elf. 'And that's why I prefer being Legless. Now, if you've quite finished, I'd like to get back to my lodgings, get washed, get changed, get to a pub, and get drunk.'

'What a lot of gets,' Glart murmured to Ugman.

'Watch it, laddie,' warned one of the gate guards, in a tone that would have been extremely threatening if he hadn't just noticed that Glart was being accompanied by a seven-foot-high cave-troll.

The three of them wandered through the gate and along the imaginatively-named Eastgate Street. It was lined with shops, stalls and barrows, and tradesmen of every description were shouting and calling in an attempt to interest the passing throng in their wares. The air was full of the scent of flowers, spices and roasting meats, and Glart thought he could just detect the comfortingly familiar aroma of burning incense wafting from some distant burner.

He stopped by a fruit stall and was surprised when the owner pressed an apple into his hands with a smile and a muttered 'God be with you, brother!' It was plain that the habit he wore was held in good esteem, for the same thing happened at every stall he approached, and five minutes later he and his two companions were walking up the street munching contentedly on freshly baked flat-bread stuffed with slices of roast lamb, their pockets bulging with fruit.

'So,' mumbled Legless, through a mouthful of meat. 'Where are you heading now?'

'There's an inn somewhere called the *Wyvern*,' Glart told them. 'That's where I must go.'

Ugman used a claw-like fingernail to dig out a large lump of meat that had got wedged between two of his teeth, and flicked it at a scavenging mongrel that was scrabbling in a knocked-over waste bin.

'There's only one pub with that name that we know of,' he told Glart, 'and I think we must have been in every *klatting* one in the city. It's a quiet little tavern down by South Gate. Used by travellers, mainly.'

They strolled along, and after a few hundred yards came to a crossroads where the road to the South Gate dived off to their left. Here they said their farewells, for Legless and Ugman were eager to get back to their lodgings and their friends. They tried to prevail upon Glart to come with them, but he refused. His visions had left him with a sense of urgency, and he knew that he had to find the woman with the long, dark hair without delay.

'Well, any time you need help, you can call on us,' Ugman told him. 'I hope you find this woman.'

'If you do,' Legless added, 'ask her if she's got a couple of friends . . .'

With that they were off, vanishing into the throng of people, and Glart turned southwards and set off in search of the *Wyvern* tavern.

Macoby was sitting at a table in a dark corner of the almost-empty tavern, drinking a double brandy and trying to stop her hand from shaking. She found she could manage this if she really concentrated hard on it, but then the rest of her body began to tremble uncontrollably, so she gave up and let the hand have its own way.

My brother is dead! she thought. *And now somebody is trying to kill me!* For a moment, grief threatened to overwhelm her, but she forcibly dragged her thoughts away from Marden. There would be time to mourn him later, but for now she had to try and analyse what was going on.

That had been no ordinary back-alley mugging! Despite the ragged clothes they had worn as a disguise, she had recognised her assailants as members of the Guild of Assassins, and she knew how much such a contract would cost. She had been extremely lucky, for without the amulet she would now be dead, stretched out on the cold flagstones of the alleyway.

But despite her escape, she was under no illusions that she was safe. The Guild would still be looking for her, and next time they found her she doubted that she would be so lucky, even with the help of the amulet. Now that three of their number were dead, they would be more careful, and she probably wouldn't even see her assassin, let alone have time to defend herself against him.

The glass rattled against her teeth as she drained the last of the brandy and wondered what to do. There could be no going back to the palace now. That was the first place they would look. She would have to solve this whole rigmarole herself, with just the help of a magic amulet that had been at the front of the queue when attitude was handed out, and a ghost who was as much use as a sundial in a snowstorm.

Macoby looked across at Darian's ghost, who was hovering by the wall with his head thrust through into the street outside. He was under strict orders to watch for assassins or soldiers, and to warn her the instant that any came near the tavern. Maybe she should get him to drift into the palace and see what was going on up there. There was a lot she would like to know, such as whether she was now officially engaged to Myal or not.

Klat! she thought. *What can I do? Where do I start?* She felt terribly alone, and had just come to the conclusion that what she needed more than anything else was to find Sarakkan again and ask his help and advice when all at once she got a horrible feeling that she was being watched. Her heart lurched and she peered round, but the tavern's few customers all seemed to be taking no notice of her at all.

Then she saw him, over by the door. He was a young monk, clad in the distinctive blue habit of the Cedrician order, and he was staring at her with the rapt, almost overawed expression of a dragon staring at a ton of best anthracite. As he met her gaze he blushed slightly, but then his face split into a wide grin and he began to walk across to her.

For a moment Macoby came close to panic, slipping her hand inside her jerkin to grasp the amulet whilst frantically scanning the monk's habit for some concealed weapon. He was carrying a dark wooden staff and she wondered whether he was about to attack her with this, but then she told herself to relax. There was something about his open, honest face that made her instinctively trust him.

She studied him as he pushed past the few customers and strode across to her table. At first she had thought that he was a mere boy, but now she could tell that he was about the same age as her. He looked powerfully built beneath the enveloping habit, but it was his face that really captured her attention. It was a face that hovered somewhere between ugly and fascinating. It was also indubitably friendly.

As he reached her table the grin widened. Macoby thought that she had seen a few big, daft grins in her time, but if there was an award for the biggest, daftest grin of the year, this one would have walked away with it. But then the young monk composed his features into an expression of seriousness, like an actor suddenly assuming a role.

'My name is Glart,' he told her. 'My lady, you are in terrible danger! There is a man who plots your death.'

Now he tells me, she thought.

'What makes you think that?' she asked him, intrigued despite herself.

Briefly, Glart told her of the monastery and of his visions, carefully skirting round the in-bed-together segment. Then he told her how the Abbot had picked him for a mission, making it sound as though the whole aim was to find Macoby and safeguard her safety.

'And so I've come to protect you,' he finished.

Macoby would have laughed out loud if she hadn't felt so close to crying.

'My brother Marden, one of Koumas's best warriors, is dead, despite knowing that someone sought to kill him,' she said. 'I barely escaped with my life this afternoon when the Guild of Assassins sent three men against me. They will try again, and they don't fail twice. How can a mere monk protect me from such dangers?'

'I don't know. I just know that I can.' Glart paused and stared at the ghost, who had pulled his head back through the wall and was listening to their conversation with interest. 'Is he with you?' he asked Macoby.

'You can see Darian's ghost?' she asked, surprised.

'Yes, I can see him. And I can sense the magic that holds him to this world. Just as I can sense the magic in that jewel you hold in your hand.'

Macoby stared at Glart in complete astonishment. Maybe he did have some hidden powers, after all. Maybe he could help. But could she dare to trust him? Marden's advice was still at the forefront of her mind.

Glart suddenly broke into another one of his infectious grins, then winked at her. All of a sudden, Macoby's mind was made up. She desperately needed someone's help and she didn't dare go looking for Sarakkan at the palace, where he would be helping with preparations for tonight's banquet in honour of Myal. Moreover, there was something about this monk that she instinctively liked.

'So what do you suggest?' she asked him. Glart peered round at the tavern's customers.

'Does anyone here know you?' he asked.

'No.'

'And no-one else knows that you're here?'

'No.'

'You're sure?'

'I'm sure.'

'In that case, I think that the safest thing we can do is stay here and have a few drinks. While we're doing that, you can tell me as much as you can about why someone should wish your death. Or is there something else that you have to do?'

'Well, I'm supposed to be attending a state banquet in honour of the man who my father wants me to marry. But I think I might just give that a miss.'

'Fine. Drinks it is, then.'

And with a confident smile, Glart turned and went to investigate the draught beers on offer behind the bar.

CHAPTER TEN

Heighway paused outside the door of Superintendent Weird's office to brush a few imaginary flecks of dirt off his trousers, then fastened up the top button of his collar. He knew that the superintendent was very big on neatness and appearance. To him, an undone collar button was like a barrel of brandy to an orc – it was an excellent excuse to go ape-shit. Heighway had a feeling that he was in for a torrid enough time already over the De Wenchas murder, without giving his boss any other reasons to berate him.

Taking a deep breath, he knocked on the door and went in. Superintendent Weird was sitting behind his desk, and Heighway swallowed nervously as he saw that his boss was reading that day's afternoon edition of the *Koumas Gazette*.

'You wanted to see me, sir?' he said.

The superintendent looked up.

'Heighway. Sit down, sit down.'

Realising that he wasn't in for one of the chief's legendary bollockings (not yet, anyway!), Heighway breathed a sigh of relief and a quick thank-you to Trann, the god of Lost Causes. Then, pulling out the chair on the opposite side of the desk to Weird, he seated himself.

'Have you read this?' asked the superintendent, holding out the newspaper.

'No, sir,' said Heighway, and taking the proffered paper he scanned the front page. Straight away he could see that the news hadn't so much broken as shattered into fragments. *De Wenchas dead!* shouted the banner headline, and beneath it Colin the Sinister had really gone to town, filling the whole page with reports, comment and speculation.

The superintendent leant across and tapped heavily on a paragraph that was headed *The Wife threw the Woods?*

'What's all this rubbish about his wife, eh, Heighway?'

'Someone knocked the colonel unconscious with one of his own bowling balls before killing him, sir. I got Raasay to spread a story saying that we think his wife threw one at him in a temper.'

'What on earth for?'

'Well, firstly, it puts the murderer off her guard if she thinks that we're on the wrong track. Secondly, it buys us some time.'

'But it makes us look like idiots, Heighway. His wife died three years ago.'

'You know that and I know that, sir, but the press haven't picked up on it yet.'

'But they will, laddie, they will.'

'Then I'll plant some more misinformation about zombies and the living dead, sir.'

The superintendent sighed and shook his head, then leant back in his chair and stared at Heighway in bewilderment, like an orc staring at someone who has just admitted to being teetotal.

'I used to think that no-one was perfect,' he said, 'but I was wrong. Heighway, you're a perfect idiot! Why the hell don't you just go out and arrest someone? Anyone will do! I mean, good grief man, the whole basement of this police station is one vast complex of torture-chambers staffed by a band of dedicated professionals who are experts at extracting confessions from the stubbornest of prisoners. There are men down there who could make a block of cement talk!'

'With respect, sir, I happen to think that it's important to arrest the person who actually did the murder.'

'You and your left-wing politics . . .' The superintendent paused, then looked at Heighway curiously. 'You said *her* guard . . . *she* thinks . . . You suspect a woman?'

'There's a female suspect who we wish to interview, sir, yes.'

'Is this anything to do with that girl who escaped from the inn?'

'What girl?'

'The one that Colin the Sinister mentions. Down at the bottom there.'

Heighway picked up the paper again and scanned the front page until he found the relevant paragraph. Under the heading *Lass in Weyr Inn*, the journalist described how a group of soldiers from Myal's personal guard had gone to that tavern to arrest a young woman, but she had somehow managed to escape from right under their noses.

'I don't think this is relevant to the De Wenchas case, sir,' he muttered.

'You don't, eh?' snorted the superintendent. 'Well, Colin the Sinister does, and he isn't often wrong. Someone must have given him a tip-off. Maybe you should find out who.'

'Sir, with respect . . .'

'With respect, nothing, Heighway. You've got three days, and then I want to hear that someone has confessed to this murder. If not, I'll have *you* arrested for it. Understand?'

'Sir.'

'Now get moving. Oh, and Heighway?'

'Sir?'

'Next time you come to see me, make a bit of an effort to tidy yourself up, will you, man? Your suit looks as though you've just slept in it.'

Heighway found Sergeant Raasay and DC Kratavan in the police canteen. Kratavan was doing the crossword in the *Koumas Gazette* and Raasay was watching, open-mouthed with amazement at the skill required and trying desperately to help. Heighway leant against the doorpost and watched.

'Four across,' read Kratavan. 'Choose a weapon as a tool. Seven letters.'

'Er . . . screwdriver?' hazarded Raasay.

'Seven letters, sarge,' Kratavan reminded him.

'Oh. Er, hammer?'

In the doorway, Heighway shook his head tiredly. To an outsider, it would have seemed incredible that Raasay was a sergeant, whilst the handsome and intelligent Kratavan was still a lowly detective constable. But then, an outsider wouldn't have known that Kratavan was the son of a poor peasant, while Raasay was a distant relative of the superintendent.

'I think it's probably pickaxe,' said Kratavan, writing the letters in.

'Coo!' said Raasay, impressed.

'Now then. Four down. Pig-like goblin in a conifer. Seven letters.'

'Umm . . . fig-tree?'

'No, it must begin with a P.'

'Pimples.'

'Porcine,' said Heighway from the doorway. 'Orc inside pine. Now here's another one with seven letters. This one also begins with a P. The clue is – Sergeant Raasay.'

'Hey, am I in the paper? My mum will be pleased!' Raasay picked up the *Gazette* and scanned the crossword clues, looking for the one that featured his name.

'The answer is – plonker,' said Heighway.

Kratavan grinned and tried to hide it. Raasay looked baffled.

'Never mind. Kratavan, get me a coffee. No, on second thoughts, make that a whisky. Raasay, go and organise a couple of burly constables to come with us. As soon as I've had a drink we're going to go and interview her ladyship.'

'Very good, sir.'

Raasay leapt up and headed for the door with a satisfied smile on his face. When it came to mundane tasks such as organising burly constables, he was in his element.

'Oh, and Raasay?'

'Yes, sir?'

'Do something about your uniform, will you? You look as though you've just slept in it. This is the royal palace we're going to, not some cardboard box in a shop doorway.'

An hour later, Heighway led Raasay, Kratavan and a couple of suitably burly constables through the gates of the grounds in which stood the royal palace of Koumas, a large, multi-towered building which was set in landscaped gardens of clipped hedges, silk-smooth lawns and winding gravel paths. They walked along a driveway that curved past a series of ornamental fountains in which various mythical stone creatures frolicked together lewdly and spewed water from every available orifice. Beyond, a wide flight of shallow stone steps led up to the porticoed front entrance of the palace.

Their official papers took them safely past several of the guards who patrolled the grounds, and Heighway led his team proudly up the steps. Five minutes later, after an increasingly angry row with a captain of the Royal Bodyguard, the furious Heighway led them back down the steps, round the side of the palace and into the stone-flagged rear yard that led to the tradesmen's entrance.

The yard was packed with carts, wagons and delivery drays, and teams of servants and porters were carrying an endless stream of victuals and supplies into the palace. Heighway weaved his way through the mass of humanity, deftly avoiding the unpleasant surprises left behind by all the delivery horses, and worked his way to the door. Here, a chamberlain was overseeing the deliveries. He had a clipboard and pen in his hands, and was making entries and marking things off on a vast list of expected goods. Heighway went to march past him, but the chamberlain grasped him by the arm, at the same time signalling to a nearby guard.

'Can I help you, sir?' he enquired, in a deceptively mild tone, and Heighway noticed that the guard's hand was resting on the hilt of his sword.

'Detective Inspector Heighway,' said Heighway, displaying his official papers. 'I'm investigating the murder of Colonel De Wenchas, and I need to ask one or two questions of the Regent and his family.'

The chamberlain looked down his nose at the inspector as though he had just been left on the step in a steaming pile by one of the horses.

'How can they possibly help you?' he enquired.

'I think that is a matter for them to decide,' responded Heighway, keeping a tight grip on his temper. 'Now, I can see that you're very busy. If you could possibly pass me on to someone who could assist me . . .'

Five minutes later, a uniformed flunkey was leading just Heighway and Raasay along a dimly-lit corridor, for Kratavan and the two constables had been deemed not high enough in rank to be allowed inside the palace and had been press-ganged into action unloading barrels of beer. They passed frantic kitchens and steam-filled, humid sculleries that seethed and teemed with servants, and Heighway would have been reminded of an ants' nest if it wasn't for the fact that this place made ants look like extremely laid-back, easy-going creatures.

Turning right, they strode down a passage that seemed to lead into the very bowels of the palace. As they came to the end, they were stopped by another guard. He too enquired as to how he could be of help, and he too spoke in deceptively mild tones whilst fingering his sword. Once again, Heighway bit down on his temper and began to explain.

'I'm investigating the murder of Colonel de Wenchas . . .'

More than fifty minutes, seven further guards and seven identical explanations later, Heighway and Raasay found themselves sitting in a luxurious anteroom on the second floor, kicking their heels and being watched suspiciously by two more of the Royal Guards. Heighway was just about to explode, he was so angry. Raasay was much calmer, but kept saying that he really needed to go to the toilet and was getting right on the inspector's tits.

But then the pair of double doors opened, and the imposing figure of the Lord Chancellor marched out to greet them. He was a tall, well-built man, dressed in purple robes and wearing a white, tightly-curled wig and an ornate gold chain that signified his office.

'Gentlemen!' he greeted them. 'Please accept my apologies. You have been kept waiting an unconscionably long time. It is unforgivable, but as you can see, there is a state banquet tonight and we are all run off our feet.'

His manner was so diplomatic and appeasing that Heighway felt his rage slipping away.

'Think nothing of it,' he said. 'We understand.'

'You are most gracious,' beamed the Lord Chancellor. 'Now, what can I do for you?'

Heighway was just about to launch into his reasons for being there when a small but desperate whimper from Raasay distracted him.

'Look,' he said, 'can my sergeant here use the toilet?'

The Lord Chancellor nodded and signalled to one of the guards, who led Raasay out of the room.

'I'm sorry about that,' Heighway sighed. 'I'm afraid Raasay is more of a defective than a detective. Now then. About my reasons for coming to the palace . . .'

Quickly he ran through the salient points of the case, and the Lord Chancellor listened quietly.

'. . . and so we have reason to believe that the Lady Macoby may be able to help us with our investigations,' finished Heighway. 'If she would grant me a short audience, I'm sure we can clear the matter up successfully.'

'I do understand your reasoning,' said the Lord Chancellor. 'However, I'm afraid that will not be possible.'

'Now, listen . . .' began Heighway, his anger rising instantly at this refusal.

'If she were here, I'm sure she would be delighted to help you,' the Lord Chancellor continued, his soft voice somehow managing to drown out the inspector's gruff tones. 'However, I'm afraid that my Lady Macoby has been missing for the last two days. The Regent is beside himself with worry, as is my Lord Myal.'

'Myal of Minas Lantan? What's he got to do with it?'

The Lord Chancellor looked round as though expecting to be overheard, then lowered his voice.

'I'm sure I can trust an officer of your standing to make sure this goes no further,' he whispered. 'Let us just say that we believe my lord Myal awaits . . . some news, shall we say . . . from my lady.'

Oh-ho, thought Heighway. *What about, I wonder? De Wenchas, perhaps? Myal led the army, and De Wenchas was the second in command. Maybe there was some professional rivalry between them . . .*

'I wonder if I might possibly have a few words with Myal,' he asked. 'I think there are one or two small items that he may be able to help me with.'

'I shall ask him,' the Lord Chancellor replied, spreading his arms wide. 'I am sure he will spare you some time. Come with me.'

And opening the double doors, he led Heighway off on another long route-march through the labyrinthian corridors of the palace.

Sergeant Raasay had been feeling unwell for most of the day, but things had really come to the boil in the past half an hour. His guts felt as though something with extremely sharp claws was trying to dig its way out from the inside, and he could tell that if he didn't make it to a toilet really quickly, things were going to get very messy.

He followed the guard along the seemingly endless corridor, trying desperately to keep control of his functions, and when at last the man indicated a door with a jerk of his thumb, Raasay flew past him as though fired from a crossbow and dived into a cubicle. Slamming the door, he sat doubled-up in pain on the seat, moaning, as all hell broke loose. It felt as though the world was falling out of his bottom.

He knew what had caused this, of course. He was even beginning to get used to it by now. The trouble was, Raasay still lived at home with his parents, and every few days his batty old grandmother would get some mad culinary urge and insist on cooking a meal for the family. Unfortunately, being several sandwiches short of a picnic, her meals were unusual, to say the least. The worst one had been last Sunday, when she had roasted a dead cat that she had found in a bin near the market-place.

This morning, he had come downstairs to find that she was bustling about in the kitchen, making breakfast. Filled with fear, he had tried to slip out of the front door, but she'd been too quick for him and had dragged him back to the table by his ear. Then she had set a plate of bacon, eggs and sausage down in front of him and told him to eat up or she'd box his ears for him.

And so, reluctantly, he had. For once, she had used the proper ingredients, and it would have been a good, nourishing breakfast if it had been cooked properly. Unfortunately, she had forgotten to light the stove, and so it wasn't so much undercooked as not cooked at all. Raasay could have coped with raw eggs, but the raw bacon and the flabby, raw sausage were another matter altogether.

It didn't help that she'd apparently been keeping the sausage in a bag under her bed for the past two months, so that it had gone a funny colour and smelt like the rear end of a dead sewer rat. And so once again, thanks to his grandmother's insanity, he had ended up as host to some demonic microbe which was ripping through his bowels like a bat out of hell.

For half an hour, Raasay sat in his own personal cubicle of torment, oblivious to the rest of the world. He didn't hear the guard telling him to make his own way back to the anteroom and then leaving. He didn't hear the two other people who came in to use the facilities but thought better of it after hearing the appalling noises issuing from the cubicle. All he was aware of was the pain in his stomach and a burgeoning desire to throw his grandmother off a cliff and then drop large rocks on her.

At last, the pain lessened. His bowels had nothing more to evacuate. He sat on the seat, panting slightly, feeling as limp as a stillborn lamb. It was then that he became aware of the world about him once more. He heard the door of the washroom open as someone entered. There was a pause, and then a match was struck. There was a loud inhalation, followed by a sigh of contentment. Then, a few seconds later, the door opened again and someone spoke.

'Ah. There you are.'

It was a low, rather threatening voice, the sort of voice that usually says things like 'Are you looking at me?' or 'Hand over your wallet.' Without even seeing its owner, Raasay just knew that he would have a shaven head, a scarred face and those mad, staring eyes that seem to focus on the bridge of your nose as though weighing up how best to plaster it over the rest of your face.

'I've been looking for you,' the voice carried on, and Raasay was just feeling extremely sorry for whoever it was that the voice had been talking to when a second voice spoke.

'Oh, yeah?' it growled, and Raasay shivered. This second voice was even worse. It was the voice of the sort of person who had enjoyed pulling the legs off spiders as a child, and who had grown up to discover that it was much more fun pulling them off people.

'Yeah. Message from the boss. There's some cops nosing around. If anyone asks, we was never at the *Weyr Inn*, right? We never tried to grab her ladyship, we never even saw her. We never saw nuthin'. Understand?'

'Right. No problem.'

'Okay.'

The door closed and Raasay sat silently in his foetid cubicle, listening to the sounds made by the second man, who appeared to be washing something in the sink. The sergeant hardly dared to breathe. He wasn't exactly the most intelligent officer in the force but even he could work out that, if two highly dangerous men have been having a conversation about not saying anything to the police, the last thing they are going to appreciate is for a policeman to walk out of a cubicle beside them immediately afterwards.

There came the sound of a plug being yanked out, followed by water gurgling away. Footsteps followed, and Raasay stopped breathing completely, for they were coming towards him. They stopped on the other side of the cubicle door, and it was only the fact that there was nothing left in his bowels that prevented them from going into immediate and noisy action. Then a still-burning cigarette-end looped over the door and landed in Raasay's naked lap.

Somehow, the sergeant managed not to react but remained silently sitting there, his pubic hair beginning to smoulder gently as he strained his ears to make out what the man was doing. There was a noisy exhalation, and Raasay could actually smell the final cloud of acrid tobacco smoke that his tormenter had breathed out. And then, to his relief, the footsteps receded, the door opened, and the man left.

Raasay was out of the cubicle like a flash. Not stopping to pull up his pants, he crossed the floor to the wash-basin in four huge kangaroo-like bounds, spurred on by the fact that small flames were licking up from his groin. And when one of the royal footmen entered the washroom a minute later to use the toilet, he was met by the unusual sight of a detective sergeant of the Koumas police sitting in a sink full of water, his legs dangling over the side, his trousers round his ankles and a blissful smile of relief on his face.

Detective Inspector Heighway took an instant dislike to Myal the moment he shook hands with him. The guy had one of those manly finger-crunching I'm-stronger-than-you-and-so-I'm-better-than-you handshakes. Add to that Myal's cold, unfriendly air, his haughty manner and his habit of looking down his nose at folk as though they were some type of lesser life-form, and the result was certainly not someone who was going to win too many Most Popular Member of the Aristocracy awards.

He had granted Heighway a short interview in the indecently luxurious quarters in which he was staying, high up in one of the palace's towers. After shaking hands, he seated himself in a padded chair of purple velvet, flanked by his chief adviser and the captain of his bodyguard. It was the only chair in the room, and so Heighway was forced to stand.

At first, the inspector phrased his questions tactfully and respect-fully. In return, Myal was icily polite, giving short but concise answers about both De Wenchas and Macoby. However, it wasn't long before this facade was ripped clean away.

Heighway had a feeling that Macoby was connected with the colonel's murder. In fact, he thought she was in it right up to her neck. So when Myal asserted that he intended to marry her, this merely confirmed Heighway's conviction, as it provided her with a possible motive. After all, she was known to be a forthright, no-nonsense individual. If Colonel De Wenchas had posed any sort of a threat to her future husband, Heighway thought that she might have decided to take the law into her own hands.

As this feeling grew, so did the intensity and directness of the inspector's questions, until at last Myal sprang from his seat with his hand on the hilt of his sword.

'Are you accusing me of having something to do with this murder?' he snarled.

'No, sir,' answered Heighway in that smug tone of voice which police officers always use when they really mean *yes sir*. 'It's just a matter of eliminating you from our enquiries.'

Myal's eyes blazed, and he half-drew his sword.

'It is you that should be eliminated,' he began, but his adviser quickly leaned forward and whispered something into his ear. Myal subsided with bad grace.

'The interview is over,' he said. 'I will not be questioned like this. Your insolence has been noted. You will be hearing more about this matter.'

'Very good, sir,' Heighway replied. 'I regret that my job has forced me to ask questions which may have seemed impertinent, and I apologise if any offence has been given.'

He made a low, sweeping bow that was perfect in its execution, then walked backwards to the door, still in the bowing position, as the stiffest of protocol demanded. Peering up, he saw that Myal was looking somewhat mollified by this display of reverence.

'If you'd be so kind as to keep me informed of your movements . . .' he added, and then turned and left the room before Myal could explode.

Outside, the guard who had guided him was still waiting, and Heighway followed him down the spiral staircase that led to the main area of the palace. *That Myal is a little touchy*, he thought. *I reckon he's hiding something, all right.*

They clattered on down the dark stone stairwell. At the next landing, a young captain of the Royal Guard was waiting for them. Heighway's guide saluted him and he returned the salute, but his eyes were on the inspector. He was a handsome man with untidy brown hair and a smiling face, but Heighway could tell that beneath this cheerful facade, he was a worried man.

'Detective Inspector Heighway?' he queried.

Heighway nodded.

'My name is Sarakkan,' he said. 'Could I have a word with you? In private?'

Instantly, the guard saluted again and trotted on down the stairs, leaving them alone.

'They tell me you're investigating the death of De Wenchas, and that you think Macoby had something to do with it,' Sarakkan said, without preamble.

'We'd simply like to establish . . .'

'Well, she didn't!' burst out Sarakkan. 'I can tell you that! I know her well, and I can tell you that she couldn't murder anyone!'

'Mister Sarakkan, nobody has accused her of murder. However, a murder has been committed, and the Lady Macoby would appear to be reluctant to come forward. Moreover, she . . .'

'She's too scared to come forward! I saw her yesterday in the city. She is hiding from something or someone. She believes that her brother, Marden, has been murdered and that the murderer is trying to kill her, too. Inspector, she's a very frightened woman.'

Heighway felt a great surge of excitement run through him. Lord Marden dead? Could this be true? He knew that Marden had ridden with the army which had fought the orcs, but no official news of casualties had yet been released. But if he *was* dead, could it have been murder? That would make two high-ups in the army who had been assassinated, and that seemed to be stretching coincidence way too far. They had to be connected.

Nonchalantly, the inspector leant against the wall. It was much colder and damper than it looked. With a muttered exclamation of annoyance he stood upright again and brushed damp, green mould off the sleeve of his coat.

'I was under the impression that the Lady Macoby disappeared two days ago,' he remarked. 'Yet you tell me you saw her yesterday?'

Sarakkan looked away, embarrassed. *Hmm*, thought Heighway. *There's been something going on between the two of them. I reckon she must have been letting him have the occasional quick one, and now the poor boy is shag-happy.*

'I told you, I know her well,' said Sarakkan. 'When she disappeared, I thought I could guess the part of town that she would hide in. I was right – I found her staying in a tavern near the old market. But she was scared out of her wits. We talked for a while and then she . . . vanished.'

'But why the hell would she run to some shit-hole of a tavern by herself when she could be living here in perfect safety, surrounded by the Royal Guard?'

Sarakkan stared at him with a strange intensity.

'Maybe she's scared of someone in the palace,' he said. 'Maybe she feels that she is in danger here.'

'But who from?'

Sarakkan said nothing, but merely looked up the stairs past Heighway, towards Myal's quarters.

'Her future husband?' laughed Heighway. 'Oh, come on, now!'

'She would not marry that man even if the only alternative was death,' said Sarakkan, softly.

Heighway stared at him, his mind racing as everything fell into place. Once again, that same urge of excitement flooded through him. He'd been chasing the wrong person! There was no earthly reason why Macoby should be in love with Myal – this was an arranged marriage. In fact, from what Heighway had seen of the man, it would be surprising if she even liked him. No, it was Myal who would benefit most from the marriage, for if Marden *was* dead, within a few years he would be the ruler of two cities. And if the Lady Macoby was right about someone wishing to kill her, what better reason could such an arrogant, self-centred man have for wishing to kill a young woman than for her to have turned him down like a bedspread, injuring his pride and ruining his plans at the same time?

'Did you know Colonel De Wenchas?' he asked Sarakkan.

'Yes. I served in his cavalry unit during the battle with the orcs.'

'Did he and Myal get on well?'

Sarakkan shook his head.

'They had several differences of opinion,' he replied, then lowered his voice. 'The colonel told me in confidence that he thought Myal had made several huge mistakes . . .'

Heighway nodded in satisfaction.

'May I ask you, sir . . . are you billeted in the palace?'

'Yes. I'm favoured, for I am a close friend of Lord Marden. I have a room in the tower here.'

'And you wish to help the Lady Macoby?'

'I would die for her!'

By the gods! thought Heighway. *He is shag-happy!*

'Then I would like you to do something for me,' he said and in a whisper he sketched out the task he wished Sarakkan to perform.

The young captain took a step backwards and frowned.

'You wish me to spy on Myal? The Regent's guest of honour?'

'Got it in one!'

Sarakkan's face broke into a happy grin.

'I'd be delighted,' he said.

Heighway eventually found his way back to the tradesmen's entrance, where Kratavan and the two constables were talking to some of the kitchen servants. They were sitting round an upturned barrel, drinking beer from a cask which had accidentally been dropped and, according to Kratavan, needed to be drunk up before it spoiled.

Heighway sent the two constables back to the station and poured himself a pint, whilst a team of scullery-boys were sent off to scour the palace and find out what had happened to Sergeant Raasay. Twenty minutes later, when Heighway was halfway through his second pint and was deep in an argument with Kratavan about whether hanging the son of the ruler of Minas Lantan would start a major war, the scullery-boys brought the sergeant back, having found him emerging from the basement toilet where he had taken refuge after a second attack of stomach cramps. He was the colour of old cheese and looked as though he'd lost half a stone in weight.

Heighway thought that his sergeant had better have a beer to cheer him up, then decided that he'd better have another one himself, as it was definitely helping his thought processes along. Then he decided that they'd better have some food as well, and so he commandeered a tray of cold meats, breads, cheeses and fruits that was meant for the banqueting-hall.

'Take it from me, Kratavan,' he said, as they began to eat, 'that man is as guilty as hell.'

'I just can't see why he'd want to murder his second in command, sir,' replied Kratavan.

'Look, let's take it from the start,' said Heighway, expansively. 'I'll demonstrate. Let's say that this boiled egg is Macoby. And this apple is Myal. Now, he wants to marry her . . .'

He placed the apple next to the boiled egg with a flourish.

'And this other apple here,' he continued, 'is Marden, her brother. He intends to stop the marriage, because he knows that his sister doesn't want it. Oh, *klatting* hell, Raasay, that's Macoby you've just shoved in your mouth!'

'Sorry, sir,' said the sergeant, through a mouthful of boiled egg.

'Okay, then, we'll say that this cold roast chicken is Macoby.'

Heighway plonked the bird down next to the apple that represented Myal.

'Nice legs,' said Kratavan.

'Shut it. Now, where was I? Oh, yes. Marden wants to stop the wedding, so Myal issues orders during the battle against the orcs which sends Marden's troop into the most dangerous part of the fighting.'

'Where are the orcs, sir?' asked Raasay, who was beginning to get confused.

'This dish of kedgeree will do. There's enough of it. Now, Marden disappears during the battle, probably killed by the orcs.'

Heighway plunged the apple into the kedgeree so that it was nearly covered. Bits of baked rice stuck to his fingers, and he wiped them absently on Raasay's shirt.

'But De Wenchas knows that there was no need for Marden's troop to be sent into that part of the battle,' he continued. 'He voices his doubts to Myal – all right, Raasay, before you ask, De Wenchas is this peach. Happy now? – and so Myal sneaks into his office unseen and kills him to stop him voicing these doubts to anyone else.'

Heighway belted the peach with his fist to demonstrate the murder, squashing it completely and splattering himself and the other two with fragments of pulp.

'But Macoby is suspicious,' he went on, 'and thinks that she might be next. So she runs away. Raasay, don't do that with the chicken. It looks ridiculous. Our next job is to find her and see if she has any incriminating evidence we can use against Myal. Then we can arrest him.'

The inspector picked up Myal's apple and took a deep bite out of it. Kratavan shook his head doubtfully, not fully convinced by Heighway's persuasive argument. Raasay carried on pretending to make the cooked chicken run on the table-top, then switched to making it do a little dance.

'I still think Macoby is involved,' said Kratavan. 'You should have seen her face when I found her by De Wenchas's body. She looked as guilty as hell.'

'No, Myal's the guilty one. I just know it,' Heighway answered. 'And he knows that I know. At one point I thought he was going to stab me.'

Raasay stopped playing with the chicken.

'That's because you were asking awkward questions, sir,' he said.

Heighway stared at his sergeant in disbelief.

'You what? How the *klat* would you know, sergeant? You spent the whole time squatting on the toilet.'

'Well, that's what the two men said, sir. The ones who were talking in the washroom.'

'What two men?'

'The ones who had been told to say that they never went to the *Weyr Inn*, and they never tried to snatch her ladyship back.'

'So that was her ladyship, was it, that lass at the *Weyr Inn*? Hmm.'

Heighway pondered on this. Had Myal tried to take his reluctant bride back by force? By the gods, they were going to have to move fast! They had to find her before he did. And it rather looked as though Colin the Sinister *had* got it right in his article, as well. Someone must definitely have tipped him off. But who? Maybe it was time to pay him a visit . . .

He stood up and looked at his watch. *Hmm, almost four o'clock in the afternoon*, he thought. *If he's anything like the other journalists I know, Colin the Sinister will be pissed in some pub by now. Ah well, I'll track him down tomorrow morning. There's no rush . . .*

'Okay, lads,' he said, sitting down again. 'I reckon we've just got time for one more pint . . .'

CHAPTER ELEVEN

When Macoby woke up the next morning, it was several minutes before she remembered where she was. At first, in her somnolent state, she was convinced that she was sleeping on a block of concrete whilst someone was slowly sawing up logs nearby. She stretched her hand out for the bell-rope to ring for her lady-in-waiting, but someone seemed to have removed it. And then she was awake, and her memory came flooding back.

She was lying fully-dressed in a room at the *Wyvern* tavern on an ancient bed that would have made granite feel comfy in comparison. The sawing of logs was issuing from the mouth of the strange young monk who had approached her yesterday. He was curled up in the chair, fast asleep, snoring his head off. When they had come up to the room the previous night, he had insisted on trying to stay awake to keep watch on her, although Macoby had told him that there was no need, as Darian's ghost was also there to keep watch and he never slept.

For a moment she lay there, watching Glart's face with an indulgent smile. He had been good company last night, making her laugh and buoying up her spirits. It was nice to wake up and find him there. She wasn't sure what use he would be if the Guild of Assassins made another attempt on her life, but he did seem to have some magical ability and she felt she could stake her life on the fact that he could be trusted. Come to think of it, that might turn out to be exactly what she was doing . . .

Hopping out of bed, she crossed to the window and peered out. To her surprise, the streets were full of people, but they all looked downcast and unhappy, and appeared to be waiting for something. On the buildings opposite, two flags hung dismally at half-mast, and Macoby wondered what was going on.

Going back to the bed, she wrapped a cloak about her shoulders and pulled the hood over her head, to disguise herself from casual glances. Then she crept silently to the door and, after beckoning to the ghost to follow her at a distance, slipped quietly out without waking the sleeping Glart, and went to discover what was happening.

Outside, she strolled quietly along the street past the ranks of people, keeping herself in the background and listening to their gossiping. Within minutes, she was up to date on all the latest news. Word of the events at the battle two days before had at last filtered back, and people now seemed to have realised that it had not been the walkover that they had expected, but a much more costly affair. Casualties had been heavy, said the rumours, and it was also said the Lord Marden was amongst the dead. As a result, there was a feeling of sadness and of mourning in the air.

These rumours came as no surprise to Macoby, but two of the others that were flying from mouth to mouth she found particularly interesting. Firstly, Myal's leadership was being widely praised. In fact, the word was that he had turned defeat into victory by his actions, and he was being spoken of as a hero. And this was why the people were out lining the streets: Myal was due to ride home at the head of the Minas Lantan contingent of the army that morning, and everyone was gathering to cheer him out of Koumas.

The second rumour was more accurate. It now seemed to be common knowledge that Myal wished to marry her, but she was relieved to find that they were not yet officially engaged. However, he was rumoured to be returning to Koumas in three days to receive an answer to his proposal. Macoby was horrified to find that, almost without exception, the people wanted her to accept.

As she listened to the almost-idolatrous gossiping, Macoby found that she was beginning to burn with an implacable hatred for Myal. But was she misjudging him? Why the *klat* was he being made out to be some sort of hero? Could Sarakkan have got it wrong?

Macoby inched closer to where a tall, burly man was talking of the battle to a small cluster of people. He was dressed in peasant gear, but from his stance and his build she could tell he was a soldier, and she guessed he must be one of the emergency militia-men who had been drafted in for the battle.

'Yes, I saw him kill five huge orcs,' he was saying. 'Our men were

101

near breaking, but General Myal fought like a man possessed! He rallied our men and led them forward until the orcs could take no more and broke. I tell you, I'm proud just to have stood near him! The man's a hero!'

The bystanders broke into animated discussion, and the man answered a couple of questions before working his way clear and setting off along the street. Deciding that she had to know the truth, Macoby chased after him and grabbed his arm.

'Did you really see . . .' she began, but then the man turned his face to her and she realised she knew him. It was the leader of the soldiers who had come to take her from the *Weyr Inn*.

'My lady!' he muttered, with a wolf-like grin. 'What a pleasant surprise! You've led us a merry dance!'

Macoby swore and turned to run, but his hand fastened round her arm and he yanked her into the shadows of a dark alleyway. She snatched her dagger from the hidden sheath, but he was too quick for her, grasping her wrist with his other hand and twisting it so that the knife fell to the cobbles.

'Ah, no you don't,' he hissed. 'I've been warned about you!'

Gasping with pain, Macoby opened her mouth to wish on the amulet, but before she could utter a word he had clamped his hand across her lower face, crushing her lips painfully against her teeth.

'Mmmph!' she mumbled.

'Huh? What?' muttered a faint voice from inside her jerkin, and Macoby realised with a thrill of fear that unless a wish was voiced out loud, the amulet could not act.

Then, to her horror, she saw that five other soldiers were waiting at the end of the alley. They were also dressed in peasant garb, and it was no longer hard to work out the source of all the pro-Myal rumours. At the sight of her, one of them spat a stream of liquidised chewing-weed onto the cobbles, and then they began to move towards her, unpleasant grins on their faces.

Realising that she was in great danger, Macoby twisted her head sharply. One of the man's filthy fingers slipped between her lips, and she bit down hard. He gasped in pain and jerked his hand away.

'You're going to wish you hadn't done that, my lady,' he snarled.

'No, I'm going to wish I was back in bed!' Macoby gasped.

There was a brief flash of light and a whirling sensation, and all at once she was lying on the ancient, lumpy bed in her room at the *Wyvern* tavern.

For a moment she lay there, half-paralysed by the horror of the assault. That look in the man's eyes as he had held her to him, his hand across her mouth . . . Macoby squirmed with revulsion as she recalled how he had stared at her. She could still feel his touch. Thank the gods for the amulet!

She pulled the slender silver unicorn out from her jerkin and stared at it. It was smirking at her and looking horribly smug.

'Honestly,' it muttered, 'what would you do without me?'

Before Macoby could reply, there was that faint *pop* which announced the return of Darian's ghost. He was hovering by the door and gave the impression of being distinctly peeved.

'I wish you'd give me some warning when you're going to just piss off like that,' he moaned. 'You've no idea how ill it makes me feel, being dragged around like a dog on the end of a lead!'

'I'm sorry,' she told him. 'Next time . . .'

'Next time,' interrupted a voice, 'you might not be so lucky.'

Macoby looked across to where Glart had been sleeping. He was stil in the same position on the chair, but his eyes were now open and he was staring at her in concern.

'What's wrong?' she asked him.

'You've been out without me, that's what's wrong!'

'Listen, friend, I've known you for less than a day, and that sure as hell doesn't entitle you to . . .'

'You don't understand!' he broke in, urgently, but then visibly held himself back. Standing, he walked across and sat next to her on the bed.

'You are in vast danger,' he continued slowly, as though explaining it as much to himself as to her. 'I can help you. But I can't do it if I'm not with you. So far, that jewel has saved you three times. But, used wrongly, it could be a bigger danger to you than anything. I can feel its power . . .'

He held out his hand in a wordless gesture, and without even thinking, Macoby placed the amulet into his palm. As it touched his skin he rocked backwards as though in pain.

'Aiee! The power in this thing!' Glart closed his fingers over it and looked up into Macoby's eyes.

103

'It was handed on to you to guard,' he continued, almost accusingly, 'and yet you have given it to a total stranger. Anyone with a little guile and a trace of the Power could have taken it from you. And with it, any half-trained magic-user would be well nigh unstoppable! Even someone like me!'

Macoby stared at the monk like a little girl who has asked a friend to hold her ice-cream while she ties her shoe, only to see the friend shove the whole thing into her mouth and swallow it.

'But it only responds to me,' she cried. 'It grants *my* wishes!'

Glart grinned at her, then suddenly his voice hardened.

'*Haec vincula inice!*' he snapped.

All at once, iron fetters appeared from nowhere about Macoby's legs, ankles and wrists. To her horror, she found she couldn't move.

'Stop him!' she yelled at the amulet in his hand. 'Free me!'

But there was no result.

'See?' said Glart. '*Illos solve!*'

And just as suddenly, the fetters vanished. Confused, Macoby rubbed at her wrists.

'Whoever holds it, wields its power,' said Glart, holding up the amulet. 'I now have it, you see, and so its power is mine.'

And with that he tossed it gently back to the surprised Macoby, who caught it and clutched it to her breast. She felt light-headed, almost faint, with relief.

'I thought you were going to keep it for yourself!' she gasped.

'By the gods! What would I want with it? No, I think you are meant to carry it – but with care!'

Macoby shook her head in bewilderment.

'This is all too much for me,' she told Glart. 'I don't even know what is happening, let alone why.'

'Maybe I can help you with that as well.'

She gazed at the young monk. He was sitting beside her with a friendly grin on his face and looked as though he was offering to help her deal with a dripping tap instead of murder, mayhem and smug magical artefacts, and she wondered how he could stay so cool, so level-headed. For an instant she felt irritated with him, but then his grin won her over.

'Okay, then, smartarse,' she said, grinning back. 'What do we do next? Any suggestions?'

'Oh, that's simple.'

'Is it?'

'Yeah. We have breakfast.'

Darian was finding it harder and harder to relate to the real world now that he was a ghost. Time seemed to run differently after death, stretching and contracting like elastic, so that at one moment people seemed to be moving in slow motion, and then a few seconds later they would be zooming around like pinballs. Occasionally they would randomly vanish or return, as though a segment of time had just gone missing completely.

There was also a strange feeling of not belonging. Things that had been important or entertaining to him now seemed to be of no interest at all. For example, if he had been offered a chance when he was alive to spy on a man and three women having a good time in a bedroom, he would have leapt at the chance and would have found it hugely entertaining. Now, it was no more than vaguely interesting. Even worse, it didn't seem to have the effect on him that such a sight should have done. Fair enough, he was dead, but some parts of him seemed to be deader than others . . .

He wondered whether becoming impotent was part and parcel of dying, or whether it was just that the living aren't very attractive when you happened to be dead. Then he began to wonder what would happen if he met a female ghost. Especially a naked one. Would she have any effect? And how did you go about meeting other ghosts? There must be others – people were always reporting seeing them when he'd been alive. Apparently, in some of the older buildings in Koumas you could hardly move without some spectre popping out of the woodwork and rattling metal chains at you.

Mind you, most of the sightings he had heard of had been single ghosts. Couples were rare. And anyway, was there any point in meeting a female ghost? Could they actually make love? As far as he knew, no-one had ever reported seeing a pair of ghosts at it like the clappers.

After a while, he decided it best to stop thinking along these lines, as it was making him feel both depressed and lonely. It was no wonder that ghosts were often reported as moaning and wailing. This haunting business was enough to make a saint moan!

He wondered what had happened to Macoby and Glart, and whether he should go and find them, but he decided not to bother. He knew that they couldn't have gone far, or he'd have been hauled after them like a dog on a leash. Then he started thinking about what Glart had said the previous night.

Apparently, he was definitely being held by a *Soul Shackle* and the young monk reckoned that this was a spell usually cast when someone wants the ghost to pass on a message. Darian thought this was probably the case with him. He was convinced that Marden had told him something he was to pass on to Macoby. The problem was, he couldn't for the death of him remember what it was. For a while he drifted round the room like a mournful raincloud, trying to force his reluctant brain into action. And then, at last, a single small memory drifted into sight like a tiny fish surfacing in a muddy pond . . .

Macoby had been much more careful what she wished for in this tavern. She didn't want to make it easy for Myal's guards to find her by leaving a trail of rough-house pubs which now served gourmet breakfasts, and so she had simply used the amulet to ensure that the landlord would provide her with something edible to eat. As a result, she and Glart had been served with eggs, bacon and sausage that were merely paddling in fat up to their ankles, rather than swimming in the stuff.

'Right,' she said, mopping up the last bit of egg-yolk with a piece of toast, 'you're the one with all the ideas. Where do we go from here?'

Glart thought for a moment.

'Well,' he said, pensively, 'we've a number of options. We could try and find out more about the amulet. I'm sure it holds the answer. The problem is, we don't know the question . . .'

'Oh, very profound.'

'I'd like to check it out, but this isn't the time or the place. No, there's other stuff we need to sort out first.'

'Such as what?'

'Ummm . . . you said that the orcs were winning the battle, yet they suddenly retreated. And they probably captured or killed your brother, yes?'

'Yes.'

'Also, you said last night that you couldn't work out why orcs should suddenly have invaded Kuhbador after all these years of peace, right?'

'Yes again.'

'So let's find out why.'

'Oh, very good. And how do you propose we do that?'

'Easy. We'll ask some orcs.'

'And you think they'll tell you? Just like that?'

'They might. It can't do any harm. I suppose the orcs have a consulate in Koumas somewhere?'

'Yeah, though I've never been there. They have wonderfully riotous parties, or so people used to say, and so Father never let me anywhere near the place.'

'Well, now's your chance. Let's find Darian's ghost and get moving.'

The ghost was in a state of some excitement when they got upstairs and was fairly whizzing round the bedroom. Talking to him wasn't easy, for he kept miscalculating and disappearing through walls, but they eventually got him to hover in one place and discovered that he had got another piece of his memory back.

'I can remember the Lord Marden telling me about the amulet,' he babbled, excitedly. 'He said that it was very old and that it came from an ancient tomb. Apparently he was in charge of an army detachment that was sent down to some archaeological digs in the south. They were to act as guards to a shipment of the riches that had been excavated from a group of First Age tombs . . .'

'That's right,' broke in Macoby, who had sat down on the bed. 'It was only a couple of weeks ago. When he came back he had changed completely. He was morose and withdrawn. And that was when he started wearing this.'

She lifted her hand to her breast, where the amulet still hung inside her jerkin.

'Lord Marden said that his men found a dead grave-robber one night,' continued Darian's ghost. 'They couldn't tell what had killed him, but Lord Marden was convinced that something had frightened the man to death. He was clutching an ancient knife and the amulet.

107

They didn't seem to be of much worth compared to the other treasures that were being excavated from the tombs, and so Lord Marden decided to hold onto them. He didn't seem too sure exactly why he did so.'

The ghost paused and looked uncertainly at Macoby, as though wondering whether he should be telling her this.

'Go on,' she urged him.

'He said it was the worst decision he had ever made,' the ghost whispered. 'He told me that strange things happened when he wore the amulet. He thought it was magical and very powerful. Then he told me that someone had stolen the dagger, and that the same person was after the amulet. Then he told me that he was going to die . . .'

'He knew?' interjected Glart, who was lounging in the chair. Darian's ghost nodded.

'He thought that someone would use the battle to ensure his death,' he went on. 'He knew that if he was killed, the amulet would be taken from him. That's why he gave it to me, so that it would be safe, for no-one knew I had it. He told me that if he died, I was to give it to you.'

There was a silence, which was reluctantly broken by Macoby. She didn't want to ask the question, but she knew that she had to.

'Did he tell you who stole the dagger?' she asked, bracing herself for the answer.

'Yes,' answered the ghost.

'Who was it?'

There was another pause, and Glart thought that the ghost was going to burst into tears.

'I can't remember,' the ghost said, at last.

'Oh, Darian!' Macoby snapped. 'You're about as much use as a hernia!'

'Go easy on him,' admonished Glart. 'It's not his fault. He'll remember in time.'

'I suppose so,' muttered Macoby, subsiding. 'Anyway, we know the answer. Myal's men seem to be everywhere. I wish I knew what he expects to get from all this.'

'Sorry, can't help you there,' came the amulet's voice from inside her jerkin.

'Maybe we'll get some clue from talking to the orcs,' said Glart, rising from the chair. 'Come on, let's get going.'

He waited for a few seconds, but Macoby showed no signs of moving, continuing to sit on the bed and picking at the stained coverlet with nervous fingers.

'What's wrong?' he asked her.

Macoby shrugged.

'I don't know,' she said uncertainly. 'I just don't feel safe going out on the streets any more. As I said, Myal's men are everywhere. And I'm no longer sure whether they're after me or this *klatting* amulet. If it's all that important, someone might snatch it.'

As she sat there looking unhappy and vulnerable, Glart felt his heart going out to her, and he felt an urge to put his arms round her and hug her. Rapidly suppressing it, he sat down on the bed at a respectable distance and fixed his most confident smile into place.

'Oh, I think we can prevent that,' he said, brightly. 'If you'll let me borrow the thing for a moment . . .'

Macoby looked at him doubtfully, but then remembered that if he'd wanted to take possession of the amulet, he could have already done so. Hauling it out, she slipped the chain over her head and handed it to Glart.

'What we need to do,' he said slowly, 'is to disguise you both. Now, let's see.'

He thought for a moment, his face screwed up in concentration, and Macoby watched him, fascinated. He had a face that was full of character, although she couldn't decide whether it was attractive or ugly. She had just decided that it was attractively ugly when he suddenly clicked his fingers.

'Ah, I know,' he said. '*Facies Barbara Plaustriterrae habe!*'

Macoby waited, but nothing seemed to happen except that the skin of her face itched briefly, and an expression almost of awe passed across Glart's features.

'Is something wrong?' she asked him.

'Now, listen,' he warned her. 'Don't panic. The spell is purely temporary. I can remove it instantly, all right?'

'What spell?'

'The spell I've just cast on you with the amulet's help. The spell to disguise you. We'll remove it the instant we get off the street again.'

Glart was now looking about as happy as a hobbit that's just been told to go on a crash diet. With a sinking feeling in her stomach, Macoby got up and walked across to stare in the small, cracked mirror that hung above the fireplace. She stared at her reflection for a long, long time.

The face that looked back at her from the mirror was the face of one of those old women who labour under the delusion that applying vast amounts of cosmetic will in some way improve the ravages of time. It looked like an action painting created by an artist who had an awful lot more paint than talent. Black mascara, blue eye shadow and red lipstick fought a pitched battle with rouge and pink foundation. It was a battle in which they were taking no prisoners.

'You had better be able to remove the spell,' she told him, 'because if not, you are going to die a very nasty death, very soon.'

'Oh, don't worry,' said Glart nervously. 'I can. And this way we can be sure that no-one will recognise you.'

Macoby glowered at him and he turned away hurriedly and switched his attention to the amulet, holding it on the flat palm of his hand.

'Right, then,' he said. 'Marden found an amulet, so Myal's men will be looking for something of that nature. And so we change this to something else . . .'

He whispered softly to the amulet, so softly that Macoby couldn't make out the words. Once again the silver metal began to change and flow, this time condensing and darkening until a simple gold ring in the shape of a lion's head lay in his palm.

'There,' he said. 'How's that?'

Macoby smiled grudgingly and extended her hand, and Glart slipped the ring over her finger. It was only when the ring began to chuckle nastily that he realised he'd slipped it onto the third finger of her left hand.

'I'm a wedding ring now, am I,' it scoffed. 'In your dreams, mate!'

Glart turned away, embarrassed, wishing he could take a hammer to the hateful lump of metal, but Macoby didn't seem to notice. She was too busy studying her reflection again.

'I suppose I should be grateful,' she said at last, turning away from the mirror, 'but somehow I'm not. Come on, let's go.'

She strode proudly to the door, then stopped.

'And you can give me my own face back before we go in to the consulate,' she told him. 'Because I tell you now, I am *not* going to sit in a room full of orcs and be the most hideous one there . . .'

The journey to the orc consulate passed uneventfully. The ghost was ordered to stay as far behind them as possible, so that no-one would associate the stream of barking dogs, hissing cats and bucking horses with them and stare too closely. But although the streets were packed with people, no-one paid them any attention, for everyone was watching the Minas Lantan contingent of the army marching out of the city with Myal at their head. He rode proudly on his horse, staring round him coldly, and almost seeming not to notice the cheering and yelling that greeted him.

Macoby and Glart stopped to watch as he rode past. At one point, Myal's gaze passed over Macoby and she flinched, but there was no hint of recogniton in his face. Her disguise was totally effective. However, the incident unnerved her a little, and she found she was trembling. Glart took her arm, and they moved away and went down a quiet side-alley to escape from the throng of people.

Five minutes later, they reached the dark, litter-strewn street in which the orcish consulate was situated. It was a run-down, dilapidated stone building with peeling whitewash on the walls and gaps in the slate roof, set back slightly from the road behind a thin strip of garden which appeared to be given over mainly to the cultivation of brambles, nettles and old beer bottles.

Everywhere was still and silent, save for two cats throwing feline insults at each other in some distant yard, but although they appeared to be the only people in the street, Macoby still felt it best to slip into a shadowy side-alley for Glart to cast the counterspell. He took the ring from her finger, whispered the incantation, then smiled at the blatant look of worry on her newly-restored features.

'Don't worry,' he said, handing her back the ring. 'You're just as beautiful as you were before.'

The sincerity in his voice was patently obvious and he almost winced, but Macoby just smiled at him. Suddenly Glart realised exactly how beautiful she did look, and he was seized with an almost uncontrollable urge to grab her and kiss her. And then, just as he was fighting the urge down, she stretched up and kissed him chastely on the cheek.

'Thanks,' she said. 'You're a pretty talented guy, and it's such a relief to have someone with me who I can trust.'

For a moment Glart thought he was going to faint. There was a loud humming noise in his ears, the sun seemed to come out, and he thought he could hear distant heavenly music. He cleared his throat, embarrassed, and the sound seemed to echo around the alleyway like a roll of thunder.

'Oh, think nothing of it,' he muttered. 'It's a pleasure to help.'

'Right, well now you can help me deal with these orcs,' she told him. 'Come on.'

They walked out of the alley and strolled up the cracked, over-grown path that led through the weeds to the battered wooden door of the orcish consulate. It was ajar, and so they pushed it open and went inside.

They found themselves standing in a single squalid room that ran the entire length of the building. It was furnished like a tavern. A bar ran along the left-hand wall, and there were a number of tables scattered about, with a few rickety chairs or stools at each. In the far corner, a flight of wooden stairs led up to the next floor. On one table stood several half-empty beer glasses, and the smell of tobacco smoke hung in the air, but the place appeared to be deserted.

For a few seconds Macoby and Glart stood by the door, listening, whilst Darian's ghost floated past them and drifted aimlessly towards the bar.

'Isn't it rather unlike orcs to be so shy and retiring?' asked Glart. 'I'd have expected this place to be a bit livelier.'

'It's not surprising they're keeping their heads down,' replied Macoby. 'Their people have just invaded our country and fought a pitched battle in which a lot of our kin have died. They're probably scared stiff of retaliation. In fact, I'm surprised a mob hasn't been here to torch the place.'

'Maybe they have.' Glart sniffed delicately. 'From the smell, I'd say the building is too damp to burn.'

He wandered across to the table with the glasses and picked one

112

up. The beer in it looked and smelt fresh. He took a mouthful and swallowed it appreciately.

'Well, wherever they've gone, they haven't been gone long,' he said.

Macoby looked upwards as though expecting to be able to see through the solid ceiling.

'Right, Darian,' she said. 'Here's your chance to be some use. Nip upstairs and see if there's anybody there, would you?'

The ghost nodded and then floated upwards and disappeared through the stained plaster. There was silence for a while, and then the ghost's head re-emerged through the ceiling.

'I think you'd better come up and have a look at this,' he told them.

They climbed the stairs, which led to a long, narrow undecorated corridor with doors along one side. Darian's ghost was waiting half in, half out of the third door.

'In here,' he told them, and disappeared through the door. Macoby opened it, and they walked in.

They were in a smallish, gloomy room that was obviously the main office of the consulate. On one side near the wall stood a large desk which was covered in papers, documents and an awful lot of empty beer glasses and bottles. Framed maps of orcish cities such as High Meneal, Great Retching and Goblin City hung on the walls. Above the small fireplace was a neatly-stitched sampler of an old orcish proverb: 'Four pints good, two pints bad.' And in front of the fireplace was a small pile of dead orcs.

There were five of them, and they had each clearly been killed by a single sword-thrust through the heart, performed so clinically that they had hardly bled. Death would have been instantaneous. Glart leaned forwards and touched one. He was still warm, and the young monk guessed that he had been dead for less than thirty minutes.

'He's beaten us to it again,' snapped Macoby. 'If only we'd got here an hour ago!'

'Look on the bright side,' suggested Glart. 'If we'd got here half an hour ago, we'd have probably joined these poor sods. Come on, let's see if we can find any clues as to who did this. Open the window, would you, and let some light in.'

113

Macoby frowned and crossed to the window. There was no glass in it, but the wooden shutter was closed tight. She thought she could hear the sounds of clattering feet outside as she undid the catch, and so as she threw the shutter back she peered out into the street below.

Several police officers were walking up the path to the door of the consulate, and one of them glanced up at her. It was the officer who had escorted her away from De Wenchas' corpse – DC Kratavan.

'*Klat!*' she swore. 'Glart, it's the police. We've got to get out of here!'

'But . . .'

'Don't argue! Where do we go next?'

'Erm . . . well, I think it might be a good idea to get you out of this town for a bit. And if we want to question some orcs, maybe we'd better go to an orc city, right?'

'Okay,' said Macoby. 'But before we head out of town, I need to go back to the palace. There's something I've got to do. Are you ready, Darian?'

'I suppose so,' muttered the ghost, mournfully.

They heard the sudden clatter of footsteps in the tavern below, and Macoby wished. There was a blinding flash, and all at once she and Glart were standing in a dark recess under some stairs. A few seconds later, there was the usual *pop* as the ghost caught up with them.

'You okay?' Macoby asked him.

'No,' answered the ghost, mournfully. 'That's a horrible way to travel. I think I'm going to be sick.'

'Well, that ought to be interesting. Listen, you two stay here and don't be seen. I'll be back in a couple of minutes.'

'What?' said Glart, who once again was filled with the urge to grab Macoby and start kissing her. It seemed to be something to do with being in dark, confined spaces next to her, and it was making him feel very confused.

'Oh, right,' he added. 'Yes. Fine.'

Macoby slipped out from the recess and skipped nimbly up the stairs. At the top was a closed door. She knocked lightly on it, hoping against hope that the usual occupant was inside. To her relief, it opened, and Sarakkan looked out.

'Macoby!' he gasped, half in surprise, half in pleasure. 'Where have you been?'

'I haven't got time to tell you, Sarakkan. Listen. Did Colonel De Wenchas tell anyone else of his doubts about Myal's handling of the battle?'

'What? Look, never mind that. What about . . .'

'Sarakkan!' she interrupted, grabbing his arms in her agitation and shaking him. 'It's important! Did he?'

Sarakkan paused and thought for a moment.

'No,' he said. 'He said it was in confidence, and warned me not to say anything.'

'Then you're in danger!' she told him. 'I think that Myal is behind all this. I think he killed De Wenchas to stop him telling people about his poor handling of the battle. He needs to be a hero to the people of this city to try and force me into marrying him! If he finds out that De Wenchas confided in you, he'll kill you, too!'

Sarakkan smiled at her, and she felt a great wave of annoyance sweeping through her.

'I'm serious!' she hissed. 'Myal is dangerous!'

'I know,' he told her, and his face grew grave. 'The police have asked me to keep an eye on him.'

He looked around as though worried he might be overheard, then lowered his voice to a whisper.

'I searched his rooms while he was at the banquet last night. Do you know what I found?'

Macoby shook her head.

'A dagger that Marden used to own, one that came from an ancient tomb in the south.'

'The one that was stolen from him?'

'You know of it?' said Sarakkan, surprised.

'Yes.'

'It may be the one that killed De Wenchas. But what baffles me is what is behind all this. Why would Myal steal the dagger? And why would he want Marden dead?'

Macoby shook her head in disbelief. Much as she loved Sarakkan, there were times when his naivety and innocence were pretty annoying.

'You idiot,' she said. 'You know he wants to marry me! It's not for love, it's for power! When Father dies, if Marden is dead, Myal and I would be joint rulers of Koumas!'

She watched as the idea took hold and horror spread across Sarakkan's face.

'We've got to stop him!' he gasped. 'We've got to find more proof!'

'Maybe I can find some.' Macoby stood on tiptoe and kissed him briefly on the cheek. 'I'll be in touch soon. Take care, Sarakkan!'

Then she turned and dashed down the stairs.

'Macoby! Wait!' he yelled, and then he dashed after her, but when he reached the foot of the stairs she seemed to have vanished into thin air, and he was left scratching his head and wondering what the *klat* she thought she was up to.

Glart was skulking in the shadows under the stairs when Macoby came dashing down them and grabbed his arm. Before he had a chance to say anything there was a blinding flash, and all at once he found that they were standing in an open field by a broad, slow river in brilliant sunshine. He blinked his eyes, trying to accustom them to the sudden change in light, and then Darian's ghost turned up beside them with its habitual faint *pop*, looking even paler than before.

'Hurp!' said the ghost.

'I'm sorry,' said Macoby, 'but I wanted to be out of there quickly.'

'Think . . . hurp . . . think nothing of it.'

'Where are we?' asked Glart.

'Right by the western borders of Koumas, near Lampa Sanda,' Macoby told him. 'You see, I've never been to the orc lands before, so the amulet reckons it can't take me there. This is as near as I've been.'

'S'right,' mumbled the golden lion's head ring on her finger. 'Sorry and all that, but you'll have to do the rest on foot. Shouldn't take you more than a couple of days to get to Great Retching, up in the mountains there.'

Glart stared westwards across the river at the grandeur of the Irridic Mountains on the other side. Then he thought about the prospect of travelling through the wilds for two whole days with Macoby.

'Ah well,' he said. 'We'll just have to do our best.' And somehow he managed to prevent himself from laughing out loud with glee.

The man was beginning to get a little worried. His plans were starting to go slightly wrong. Nothing too serious so far, but with the police getting involved he had to be careful. That moron Heighway was no problem, but he hadn't expected Macoby to disappear like this. Now he hadn't the faintest idea where she was. If she found out that he was behind all this, wild horses wouldn't get her to marry him. Better speed up his plans. Force the issue. Exert a bit of pressure and marry her quickly. After that, it wouldn't matter, for she was expendable . . .

CHAPTER TWELVE

Heighway awoke with the muzzy head and sour-tasting mouth that told him he might have overdone it a little the previous day. He lay for a while in his lonely bed, wondering what time it was and thinking that he probably ought to be at the police station by now. Most of his officers had wives who got them up for work on time (and Sergeant Raasay had his mum), but Heighway was a lifelong bachelor who had discovered from years of experience that the best cure for a hangover is sleep, and so he was habitually and unapologetically late for work.

He was thinking about the facts of the current case. The more he thought about it, the more he was convinced that Myal was behind it all. He reckoned that it wouldn't be too difficult getting enough proof to convince the superintendent. No, the problem would be in getting him to agree to the arrest of such an important man. Still, time enough to face that problem later. For the moment, he still had to find the proof.

The muzziness began to dissipate after a while, and so Heighway rose and got dressed. Then, with a piece of toast in his hand, he left the house and set off for the headquarters of the *Koumas Gazette* in Malthouse Lane. He had decided that his next move should be to track down Colin the Sinister, for the journalist seemed to be finding out facts before the police. He obviously had a useful source of information which, hopefully, he could be persuaded to share.

Heighway stopped at the bottom of the street to buy the morning edition of the *Gazette*, curious to see if Colin had come up with anything new. At first, he thought that the journalist had dropped the case altogether, for the crime page was given over almost entirely to the murder of one of the village elders at a nearby hamlet. The man, who was the local priest, had been found stabbed to death minutes before he was due to conduct a mass, and under the banner headline *Service Off – Elder Dead!*, Colin the Sinister, painted his usual accurate but lurid picture of the crime.

But then right down at the bottom of the page, under the heading *Lass Bust or Wood Stocks*, Heighway found a small paragraph that caused him to stop dead in the middle of the street and curse violently.

Yesterday evening, the paragraph ran, *Superintendent Weird of the Koumas Urban National Troopers announced that the arrest of a woman in connection with the murder of Colonel De Wenchas was imminent.*

'Detective Inspector Heighway is hot on the trail of a suspect,' the Superintendent told our correspondent. 'He has orders to arrest the lass responsible in the next three days, or else I've told him that he will be locked in the old wooden stocks on Felonsgate where you can all go and throw refuse at him!'

Heighway crumpled up the paper and hurled it with venom at a nearby stray dog. He had come across some bizarre forms of motivation during his career, but without a doubt, the strangest was the superintendent's habit of treating his subordinates like criminals unless they came up with some real criminals for him to treat that way instead. He had no doubt that, unless he arrested someone within three days, the chief would carry out his threat as promised.

Nor was the chief going to be too pleased when he heard who the main suspect was. He had been bad enough when he heard that Heighway wanted to question the Lady Macoby. He was going to go completely berserk when he heard that Heighway now wanted to arrest the eldest son of the ruler of Minas Lantan!

Cursing himself for not keeping the superintendent up to date with the case, Heighway turned and headed for the police station with a sinking heart. All of a sudden, he had a feeling that this case was going to go sadly wrong.

It took a couple of stiff whiskies in the police canteen before Heighway felt he'd summoned up enough courage to go and face his boss, and even then he dithered nervously outside the superintendent's office for several minutes before knocking on the door. But when he did eventually enter, he found that his boss was in an unusually good mood.

'Morning, Heighway,' he boomed. 'God, man, you look as though you've slept in those clothes. Arrested Lady Macoby for the De Wenchas murder yet?'

'No, sir. I don't think she did it, after all.'

'Don't you? Don't you now?' The superintendent leaned back in his chair and cupped his fingers behind his head. 'DC Kratavan does.'

'Kratavan's wrong, sir.'

'Is he, indeed? So, who did it, then, Heighway?'

The inspector swallowed nervously then took the bull by the horns. 'Myal of Minas Lantan, sir.'

'Tell me you're joking!'

Quickly, Heighway ran through his reasons for suspecting that Myal was a murderer.

'He expects to end up ruling both cities,' he finished. 'But De Wenchas could have prevented that. I've got a man in the palace watching him, an army captain called Sarakkan. He can vouch for the fact that there was mistrust and suspicion between Myal and De Wenchas. I've just got a couple more lines of inquiry to check out, and then I'd like to detain Myal for questioning, sir.'

The superintendent began to laugh, slapping the desk with the flat of his hand in his mirth.

'You'll have a job!' he gasped. 'He's just ridden out of Koumas at the head of several hundred soldiers who worship the ground he treads on. I suppose you could chase after him, but if you tried to arrest him they'd cut you into tiny fragments. And if they didn't, I would!'

Suddenly the superintendent was no longer laughing. He sprang to his feet, marched round the desk and lowered his face until he was staring into Heighway's eyes from a range of about six inches.

'So you suspect that Myal is a murderer, eh?' he shouted. 'Well, I suspect that one of my detective inspectors is a total prat and a complete dick-head! What the hell are you trying to do, man? Plunge this city into war with its closest neighbour and ally? Myal's a *klatting* hero!'

'With respect, sir, he's a *klatting* villain.'

The superintendent prodded Heighway firmly in the chest with one finger.

'You are not arresting Myal. Find someone else who we can accuse. What about this what's-his-name, this Sarakkan? You said he's an army man?'

'Yes, sir.'

'Well, he'll do. Are his parents at all influential or well-known?'

'I don't think so, sir. He's of peasant stock.'

Heighway paused, wincing inwardly at his use of the word *stock*. The last thing he wanted to do was to remind the superintendent about his promise to Colin the Sinister.

'Excellent. No-one to complain about his arrest and cause ructions.' The superintendent stood upright and rubbed his hands together happily.

'Although he said he's friendly with Lord Marden,' Heighway added. 'And I think he's been shagging the Lady Macoby.'

'Even better! We can say he's been trying to frame Myal to prevent him from marrying her, out of jealousy. Well, there we are, then, inspector. Case solved. Congratulations. Looks like you won't be spending several hours in the public stocks after all.'

The superintendent shook Heighway's hand and then led him to the door.

'Let me know when you've made the arrest, won't you,' he said, and Heighway found himself out in the corridor with the door shut behind him.

Shaking his head in frustration, he wandered off in search of Sergeant Raasay. As he did so, he thought about the superintendent's suggestion of arrresting Sarakkan. The temptation was almost overwhelming, but Heighway still retained some of the idealism that had caused him to move to Koumas in the first place, and so he ruefully put it to the back of his mind. He had a duty to arrest the right man, if possible. Moreover, if Myal was indeed the murderer, then he was not fit to be Macoby's husband and was a threat to the whole of Koumas. In fact, if Heighway could only find enough cast-iron, impossible-to-ignore evidence, the chief would be forced to arrest Myal out of sheer patriotism. But if he couldn't, and he was in imminent danger of being sent to the stocks, then and only then might he be forced into framing somebody such as Sarakkan . . .

*

121

Heighway eventually found Sergeant Raasay in the sick-bay. He was having his stomach pumped, and looked desperately ill.

'Good morning, sergeant,' Heighway greeted him. 'Don't tell me, let me guess. Your grandmother's been doing the cooking again, right?'

Raasay nodded unhappily.

'What was it, this time?' Heighway asked.

'Last night's pie, sir. Apparently she's been saving up cockroaches and bed bugs for months, and . . .'

'That'll do, Raasay. Spare me the details.' Heighway shut his eyes and waited until the queasy feeling had gone. 'Have you any idea where Kratavan's got to?'

'I think he's gone to the orcish consulate, sir. We had a tip-off that there's been a bit of unpleasantness down there.'

'Hardly surprising after the invasion. You'd have thought they'd have had the sense to pack up and leave town for a while. Ah well. I'd better stop off there and see what's happened, I suppose.'

The inspector arrived at the consulate just as the police pathomancer was leaving. Once again, it was the stout, black-draped figure of Madam Min.

'Morning, Min,' he greeted her, hoping against hope that she wasn't in one of her garrulous moods.

'Morning, inspector.' Madam Min paused and seemed to be staring through him absently, as though receiving some astral message. 'I see you had toast for breakfast.'

'Very good,' he answered, impressed despite himself. 'Your psychic powers are sharp this morning.'

'Psychic powers be buggered! You've got crumbs all down your shirt and butter smears on your chin.'

'Ah,' said Heighway, removing the evidence with his hand. 'Had a working breakfast on the hoof. You know how it is. So, what's happened here? Surprise me, Min.'

'Orcs.'

'In an orcish consulate? Get away!'

'No need to be like that, just because you've got a hangover.' Min paused again and pressed the back of one hand to her forehead. Her eyes closed, and her other hand began making vague sketching movements in the air. 'Oh, what is this coming through . . . ? I see you, in the near future . . . There's a connection with wood . . . you seem to be wearing wood around your wrists and ankles . . . you're sitting there . . . people are laughing . . . I see an awful lot of very ripe tomatoes . . .'

Heighway had gone quite pale.

'Fine, well, I must rush,' he muttered. 'Got a lot to do. 'Bye, Min.'

He strode off up the path and pushed past the burly constable who was on duty at the door. Min opened her eyes and chuckled happily to herself. That would teach the crabby old bugger to make sarcastic remarks! It was a help sometimes, being a psychic, but it was even more of a help that she'd read the superintendent's comments in Colin the Sinister's column last night . . .

The dead orcs had been laid out in a row in front of the desk when Heighway got upstairs. Kratavan was sitting on the desk flicking through some pornographic manuscripts that he'd found in one of the drawers. He leapt up, and the inspector could tell that he was bursting with some item of news, but he waved the detective constable to silence and bent down to look at the corpses.

'Not too difficult to tell what killed them, eh, Kratavan?'

'No sir. But guess who . . .'

'What did Madam Min have to tell us?'

'Er . . .' Kratavan bottled up his excitement with obvious difficulty. 'Well, they were all killed by experienced swordsmen, most probably army veterans. And each orc was killed by a different sword, so there were at least five soldiers here.'

'I can count, man! Go on.'

'Death was instantaneous. And the spirit of the second orc from the left is extremely unhappy, Min reckons. Apparently he had just won a lot of money off the others in some form of gambling game, but they were all killed before they could pay up. The spirit would like us to transfer some money from the others' purses into his, so that he can rest in peace.'

'Well, the spirit can go and shag himself. Time of death?'

'About an hour ago.'

'Anything else?'

'Erm, yes,' answered Kratavan. 'She said to make sure I said exactly this.' He cleared his throat, and then recited carefully, '*Be careful you get the right person for the murders, Heighway, or you could be in trouble. You need to take stock of the situation.*'

Kratavan stopped and looked at the inspector, puzzled. 'What exactly does that mean, sir?'

'It means that I am going to go round to that old biddy's house and piss in her cauldron if she doesn't stop taking the mick,' the inspector raged. 'Come on, Kratavan. You've been bursting to tell me. What have you found?'

'Well, sir. It was as we were just getting here. Someone was still in this room. They opened the window. I was on the path outside, and I got a clear view of their face.'

'Anyone we know?'

'Yes, sir. The Lady Macoby, sir!'

Heighway stared at Kratavan in disbelief.

'Are you sure, man?'

'Positive, sir!'

'Hm.'

Heighway thought for a moment, then brightened. This didn't affect his theory at all. In fact, in some ways it helped to strengthen it.

'Listen, Kratavan, this doesn't mean that she had anything to do with murder.'

'But sir! She was in this very room . . .'

'And they were all killed by veteran soldiers, not by small female members of the royal family. We know that Macoby has been hiding somewhere in town, scared stiff that someone's trying to kill her. And Colin the Sinister found out that someone tried to snatch her from that tavern. What better place for her to hide than in the orc consulate? No-one would look for her here. But she must have been betrayed. The same soldiers came down here, killed everyone and took her off with them. Couldn't you have stopped them?'

'We didn't see them, sir. We came straight up the stairs, but they'd vanished. There's no other way out. It must have been magic, sir!'

'Well, there you are, then. There's something deeper than we thought going on here. I hope that poor girl's all right.'

Heighway looked down dispassionately at the dead orcs, then began to pace back and forth, thinking deeply.

'Look,' he said eventually. 'We need to know what we're dealing with here. Get Madam Min back and find out if magic played any part in all this, then let me know. If we're up against some powerful magic-user, we could be way out of our depth.'

'Right, sir. Where will you be?'

'I'll be talking to Colin the Sinister. He seems to be the one man who's found out more than we have.'

'So where will I find you both, sir?'

Heighway looked at Kratavan and shook his head impatiently.

'He's a journalist, for God's sake. Where do you *think* you'll find us? In a pub, man! In a pub!'

Colin the Sinister knocked back his remaining half-pint of Old Pustule's Bitter in one vast swallow, and then held out his glass to Heighway.

'As you're picking my brains, inspector,' he said, 'I'll have another pint of the same.'

Heighway sighed and took the proffered glass, then went to the bar and bought a refill, plus one for himself. He took them back to the small table by the fireplace, plonked them down and then seated himself opposite the journalist and repeated his question.

'How did you find out about the attempt to kidnap that girl at the *Weyr*?'

'Well, I'd like to say that it was all down to a mixture of journalistic intellect and investigative brilliance,' said Colin the Sinister, after down half his pint. 'But sadly, that's not the case. The *Weyr*'s scummy landlord turned up at the office, said some soldiers had burst into his tavern and tried to make off with this pretty young girl, and would we like to buy exclusive rights to the story for cash. I said no, but I'd buy him a couple of pints for it.'

'So why did you link it to the De Wenchas case?'

'Wishful thinking, really. The soldiers in question were from Myal's personal guard. There's a rumour going round saying that Myal and De Wenchas didn't get on too well . . .'

Colin the Sinister swished his beer around in its glass for a moment and watched it as though looking for omens. Then he smiled lazily and looked straight at Heighway. The inspector realised that although the journalist looked shabby and down-at-heel, there was a piercing intelligence behind the world-weary eyes.

'Let's just say that I don't want to see this marriage come off. I don't trust Myal, and I don't want to see him ruling this city. If I can do something in my small way to show the public an unpleasant side to this seemingly heroic figure, then I will.'

There was a pause as the journalist gazed at the policeman. Heighway thought that the man's thin features, hypnotic stare and beak-like nose gave him the appearance of some dangerous bird of prey. He could understand how he had come by his name, and all at once he felt like a small boy who is being interrogated by his irate headmaster.

'You wouldn't have any interest in Myal, would you, inspector?' Colin added, his head on one side. 'You wouldn't have any reason to think he's connected to the De Wenchas murder, by any chance?'

'Would I be likely to arrest such a prominent figure?' parried Heighway. 'Anyway, I'm told he's gone back home to Minas Lantan.'

'Rumour has it he's coming back in a few days. If you are planning to arrest him, it would make a hell of a story. And in the hands of the right journalist, the arresting officer would become a hero.'

'I'm afraid our investigations still have some way to go.'

'In other words, you want to make damn sure that you've got a whole stack of watertight evidence before you move against Myal, because if you screw up, you're likely to end up with your head stuck on a spear outside the gates of Minas Lantan. Right?'

Heighway smiled sourly.

'Something like that.' The inspector paused for a moment, thinking over Colin the Sinister's blatant offer. Make sure that he gets exclusive coverage in return for a favourable front-page write-up. There was something decidedly attractive about the proposition.

'Off the record . . .' he began.

The journalist leaned forward eagerly.

'. . . and I mean off the record,' Heighway told him, 'or else you'll be paying a little visit to Sergeant Hogman and his unpleasant mates in our luxurious and well-equipped pain amplification facility, down in the police station basement . . .'

'You've got my word, for what that's worth.'

'Then I think Myal is in it up to his neck. And I think that the poor girl whom Myal's men have been chasing after is the Lady Macoby.'

'Seven shades of shite! Why?'

126

Quickly, Heighway ran through his reasons. As he did so, a flame of excitement began to burn in the journalist's eyes, and his finger-nails began to beat out a restless tattoo on the table-top.

'So,' Heighway finished, 'if I could just lay my hands on one of his minions, Hogman's boys would drag the truth out of him in minutes. But as they've ridden home to Minas Lantan . . .'

'Myal might have ridden home,' interrupted Colin the Sinister, 'but he must still have men in Koumas! You've heard all the pro-Myal bollocks that's sweeping through the streets. Someone is engineering it. He's got a little clique of his people still working for him here, spreading rumours and stoking up the feelings of the populace!'

'That's not all they're doing, either. They've massacred the staff of the orcish consulate. And we think they've succeeded in grabbing Macoby this time.'

'What? When was this?'

Colin the Sinister was on his feet, hands fumbling for his notebook, all ready to dash off. Heighway grabbed him by the arm and dragged him back.

'Listen,' he told the eager journalist, 'you can have the story, but I want you to sit on it for a couple of days. I don't want Myal's men tipping him off, I want the evil sod to ride back to Koumas thinking that he's in the clear. Print whatever story you want to on the day he comes back, but wait until then. And I'll make sure that we don't release the news to any other journalists.'

Colin the Sinister stared at Heighway for several seconds, then nodded unwillingly.

'All right,' he said. 'Two days. But if I get the faintest whisper that any other paper has the story, I run it. Okay?'

'Okay.'

Heighway released his grip, and the journalist hastened out of the tavern without even finishing his beer. Absently, Heighway reached across and poured it into his own, nearly-empty, glass. He picked up the bar menu and studied it, vaguely wondering whether or not to have a sandwich. And then he sat back in his chair and thought about his next move.

Plainly, he didn't have much time. The only way he could get the information he needed would be to find one of Myal's underlings in Koumas and break him. And there wasn't enough time to break him in the proper ways, through a rigorous, crafty but humane interrogation. Heighway realised with regret that he was going to be forced to use the services of Hogman and his gang of sadists in the torture chambers.

Oh, well, he thought. *You can't make an omelette without breaking some eggs. Although it's a shame that Hogman believes you can't make prisoners talk without breaking a few heads. And some ribs. And fingers and toes. And testicles. Most especially testicles. Hogman's very big on breaking them . . .*

Sighing heavily, Heighway put the menu back on the table and stood up to leave. All of a sudden, he seemed to have lost his appetite . . .

CHAPTER THIRTEEN

The sky was cloudless. There was no moon tonight, and the countless stars twinkled and shone with an almost magical brilliance. Glart lay on his back and stared at them, trying to pick out the constellations. He was further south than he had ever been before, and there were one or two in the south-eastern sky that he was seeing for the first time. Just above the horizon he could make out the distinctive shape of Herpes Major, and nearby the small cluster known as The Haemorrhoids glittered with a reddish malevolence.

He sat up as Macoby walked back into the hollow where they were camped. She bent down to place another armful of sticks onto the fire burning on a hearth of stones that Glart had built, then sat down beside the novice monk.

'That will have to do,' she said. 'If there's another stick within half a mile of here, I'll be amazed.'

Glart nodded. They were high up in the mountain passes now, and few trees grew up here. It had taken them over an hour to collect enough wood to start a fire.

'How's the ghost?' he asked.

'Darian? Oh, he's fine. He seems quite happy to be on guard duty up there, as he doesn't appear to need sleep and he doesn't feel the cold.'

The hollow was fifty yards away from the main road that ran from Lampa Sanda to Great Retching, the subterranean orc city beneath the Irridic Mountains. It was a road that was seldom used by travellers, and so far in their journey they hadn't met a living soul (although they had passed several corpses of orcs who had accidentally got killed during some of the more exuberant party games with which orc armies like to pass the time). However, it was only sensible to mount a guard at night.

Macoby rubbed her hands together in front of the fire to warm them, then wrapped her blanket about her shoulders.

'I wish we had more firewood,' she said. Instantly, there was a rumbling sound, and then a deluge of small logs poured over the northern edge of the hollow and came bouncing and rolling down towards them.

Leaping up, Glart and Macoby grabbed their backpacks and scrambled round to the other side of the fire, out of the way. They stood watching until at last the deluge died down to a trickle and then finally dried up altogether. Luckily, the torrent of wood had stopped short of the fire, but the other half of the hollow now seemed to be completely full of logs.

Glart leant forward to pick up a couple and dropped them onto the flames. They blazed up satisfactorily and he sat down again and grinned up at Macoby.

'You need to be ever so careful what you wish for,' he told her. 'If you ask for the wrong thing we could be dead before you get a chance to change your mind.'

Cursing inwardly, Macoby pulled the lion's head ring off her finger and stared at it. Once again, it seemed to be looking unbearably smug.

'I wish I knew who the hell made you,' she ground out. The ring became, if anything, even smugger.

'I'm sorry,' it said piously. 'I'd like to help you, but it's just not allowed, I'm afraid. Rules, and that.'

Glart stretched his hand out.

'Could I have another look at that thing?' he asked. Macoby nodded and handed it to him. He took it and turned it over in his hands, and the gold glinted in the firelight.

'You're a very powerful object, but then I guess you know that,' he told it. The ring tried to look modest and failed miserably.

'Well, you know,' it said. 'I do my best.'

'I reckon that you must be familiar with just about every magical spell that there is. And not only do you know them, but you can perform them as well. I've never heard of anything that had that much ability.'

He paused while the ring had another go at looking modest. It still didn't seem to have acquired the knack.

'I reckon that the man who made you must have put all his power into you,' Glart went on. 'He must have done that for a purpose.'

'Stands to reason,' said the ring.

'I've got a feeling I know why he did so,' said Glart. There was a long pause.

'Well, come on, then,' urged the ring, impatiently. 'If you're so clever, tell us why.'

'I think he was getting old, and was finding it difficult to remember all his spells. And so he used every last vestige of his incredible powers to put them all into you, to make what was virtually an interactive magical encyclopaedia.'

'Very good,' said the ring. 'Very good indeed.'

'So how old was Adomo when he forged you?' asked Glart, casually.

'Well into his seventies,' answered the ring, 'although he was still . . .' Its voice trickled into silence like a stream drying up. 'Oh, you crafty sod!' it said, and they could hear the reluctant admiration in its voice.

'So it *was* Adomo who made you!'

The ring said nothing. It looked as though it was sulking.

'Who was Adomo?' asked Macoby. The ring still refused to speak, and so Glart began to tell her the full story of Brother Benidormus's discovery.

'The abbot thought that Adomo himself was coming back from the dead,' he finished. 'But, if I remember correctly, the book only spoke of his magical powers being unleashed. And the amulet is his magical power. That is what the prophesy was referring to. If it falls into the wrong hands . . .'

He looked down at the lion's head ring and then handed it back to Macoby.

'We have to find some way of destroying it,' he said. 'But, until then, I think that you are meant to be its guardian.'

'Surely that can't be too difficult,' Macoby replied. 'I mean, can't we melt it in the fire, or something?'

Glart shook his head.

'You still have no idea how powerful it is,' he replied. 'We couldn't even dent it. Maybe it could destroy itself. I don't know.'

'You mean, if I ordered it to self-destruct, it would do so?'

'Hey, now hold on,' said the ring in an aggrieved tone. 'I mean, forget it, guys, okay? Rearrange these three words to make a meaningful sentence. Yourselves, screw, go.'

Macoby scowled at the ring.

'Can I ask you something?' she said to it.

'Fire away,' it answered begrudgingly.

'Why the hell did this Adomo give you the power of speech? I mean, forgive me if I seem a little dense, but I can't see a single advantage.'

The ring seemed to be pondering whether it should answer the question, but eventually seemed to decide that there was no reason why it shouldn't.

'Well, if you must know, originally he didn't. I was mute. But then he lost me one day. He was always losing things by that stage, putting them down and then forgetting where he had put them. I spent three months down the side of the settee. So when he eventually found me again, he created a voice for me so that the next time he lost me, I could tell him where I was. And I might tell you that he never regretted it . . .'

The ring's voice had gone dreamy, almost nostalgic, as it thought about the past.

'We used to have such fascinating debates,' it murmured. 'Well, not really debates, I suppose. More like arguments. Along the lines of yes it is, no it isn't, you did, I didn't, did, didn't, shut up, no you shut up. He was a cantankerous old git, truth be told.'

It sighed fondly, then made an obvious effort to drag itself back to the present.

'Still, at least he had something approaching an intellect,' it muttered bitterly. 'At least he wasn't somebody who thought that debate was de thing on de end of de fishing line.'

Macoby glowered at it and yanked it back onto her finger.

'You know that you can change your shape and appearance at will . . .' she growled.

'Mmm?'

'Can you also change your personality?'

The lion's head scowled.

'What's wrong with my personality?' it whinged. 'I'll have you know that when my master . . .'

'Change it!'

There was another silence.

'Well?' asked Macoby.

'I have had the honour of carrying out your enlightened instructions, as ordered,' the ring intoned in a rich, plummy and slightly slurred voice that sounded like an elderly classical actor who's been at the sherry again. 'Is there anything further that your revered highness requires?'

'Er, no.'

'Then, oh beauteous one,' the ring began to intone, 'oh most magnificent lady, oh most wonderful and incomparable . . .'

'SHUT the KLAT up!'

The ring lapsed once again into silence.

'We shouldn't blame it,' said Glart. 'Adomo must have imbued it with the types of personality that he wished to deal with.'

'Then he must have been a really sad old man!' snapped Macoby. Rising, she snatched up a couple of logs and rammed them into the fire with feeling. Then she sat down again beside Glart, tucked her knees up under her chin and stared into the flames.

'I'm sure there must be a way to get this *klatting* jewel to tell us what's going on and who's behind it all,' she said, 'instead of poncing around out here in the back of beyond on a wild goose chase.'

Glart looked at her almost with awe. When he had first met her and had discovered that she was the Regent's daughter, he had expected that she would be a prim and proper young lady. But Macoby had turned out to be a down to earth, no-nonsense young woman who was good fun to be with. And, *klat!* was she beautiful! Glart looked at her mud-stained leggings and wondered what she'd look like if she was wearing a dress. Then he began to wonder what she'd look like if she wasn't wearing a dress . . .

'What are you thinking?' she asked him, and Glart almost swallowed his tongue.

'Oh! Erm, I was trying to work out what we should do when we get to Great Retching,' he stammered. 'I mean, what with you being the daughter of the Regent of Koumas, we should get an audience with the orcs' mayor without any difficulty. But what are we going to ask him? I mean, he's hardly going to break down in tears as soon as he sees us, confess all and tell us everything he knows, is he?'

133

'I've been thinking about that,' Macoby told him. 'I think we should try and find some of the orcs who took part in the battle. Maybe question the commander, and find out why they retreated. And there must be one somewhere who saw my brother die, maybe even the one who killed him. If we could only find that orc, just to ask him what happened to the body . . .'

Her eyes filled with tears, and Glart wanted to put his arms around her and hug her. Instead, he reached out a hand to cover one of hers and squeezed it.

'Maybe Adomo's jewel could help us,' he suggested.

Macoby held her hand up and studied the ring doubtfully.

'Could you show us the face of the orc who killed Marden?' she asked it.

'Well, that depends on what you mean,' answered the lion's head. 'If you want me to transport him here now, then yes, I could do that.'

'Then do it!' she snapped, before Glart had time to stop her.

There was the faintest whisper of displaced air, and all at once an orc was lying in the hollow beside Macoby. It was a large orc, probably one of the *Uttuk* tribe, with long, bowed legs and powerful muscles. It was also indisputably dead. A sword or an axe had cleaved down through the joint between shoulder and neck, smashing through the collar-bone and carving into the ribs and lungs, leaving a huge, gaping wound.

Glart guessed that the orc had been killed during the battle, and had been left lying on the battlefield. Whatever had happened, it had obviously been dead for a day or two. It wasn't the fact that something with a liking for eyeballs had been feeding off it that gave this away, nor was it the blowflies that were crawling in and out of the festering wound. It was the smell, the hideous, mephitic, rotting-meat smell of decay.

'Get rid of it!' gasped Macoby, and the corpse vanished instantly. There was a stunned silence, broken only by the bemused buzzing of a couple of bluebottles that had got left behind, and then Macoby burst into floods of tears. She cried as though her world and her heart was shattered, and Glart wrapped his arms around her and drew her to him, holding her close to comfort her until, at last, the sobbing died down, and she fell into an exhausted and troubled sleep.

When Glart woke up it was already daylight. The sun had presumably risen, but it was hiding somewhere behind the huge bank of threatening grey clouds that were looming around the mountain peaks. A cold wind was blowing, seeping over the top of the hollow and scattering the cold ashes of the dead fire.

He sat up and looked around. Macoby was already awake and was sitting on a stone nearby, carving slices off a strip of dried meat with her knife and popping them into her mouth. He could tell she had been up and about a while, for his water bottle was sitting beside him, full of clear, fresh water.

Raising it to his lips he drank deeply, then splashed a little into one hand and scrubbed ineffectually at his face.

'That's better,' he said. 'I want to look my best for the orcs.'

'That's your best?' responded Macoby. 'Then I'd hate to see you looking your worst.'

Glart grinned at her, pleased to see that she was obviously feeling better, but she refused to meet his eyes and looked almost embarrassed.

'Listen,' she began. 'About last night . . .'

'Forget it,' Glart interrupted. 'If you hadn't started crying, I would have done. That corpse was horrific. And you've been through enough in the past couple of days to start a dragon weeping.'

'But . . .'

'But nothing!' Glart stood up and stretched. He looked round at the towering mountains and the scudding clouds, thinking how beautiful it all was, then looked back at Macoby.

'When all this is over,' he continued, 'I'm going to end up spending the rest of my life inside the enclosed walls of a monastery. But when I'm old and grey, which will be in about three years time if yesterday is anything to go by, then I will be able to look back to the night when I comforted a brave, beleaguered woman and held her in my arms. And it will give me a warm glow all over.'

He grinned to show that he was joking and prayed that she wouldn't realise he was speaking the literal, desperate truth, and she smiled a little shamefacedly and held out a slice of dried meat for him to take.

'So how's Darian this morning?' he asked. 'Still keeping his spirits up?'

'Oh, he's fine. He's up by the road, keeping an eye out for passers-by.'

'It's a shame he didn't get a chance to look at that orc corpse last night. Maybe he could have told us something.'

'As a matter of fact, he did,' said Macoby. 'I got the jewel to fetch the body back this morning so that he could have a look at it.'

Glart stared at her with respect. He doubted if he would have had the courage to do that.

'And?' he prompted.

'And he could tell when it died, just like with De Wenchas.'

'During the battle?'

'No – about two hours after it. That orc must have been butchered by his own folk. It looks as though someone has been very careful about tying up any loose ends.'

Glart furrowed his brow and thought about this for a moment. Someone was being very, very careful indeed and had done an awful lot of planning.

'I hope we're not walking into a trap,' he muttered, but Macoby shook her head.

'No-one could possibly have known that you would turn up out of the blue,' she told him. 'Whoever is behind all of this, they can't have allowed for that. You're my trump card, my ace in the hole.'

Glart turned away, pleased but embarrassed, for this last phrase was uncomfortably close to a few of the raunchy fantasies that he'd tried to prevent invading his mind whilst he had held her the previous night.

Macoby sighed, and a faraway, dreamy look crossed her face.

'I do hope Sarakkan is all right,' she murmured, and reality swept through Glart like a flood of ice-cold water.

'I'm sure he is,' he muttered gruffly, and stooping, he began to stuff his sleeping-roll into his backpack with a good deal more force than was strictly necessary.

*

The road wound on ahead of them up into the mountains, a broad flat track of beaten earth and smooth, well-trodden stone. It had been constructed in the First Age, when roistering orc armies under the leadership of famous kings such as Udok Greenfang and Zagash the Flatulent had come marching along it to lay waste the rich, decadent cities on the plains of ancient Qital.

Now it was clearly not much in use, for plants and grasses had begun to overgrow it, although these had been trampled and flattened by the recent passage of the orc invasion force. But there was a silence that hung above the old road now, a quietness, as though it knew that its best days were behind it and it had accepted that it was slowly going to merge with the landscape until, once again, it was just a part of the mountain terrain.

Macoby and Glart paced slowly along with their hoods pulled over their heads, for there was a cold wind blowing and a soft rain like floating mist was settling upon them. The ghost was drifting along some forty feet ahead of them as a spectral advance guard, with instructions to let them know if it saw the slightest sighs of life, but so far they hadn't come across a living soul. Dead souls, yes, for every now and then they would pass the bloated corpse of yet another orc lying sprawled at the roadside, abandoned by its comrades, the victims of battle wounds or of some barbaric orc game.

Macoby was getting a little worried about the ghost. Darian was becoming more and more withdrawn by the hour. He seemed to be turning in on himself, as if the world of mortals held no further interest for him. He was also brooding on his inability to remember exactly what message Marden had given him. Macoby had told him that this no longer mattered as they now knew that it was Myal who was behind the plotting and the murders, but the ghost was still convinced that there was something he had to remember before the *Soul Shackle* would be broken and he was free, and it was preying on his nerves. However, Macoby had told herself that they might well hear something from the orcs which might jolt his memory, and so for the moment she had shelved the problem.

On they trudged for mile after mile, while the rain drifted down and soaked them to the skin. They were splashing through puddles now, and the occasional roadside streams that they passed were changing from small, clear runlets of water into gushing, spouting muddy torrents. Macoby had thought the previous night, when the orc corpse appeared, that life couldn't get any worse. She'd been sadly wrong.

At one point, Glart stopped beside one of the abandoned orc corpses and bent down to examine it. The orc had been a small, ugly brute, and had obviously died whilst playing a typical orc game such as Catch-the-dagger, for a small, sharp playing-knife was still protruding from one eye socket. Glart reached down and removed something from around the creature's neck, then turned to Macoby. He was holding a revolting orc pendant, a black metal figurine in an extremely obscene pose.

'Here,' he told her. 'Put this round your neck.'

'You're joking!'

'No, listen. If we're walking into a trap, the orcs could have been told to search you for an amulet or a pendant of some kind. This might fool them into overlooking the ring.'

Macoby nodded grudging acceptance. Taking the foul object, she pulled back her hood and looped it over her head.

'Well, all right,' she said. 'But if you dare tell me it suits me, I'll shove it up your nose.'

'Who me?' said Glart, who had been on the point of saying exactly that. 'I've got more sense than that!'

Macoby reached into her backpack and pulled out some bread. Although the rain had soaked through most of the clothes she was wearing, the stout leather pack was of elven manufacture, and had kept the food inside dry. She broke the bread in half, handed a piece to Glart, and then they set off again, chewing as they walked.

Late in the afternoon they came to a crossroads. Here, a road ran south to the orc cities of East Retching and Zahm. Another branched off northwards, snaking through the mountain passes to run down to a vast, marshy area in an angle of land between the Alovaq River and the Great River Leno, and eventually leading to the swamp-side orc town of Little Retching in the Bog. But the road ahead was the one they chose, for they knew that just a few miles further on lay their goal, the subterranean capital of the Irridic orclands, Great Retching. And so, after pausing to replenish their water bottles at a stream that came plunging almost vertically down the mountainside, they trudged on.

The light was beginning to fade when they breasted a rise in the ground and saw that they had at last reached their target. The road ahead of them snaked left to twist around a spur of the mountain before climbing westwards towards the highest passes, but where it bent left, an offshoot ran straight towards a cliff face to disappear inside the wide, dark tunnel that was the entrance to Great Retching.

As they drew nearer, they could see that someone had posted guards. A group of small, sulking orcs armed with spears was crouched at the side of the road just inside the tunnel entrance, playing a game that involved throwing dice, shouting a lot and hitting each other with the butts of their spears.

Although Glart had never visited an orc community before, he had been thoroughly schooled in the ways of the various races. He knew that, these days, orcs never bothered with such trivialities as guards, for they knew quite well that no-one in their right mind would go anywhere near an orc city. The orc mayor must have been worried about reprisals for the raid. Either that or he had been warned to be on the look-out for a couple of visitors . . .

Macoby caught up with Darian's ghost and whispered to it to keep under cover and as far behind them as possible, and then she and Glart strode boldly towards the orcs. They were so engrossed in squabbling over their game that they didn't notice the human couple approaching until they were a mere thirty yards away, but then they all straightened up to formed a ragged line that bristled with spears, suspicion and halitosis.

'Ere, wot do you two want?' snarled the biggest, who appeared to be their leader.

'We are an official delegation from the city of Koumas. Please present our compliments to your mayor, and tell him that we request an audience.'

'Why, are you a pair of stand-up comedians?' snarled a second orc, and the others all laughed. It sounded like a pack of hyenas fighting to the death.

139

'Most amusing,' said Macoby, in a voice like ice cracking. The laughter died away.

'So why would Mayor Bogbreath want to see an official delly . . . duli . . . degil . . . what you said, eh?' asked the orcs' leader.

'Why don't you ask him?' Macoby suggested, sweetly.

The orcs looked at one another. Although they had been put on sentry duty, it was obvious that no-one had told them what to do in the event of someone actually turning up.

'Yeah. Well, okay,' said the leader. 'Bleb, Megrim, stay here on guard. The rest of you, come with me.'

He snarled some further comment under his breath, and the others all laughed again and looked speculatively at Macoby. And Glart had a feeling that it was a good job that Macoby hadn't caught what was said, for he reckoned that she wouldn't have liked it one little bit.

The tunnel ran as straight as a die into the heart of the mountain. It was a good fifteen yards wide and ten yards high, and was lit by smoking, foul-smelling torches that were thrust into rough-hewn stone sconces in the walls on either side. As they walked along, Macoby could hear a distant sound, a continuous roar that sounded like thousands of far-off voices all shouting at once. It was a bit like an enormous and extremely raucous party taking place half a mile away. Which was more or less exactly what it was.

In orc society, no-one wastes any time in the pursuit of riches or possessions. Orcs are only interested in one thing: having a good time. Their life is one long party, fuelled by vast amounts of alcohol. They have a very straightforward way of ensuring that necessary tasks such as building, cleaning, or food and drink production are done; the larger, more vicious orcs simply pick on the smaller, weaker ones and threaten them with extreme violence unless they do the work. Then the large ones sit back and enjoy themselves, while the small ones get on with the task in hand and then join in with the party.

What Macoby could hear was the sound of a whole city of orcs drinking, shouting, fighting, singing, feeding, farting, belching and then drinking and shouting some more. And the further they walked down the tunnel, the louder it got, until by the time they came to the first of the vast caverns that made up the city, the clamour was indescribable.

Glart turned to her and said something, but she couldn't make out what it was. Shrugging, she pointed to her ears and he nodded his understanding. He still had a grin on his face and she marvelled at his calmness and self possession. She was really, really glad that he was with her, and she reached her hand out and took hold of his.

The orcs turned into a low side-passage and scurried down it, then took a bewildering series of turns into other side-passages and tunnels until Macoby was totally lost. Eventually they found themselves being escorted down a long, straight corridor that led to a circular doorway blocked by a snugly-fitting door which looked just like the top of a vast beer barrel, mainly because that's what it was. The noise was slightly less here, and it was possible to hear what someone said if they cupped their hands and shouted straight into your ear.

'Nice place for a holiday,' yelled Glart.

'I'd prefer somewhere a little livelier,' Macoby yelled back.

The largest orc stopped in front of the door and jerked one grubby, taloned finger at Macoby.

'Mayor Bogbreath will see you,' he yelled at her, 'but not the monk. He's to come with us while you have your, er, your audience. Bogbreath would like you to wait in here, and he'll join you as soon as he can.'

Macoby looked doubtfully at Glart, but he smiled encouragement at her.

'Go ahead,' he yelled. 'I'll see what I can find out from these lads here.'

Taking a deep breath (and then wishing she hadn't, for the orcs smelled as though their idea of personal hygiene was to wash themselves daily in barrels of rotting fish intestines), she stepped forwards, knocked on the door, and went inside.

She found herself in a bare, circular stone cave that was about twenty feet across. It was lit by a single candle-stub resting on the rickety chair which was the one item of furniture that the room possessed. Before she could ask what the hell was going on, the door closed behind her and she heard someone bolt it.

Right, she thought. *I'll give this Mayor Bogbreath exactly one hour . . .*

And ruthlessly putting aside any doubts or fears about whether she'd be able to do anything at all, she moved the candle and sat down on the chair to wait.

In fact, it was about fifty minutes before the door suddenly opened and a large, grinning orc shambled in. He was wearing jet-black clothes that appeared to have been made from the warty hide of some creature better left unguessed, and in his left hand he was holding a sword that had a long, wavy blade.

'Good evening, my lady,' he said, extending his right hand. Macoby gritted her teeth and shook it as diplomacy dictated, trying not to shudder.

'I bring you greetings from the Regent of Koumas,' she said. 'After the recent . . . unpleasantness between our two cities, we feel that it is time to begin the healing process. Many of our people suffered sad losses in the battle. Others, myself included, have loved ones who are missing. I have come here seeking news of these missing folk, and I would like your permission to talk to those of your people who fought that day, and in particular your general.'

Bogbreath strolled around her in a circle, so that she was forced to keep turning in order to face him. She felt like a lot in some unspeakable auction.

'I'm afraid that won't really be possible,' he told her. His voice was a deep snarl that was full to the brim with the orc equivalent of unctuousness. 'You see, General Kala-azar has been demoted. In fact, demoted quite a long way. But I'll tell him that you asked after him.'

Macoby took a step forward, about to remonstrate with him, but as she did so he raised his sword to point threateningly straight at her, and she froze.

'In the meantime, perhaps you would like to rest a while,' he suggested. 'I hope you find your quarters . . . adequate.'

'My *what*?'

'Oh, didn't anyone tell you? How remiss of them.' Bogbreath gestured at the bare walls of the cavern with his sword. 'This charming room will be your quarters for the next few days. Your friend will be along later to share them with you . . . if he survives.'

Bogbreath laughed out loud at the expression of horror on Macoby's face, then gently lifted his sword until it rested against her throat. With a quick flick of his wrist he jerked the tip of the blade backwards, and the pendant that Glart had taken from the dead orc flew through the air and into his hand.

'Thank you,' he growled. 'Pleasant dreams.'

And then he backed out of the room, slamming and bolting the door behind him, and Macoby was left alone.

CHAPTER FOURTEEN

The morning sun was blazing through the curtains when Heighway woke up. He lay there for a few seconds, staring at the faded, peeling wallpaper and wondering whether he should stay in bed a bit longer to get rid of his hangover. But then he realised that, for once, he didn't have a hangover, and so he got up straight away. He was too restless to stay in bed without a good reason, for today could well be the day that he cracked the De Wenchas case, and he was itching to be up and at it.

Not even bothering to make toast or boil the kettle, he dashed out in search of a newspaper. He was half-expecting to find that Colin the Sinister had reneged on his promise and had splashed news of Myal's guilt and of the orc consulate murders all over the paper. But when he bought his copy of the *Koumas Gazette* from the shop on the corner of the street and opened it with nervous, fumbling fingers, it was to find that the journalist had kept his word. There wasn't a single mention of the De Wenchas case.

Instead, the lead story was about the arrest of a well-known female ballet dancer who had been moonlighting as a high-class prostitute. One of quins born to a minor nobleman, she had lured interested clients by performing on stage without underwear, a fact that became obvious when her skirts flared out during the faster pirouettes. Colin the Sinister had splashed the story across two pages under the heading, *The Siren Twirl of Knickerless Quin*.

Heighway read the whole lot with relish whilst strolling along in the street. He was so engrossed in the story that he was nearly run over by a couple of carts. But then, he had always found something fascinating about the sleazier aspects of police work, and had more than once thought of applying for a transfer to the vice squad. As he walked through the front door of the police station, he wondered if it was too late to apply. If he screwed up on the De Wenchas case he was going to need another job . . .

Grabbing a cup of coffee from the canteen, he let himself into his office and sat down at his desk to work out what he was going to say to his men. He'd pulled twenty officers off various other cases and ordered them to attend a briefing that morning, for he urgently needed to arrest one of Myal's agents for questioning.

But how the hell were they going to find one? Now that the rest of the Minas Lantan soldiers had marched home, all the undercover guys would have ditched their uniforms, and would be hidden amongst the teeming throngs of everyday humanity. It would be like looking for a straw-coloured, straw-shaped needle in a haystack.

Maybe I'll be lucky, thought Heighway. *Maybe one of them will be stupid enough to be still wearing the uniform of the Minas Lantan Guards. No. Dream on, mate, dream on. Nobody is going to be that much of a cretin . . .*

Private Boron of the Minas Lantan Guards was extremely proud of the fact that he had been picked for special duty serving with Lord Myal's personal guard. This was the first time in his three years in the army that anyone had shown the slightest faith in him. But then, that wasn't surprising. He was thin, weak, indecisive, and a natural-born coward. The only thing he had going for him was a desperate eagerness to please, and anyone who looked at him could tell that he wasn't cut out to be a soldier, let alone an officer.

Anyone except his poor old widowed mum, that is. Determined to give her only son a decent start in the world, she had picked on the army as a worthwhile career and had scrimped and saved until she had enough money to buy him a commission. And so Boron had become a lieutenant in the Guards.

Three years, umpteen disasters and four demotions later, he had attained the lowly rank of private. He would have slipped even further down the ladder if that was possible, but that would have meant creating a new supremely low rank especially for him, and so his superiors had contented themselves by handing him the most menial jobs possible, such as peeling potatoes in the cookhouse.

However, they'd been forced to rethink this strategy after Boron accidentally dropped a grenade into a vat of peeled potatoes without

145

noticing. It had been impossible to pin the blame for the resulting explosion on him, especially as his supervising sergeant had been amongst those killed, but no-one had any real doubt who had been responsible.

Boron had spent an unhappy couple of weeks confined to a cell and wondering what degrading post the army would find for him to foul up next. He had already spent two months looking after the mules, until they all died. He had spent a week in charge of the latrines, until several officers were poisoned by an escaping cloud of hydrogen sulphide. He had been a warder in the prison block, until the great escape left him with no-one to guard. There didn't really seem to be anything left for him to do.

But then, one night, a sergeant called Gutslash had slipped quietly into his cell and had asked him whether he'd like to transfer to Lord Myal's guards. Ruthlessly suppressing the fear that this might be a bit dangerous, Boron had jumped at the chance. He'd reckoned it was about time he did something to make his mother proud of him.

He'd been surprised when Gutslash had hustled him quietly out of a rear door to where a small group of horsemen were waiting in the dark, but he'd asked no questions. He had been even more surprised, and very worried, when they rode out of Minas Lantan, but as they rode, Gutslash had explained that Lord Myal had work that needed doing in the city of Koumas. He would be arriving soon, Gutslash had said, but in the meantime, selected members of his guard were to prepare the way for him.

Boron had been delighted to find that all the work had entailed was talking to people in the bars and taverns of Koumas and telling them what a good chap Myal was. All he'd had to remember was not to let on that he was a member of Myal's personal guard, and Gutslash had given him a nice, heavy purse stuffed with gold to buy himself and other people lots of drinks.

But then came the orc invasion. Myal had arrived in Koumas at the head of the Minas Lantan troops, and Boron had been delighted and terribly proud to pull on the guards' uniform for the first time and to wear the red cockade on his helmet. This had been tempered by the fear of going anywhere near real fighting, but, to his delight, Gutslash had told him that he was needed for more important work.

When the army marched out, a day later, Boron and a few of his confederates had stayed behind undercover in Koumas. They had reverted to plain clothes, and Boron had spent another happy twenty-four hours in taverns, buying people drinks and telling them not to worry, for that Myal was a brilliant leader, he knew what he was doing, he'd soon send the orcs packing, et cetera, et cetera.

The army had returned, ragged, weary, but victorious, and Boron's orders had changed. Now he was to mingle in taverns and tell everyone that it was General Myal who had saved the day, that the man was a hero, and that it would be a damned good thing for Koumas if the Lady Macoby accepted his proposal of marriage. Boron had been ordered to remain in his disguise of plain clothes to do this, and for the first day, he had reluctantly done so.

But, that night, he had sat in his lodging room, looking at his uniform, stroking the red cockade, and realising that for the first time in his life, he felt proud of himself. It had seemed a shame not to be able to wear it. In fact, it had seemed pointless, as well. After all, he was supposed to be telling people that he had fought next to Myal, so why shouldn't he wear the uniform of his personal guard? Surely it would just back up his story.

And so it came about that, on the day when Inspector Heighway was to issue orders to his men to arrest anyone they saw who was wearing the uniform of Minas Lantan, there was just one man in the whole of Koumas who was doing so . . .

After a night in the police station sick-bay, Sergeant Raasay was feeling a whole lot better. For the first time in weeks he'd been able to look forward to eating breakfast in the knowledge that, while the canteen-cooked porridge wasn't exactly a gourmet meal, it would at least be cooked, and would be warm, filling, and comparatively safe to eat.

After breakfast, the police doctor put him through a set of rigorous tests that consisted of making him stick his tongue out, checking his pulse, and asking him if he'd pooed his trousers in the past twelve hours. He was then declared fit for duty, and was told that Inspector Heighway wanted to see all available officers in the briefing room at half past ten.

Raasay was a few minutes late getting there, as the briefing room was on the second floor and he was so weak he had to keep stopping after every four or five stairs to have a sit down. He opened the door to find twenty officers listening to Inspector Heighway, who was outlining the need to find and interrogate a member of Myal's personal guard.

'If you think you've spotted one,' he was saying, 'follow him, but be discreet. Don't let him catch on. Work in teams, listen and watch. When you're sure that he's one of Myal's men, arrest him and bring him . . . seven shades of suffering shite!'

Heighway had seen Raasay and was staring at him in disbelief. Twenty heads swung round to see what he was staring at, and twenty faces stared in shocked disbelief. Raasay stared back at them, a little discomfited. He'd realised that he probably didn't look too healthy after the experiences of the past thirty-six hours, but he hadn't expected that he'd produce this reaction.

'By the gods, Raasay!' muttered Heighway. 'Are you all right, man?'

Raasay nodded.

'Yes, sir. Fine. Well, er, not as bad as yesterday, anyway. And the doc says I'm fit for active duty, as long as I stay within easy reach of a toilet.'

'Fit? You look as though you've died, been buried, and been dug up again a week later.'

Raasay grinned weakly, then shuffled across to a chair at the back and sat down. The inspector shook his head and then carried on with his briefing, and Raasay snuggled down in his chair and luxuriated in his surroundings.

The hard wooden seats, the Koumas street-map on the wall that was stuck full of coloured pins representing God knows what, the irreverent comments and ribald jokes of his fellow officers, the sour sweaty smell of twenty male bodies in a small room, all of these things gave the sergeant a far greater sense of belonging than he got in his parents' house. This was his home, the police station, this was where he belonged, and he revelled in it.

After about twenty minutes, the meeting broke up. All the other officers filed out, and Inspector Heighway wandered across to a chair in the row in front of Raasay and sat down astride it, resting his folded arms on the back of the chair.

'You sure you're up to this, sergeant?' he asked, not unkindly. 'I've seen maggots that look fitter and stronger than you do at the moment.'

'No, I'm fine, sir, honestly. I just want to get out there and do my duty.'

Heighway pursed his lips dubiously.

'Well, all right,' he said. 'But don't do too much. Find a busy tavern, sit in it and keep your ears open. If you think you've found one of Myal's guards, go and fetch one of your colleagues and get him to do the arresting. Now get out of here before you slide between two of the floorboards, man.'

Raasay saluted and tottered to the door. He felt touched by the inspector's obvious concern and, it had to be said, a little surprised, for Heighway's usual method of sympathising was to belt someone on the back, tell them not to be such a wimp, and order them to go down to the pub and get pissed. He opened the door, then paused.

'You can rely on me, sir,' he said. 'I won't let you down.'

And with a feeling that, at last, things were starting to go well, Sergeant Raasay staggered off to do his duty.

Private Boron looked at his reflection in the cracked, stained mirror of his lodging room and swelled with pride. He had always thought that there was something incredibly macho about black leather, and the uniform of Myal's personal guard used reams of the stuff. The only hint of colour was provided by the red cockade in the burnished metal helm.

Boron turned sideways and struck a pose, then turned the other way, struck another pose, and banged his elbow badly on a cupboard door. But that didn't matter. Other people might only see a scrawny, thin wimp inside a black leather uniform two sizes too big, wearing a metal helmet that sat on his head like a coal-scuttle, but as far as he was concerned, he was the bee's knees. The dog's dangly bits. The crème de la *klatting* crème.

With pride in his heart and a nasty bruise on his elbow, Private Boron set off to meet his nemesis.

Sergeant Raasay sat in the bar of the *Blue Cockatrice* and thought to himself (again!) how clever the inspector was. He was forever telling people who were unwell that all they needed was a few drinks inside

149

them. Raasay had always thought that this couldn't possibly be true, but now, with three pints of Gobbo's Pearly Light Ale inside him, he was feeling better than he had done for days.

All of a sudden he remembered that he was supposed to be on duty. Dragging his gaze away from the barmaid's cleavage, he stared round the pub. He was just wondering how he was supposed to recognise an agent of Minas Lantan if they weren't wearing a uniform and was wishing that he'd payed a bit more attention at the briefing, when suddenly he realised that the man at the next table *was* wearing a uniform. Moreover, Raasay was sure that it was the uniform of Myal's personal guard. He'd seen several of them during the trip to the royal palace, a trip that would be etched into his memory for as long as he lived.

The sergeant stood up, mindful of Heighway's instructions that he should go and find one of his colleagues to make the arrest, but then he noticed that the man had nearly finished his drink. *He could have disappeared by the time I get back here*, he thought. *I'd better arrest him myself.*

He took a deep breath, bracing himself. Although he felt a lot better, he was still extremely weak, and even though the guy at the next table looked pretty thin and weedy, he'd only have to flick Raasay with his little finger to knock him down. Still, Raasay felt that he had to do his duty, and so he finished off his drink in one go and then tottered determinedly across to the next table.

Although he had come out in his uniform, Boron had immediately suffered a severe attack of doubt. One thing that three years in the army had taught him was the inadvisability of disobeying orders. If Sergeant Gutslash caught him dressed like this he'd probably get court-martialled again, and so he'd decided to have a quick drink and a pose in a quiet tavern before going home and changing.

He had chosen a place called the *Blue Cockatrice*, just round the corner from his digs, but he hadn't enjoyed the drink. Every time the door had opened, he'd expected it to be Gutslash. He was just about to finish his beer and go home to get changed when a pale, thin and extremely ill-looking man staggered across to his table, leant on it for support and stood there peering down at him forlornly.

150

'I'd like you to accompany me to the station,' said the man.

If Boron had realised that this guy was in fact a police sergeant, he would have been out of the door and off down the street in a flash. But the man looked desperately ill. His face was dead white and he was sweating. He obviously needed someone to help him get to this station, wherever it was, and Boron was at heart a kind and generous man.

'Okay,' he said. 'You tell me where it is and I'll help you get there.'

Sergeant Raasay could hardly believe his ears. On the previous occasions that he had arrested someone, they had been violently opposed to it, and he had suffered injuries ranging from a black eye to a broken finger. But now, here was this Minas Lantan spy agreeing to be arrested and offering to help him back to the police station. Such generosity of spirit almost moved him to tears.

'Thank you,' he said. 'I appreciate this.'

'You're welcome,' said Boron, and together, the two of them shuffled out of the *Blue Cockatrice* and headed off up the street towards the police station.

DC Kratavan was standing by the stairs in the main foyer of the police station building, trying to brief Sergeant Hogman on how Inspector Heighway wanted the interrogation of the prisoner to be carried out. It was a task that was made more difficult by a number of factors.

Firstly, Kratavan had an intense dislike for torture, sharing Heighway's belief that it was inhuman and degrading. Secondly, he had an intense dislike for the torturers themselves, and in particular for Hogman, whom he thought was a fat, sadistic unintelligent bully. And thirdly, Hogman was a sergeant whilst Kratavan was merely a detective constable. This meant that he had to be polite to the fat slob and listen in silence when Hogman voiced his intention of setting about the hapless prisoner with a vengeance, when what he really wanted to do was to tell him that if he didn't follow his orders to the letter, Kratavan would tie him face-down on one of his own benches and set about him with a red-hot poker.

Kratavan was feeling really pissed off.

'Anyway, who is this lucky boy?' asked Hogman.

'We don't know yet,' answered Kratavan. 'We're looking for some-one in Myal's personal guard. As I told you, Inspector Heighway said that *if* we arrest someone, he specifically wants you to . . .'

'Is that him, with Raasay over there?'

'. . . make sure that you don't overdo it. What? Who?'

Kratavan swung round and stared at the odd couple who were struggling up the steps and in at the main door. One of them was Sergeant Raasay all right, and with a sinking feeling Kratavan saw that the other guy was wearing the black uniform of Myal's personal guard. *Klat!* He'd been half hoping that they wouldn't arrest anyone, so that they wouldn't have to go through the horrors of watching Hogman at work in the basement.

'Yes,' he sighed. 'I'm afraid it is.'

Boron helped the poor, sick guy across the wide hallway to a desk at one side, and it was only when they had got there that he looked around him and realised to his horror that they were in the foyer of a police station.

'Listen,' he gabbled to Raasay, 'I'm sure they'll look after you here, but I've got to be going.'

'But you can't,' said Raasay, in surprise. 'I've arrested you.'

Boron looked at him in horror. He felt like someone who has rescued a drowning lamb, only to have the poor little creature bite his arm off at the elbow.

'Yes, I bloody can, you rotten bastard,' he said. 'Just watch me!'

Raasay grabbed him by the sleeve. It was like being restrained by tissue paper. Boron shook him off, then gasped as something grabbed him by the neck and lifted him into the air.

Screwing his head round, he found that he was staring into a fat, perspiring, leering face. Small, piggy eyes stared almost lustfully at him from between rolls of flesh, and foul breath emanated from a grinning mouth that was literally drooling with anticipation.

'I'm Sergeant Hogman,' said the mouth. 'You and I are going to have a little fun together. Come with me, and I'll show you my toys.'

Boron wriggled like a worm on a hook, but it made no difference. The hand clamped round his neck was like a vice. All of a sudden, he was being carried towards a staircase that led down to a dark passageway, and he could tell by the expressions on the faces of the watching police officers that he was not going to like what he found down there one little bit. And then he heard one of them mutter the word 'torture'.

Instantly, Boron froze. Desperately, he tried to lash his brain into motion, urging it to come up with some cunning plan of escape, some way out of this nightmare. For a moment it stuttered ineffectually, but then all at once it came up with a course of action and put it into immediate effect.

Boron fainted.

Inspector Heighway paused at the top of the stairs leading down to the basement and dragged a finger around the inside of a collar that suddenly seemed several sizes too small. He glanced sideways at Kratavan and Raasay, and was pleased to see that they shared his revulsion.

'Come on, sir,' Kratavan urged him. 'We'd better get down there. Hogman's only had him for ten minutes, so the guy might still have some entrails left.'

Heighway nodded, gripped the handrail and began to walk down. He hated this staircase. It had been designed by somebody who knew an awful lot about human fear and dread. It began in the brightly-lit foyer as a normal, friendly flight of wide marble stairs, but after ten steps it bent back on itself, curving downwards anti-clockwise and narrowing to become a slippery, uneven spiral staircase. The walls faded from a cheery white through grey to a black, damp stone that dripped moisture. And the lighting diminished to a threatening, dull reddish hue. The overall efect was to make you realise that you were walking down to somewhere very unpleasant indeed.

At the bottom was a single heavy wooden door studded with metal bolts. Heighway pushed this open and led the others along the dark, stone-flagged corridor that led into the heart of Hogman's domain. He didn't need to guess where the interrogation of the new prisoner was taking place. They could tell by the screaming.

Heighway flung open the third door on the right and marched in, with Kratavan at his heels and Raasay hovering nervously behind. This was the source of the screaming, all right. The man whom Raasay had arrested was strapped into an interrogation chair. His black uniform was stained with sweat and with urine where he had wet himself. His eyes were wide and staring, and from his open mouth poured a ceaseless stream of screams, crying, pleading and babbling.

Behind him, Hogman and two of his brutal acolytes were preparing a set of equipment that even the Marquis de Sade would have considered a bit over the top. Pokers and pliers rested on the coals of a red-hot brazier, and on a nearby table were an interesting collection of probes, knives, and scalpels.

'By the gods, Hogman!' yelled Heighway. 'What the *klat* have you done to him?'

'Nothing, sir. We haven't even touched him yet. We just strapped him into the chair and told him what was going to happen and he started yelling. He won't shut up, sir.'

Shaking his head, Heighway leant forwards and rested one hand on each arm of the prisoner's chair, bringing his head down to look the terrified man straight in the eyes.

'It's all right,' he told him. 'Nothing will happen to you if you co-operate.'

'I'll co-operate,' the prisoner told him, with all the fervour of a recent convert to one of the more exuberant religions.

'Good. All we want you to do is answer a few questions. Now then. What's your name?'

'Boron!'

Hogman cuffed the prisoner round the back of the head with a fist the size of a leg of ham.

'Don't you call the inspector names,' he warned him.

'It's my name! Boron is my name! Honestly!'

'Okay, okay! Right then, Boron. That's an interesting uniform. Is it yours?'

'Yes!' Boron nodded his head so vigorously that a small snowstorm of dandruff floated down into his lap.

'Who do you work for?'

'Myal of Minas Lantan. I'm in his personal guard.'

'Good. Very good. Now, will you tell me everything about the work you've been doing recently?'

'Not half!'

Boron's face was a mask of sheer truthfulness and honesty. Satisfied,

Heighway stood upright and turned to Hogman, who had been listening to these exchanges with growing apprehension.

'I don't think your talents are going to be required after all, sergeant,' he told him.

'What?' Hogman looked devastated.

'You heard me.'

'Not at all?'

'No.'

'But . . . can't I just torture him a little bit?'

'Just for fun, you mean?'

'Yeah.' Hogman grinned. He hadn't realised that the inspector understood.

'Hogman, you're a sadistic, nasty, uncivilised, brutal thug.'

'Thank you, sir!'

Heighway shook his head, tiredly. The sooner he was back in his own room, away from the claustrophobic terror of this foul basement, the better.

'Kratavan, untie the prisoner and bring him to my office,' he ordered. 'And I don't want to see a mark on him. Hogman, you see the red-hot poker that one of your minions has just pulled out of that brazier?'

Hogman looked round.

'Yes sir?'

'Sit on it and swivel. And that's an order.'

Ten minutes later, Heighway was sitting at his desk with Boron sitting nervously opposite him in a chair. The prisoner's small, weedy frame was shaking with fear, and he looked as though he was going to burst into tears at any moment. Not for the first time, Heighway wished that he was involved in a cleaner, more wholesome line of work.

'Right, sunbeam,' he said. 'You've seen what those bastards down-stairs would like to do if they get their hands on you. But if you tell me everything you can, then I can keep them off your back. And off your testicles. Now, exactly what have you and your friends been doing?'

Boron started talking, and didn't stop for nearly half an hour. It

155

wasn't long before Heighway realised that the guy was a mere menial, a non-too-bright foot soldier who knew very little of the plot in which he had been involved. But even so, he had a lot of useful information which helped to back up the inspector's theories.

'So you don't know where this Gutslash or any of the others are lodging?' he asked, when Boron had eventually run dry.

'No. But I'm supposed to meet some of them in a tavern in two days time.'

'And you never heard them mention Colonel De Wenchas? Or anything about killing anyone?'

Boron hesitated briefly at the thought of what Gutslash would do if he ever caught him, but then the memory of those thin metal probes which Hogman had been caressing floated before his eyes.

'Well, one night in the pub they were talking about killing someone. But it wasn't humans, it was orcs they were going to kill. I thought it was just something to do with the battle.'

Heighway breathed out a gentle sigh of relief. At last! A link between Myal and the murders. Now the superintendent would have to act.

'Okay,' he said. 'You've done very well. Now, let's run through this killing the orcs bit. Tell me every single thing they said . . .'

Superintendent Weird was sitting behind his desk reading through an official-looking parchment when Heighway strode into his office. He gestured at a chair without looking up, and so the inspector sat down and waited until his chief had finished reading the document. After a while he shook his head irritably and rolled up the parchment, and then he looked up and stared blankly at Heighway.

'Arrested this what's-his-name, this Sarakkan yet, have you, inspector?'

'No, sir.'

'No? Why the *klat* not?'

Heighway winced inwardly. The chief was clearly not in the best of moods.

'Fresh evidence, sir. We've been interrogating one of Myal's guards. Just the sight of Hogman was enough to set him singing like a canary, sir.'

'Oh, wonderful.' The superintendent began to thwack the rolled-up parchment into the palm of his hand. Heighway got the distinct impression that his chief would prefer to be thwacking him in the face with it, instead.

I have here,' the Superintendent continued, 'a letter from the royal palace. Apparently a messenger from Minas Lantan arrived in Koumas a couple of hours ago. They have made an official complaint at the treatment Myal received at the hands of, and I quote, "an over-zealous, rude and insolent police officer". The palace has indicated that, henceforth, Myal is to be treated with the utmost deference. And you have been subjecting one of the man's personal guard to the tender, loving care of Sergeant Hogman? Tell me it isn't true.'

Inspector Heighway had a sinking feeling in his stomach. This wasn't going at all how he'd hoped. Still, he had to press on.

'Myal's guilty, chief. He's behind the murder of five orcs, as well as Colonel . . .'

'I don't care if he's behind the murder of a gross of orcs, several colonels, twenty majors and your dear little grey-haired old mum! We are *not* arresting him and starting a war between our two cities! Now, get out there, pick on some other poor innocent, and charge him with the murders. Do you understand me?'

'Yes sir,' muttered Heighway. He stood up and marched to the door with as much dignity as he could muster.

'And Heighway,' added the superintendent. The inspector stopped and looked back.

'Myal's due at the palace the day after tomorrow. I want someone else arrested by then, or you'll be a sergeant, and you'll be in the stocks. Understand?'

'Sir.'

Heighway closed the door and stomped off down the corridor, deep in thought. It looked as though he'd better start making arrangements to arrest Sarakkan, after all. Or, at least, that was what he'd tell everyone else in the department . . .

Heighway smiled to himself. He had another plan, a plan that he would have to keep secret until it was time to put it into action. And when Myal rode back into the city, he was going to be in for the shock of his unpleasant young life.

CHAPTER FIFTEEN

When the door closed behind Bogbreath, Macoby knew for sure that they *had* walked straight into a trap after all, but she refused to panic. So she was locked in an underground cavern whilst Glart had been taken away to face some unknown trial. So what? *He will be along later – if he survives*, Bogbreath had told her, and from everything that Macoby had so far seen of the young monk, she reckoned he was a born survivor. So he would be back soon. That was what she had to believe.

She knew that she had one major factor in her favour, thanks to Glart: Adomo's jewel. She looked down at the ring, which was still sitting quietly around her finger and wondered whether she should use it now or wait a while. She knew that she could be out of this prison in a second if she utilised its power, but Glart's warning and the misadventure with the orc corpse had convinced her only to use it with the greatest of care. Still, there was someone else who might be able to help. That is, if he hadn't been captured as well . . .

But she needn't have worried. A short while later, Darian's ghost came oozing through the door and drifted towards her.

'Boy, am I glad to see you,' she told him. 'I was really worried! I thought you might be visible to the orcs, and they might have found some way of catching you.'

'No, apparently not,' the ghost whispered.

'Have you any idea where they've taken Glart?'

'No. I tried to follow but they've gone too far away, and I'm still tied to that jewel.' The ghost looked upset, as though he felt he had let Macoby down.

'Don't worry,' she told him. 'Look, why don't you have a scout around? Check out all the other caverns and rooms you can reach, see what you can hear.'

The ghost nodded mournfully and drifted up through the ceiling, and Macoby sat down on the floor again and wondered what she should do. After a little thought, she decided that the best thing would be to wait until Glart was brought back before trying to escape. But how could she be sure that he was indeed all right? A little nervously, she tapped the lion's head ring with one finger.

'Are you awake?' she whispered.

'Indeed I am,' answered the ring in its new, resonantly plummy voice, 'oh most beauteous flower of . . .'

'Can it! Good grief!'

'If silence is the thing most desired by your munificence, then I shall most certainly . . .'

'I said CAN IT!'

The ring ground to a halt and Macoby glowered furiously at it.

'Two things. Firstly, can you please go back to the previous personality that you had?'

'You got it, sweetheart,' replied the ring, smugly. 'I knew you'd see sense in the end.'

'Secondly, is there any way in which you can find out how and where Glart is at the moment?'

'Several ways. But if you want to know exactly how he's feeling, probably the best would be a *Mind-meld* spell.'

'What is that, exactly?'

'Well, the *Mind-meld* was invented by a First Age wizard called Bagazald in the year 474,' the ring told her. 'He invented it so he could keep tabs on his much younger and extremely pretty new wife, whom he suspected was playing around with the king's youngest son.'

'Did it work?'

'Apparently. Bagazald was put to death a couple of months later for Blowing Up with Malice Aforethought the Fifth in Line to the Throne with a Fireball.'

'Oh, dear. So how does it work?'

'Well, I would cast the spell and link minds with Glart, and then give you a running commentary of what he is seeing and how he is feeling.'

'Will he realise what you're doing?'

'If he's got any magical knowledge at all, yes.'

'Sounds perfect. There's no side effects that you're not telling me

159

about, are there? Glart isn't going to end up senile or mentally impaired?'

'No more than when you met him.'

'Okay. Let's do it.'

'Right, then. Now, let's see . . . Here we go. Establishing contact . . . woooo!'

The ring's voice suddenly changed, becoming slurred and giggly.

'I'm shat . . . I mean, sat . . . in a vasht bar with a load of . . . lotsh and lotsh of orcs. By the gods, there's a lot of them. Lotsh and lotsh and lotsh . . . hic . . . More orcs than you've . . . than you've . . . well, if you took the biggest number of orcs you can imagine and mulpity . . . mulpit . . . multiply it by ooh . . . five, then you'd have . . . you'd have . . . er . . .'

Macoby suddenly realised that Glart must be drunk.

'Are you all right?' she asked with concern.

'I'm fine. Fine. Fine fine fine fine fine. They've given me lotsh to drink and they're questing me with pumptions . . . pumping me with questions. But I knew what they were up to an' I've used a little shpell . . . spell . . . on them. I've learned more than they have . . . hic . . .'

There was a long pause, and when the ring spoke again it was in a voice that was brimming with distaste.

'Well, there you are, then,' it said. 'We're locked in here, and your friend is off with all those orcs and having the time of his life. Uncaring, some might call it.'

'As long as he's all right,' said Macoby.

She sat down on the floor and unpacked her bedroll. She was pretty sure that Myal's men were the ones who were after the amulet and that Bogbreath had taken it for them, not for himself. That was the advantage of a magical jewel that could change shape at will: no-one really knew what it looked like. The orc pendant would probably get as far as Myal himself before he realised it wasn't Adomo's amulet. Macoby reckoned that she probably had at least twenty-four hours grace before the orcs found out that she must still have it. She might as well get some rest.

And so, stretched out her bedroll, she lay down, blew out the candle and closed her eyes.

*

It was pitch dark when something woke Macoby, and she sat up with a start. She could hear distant laughing and snarling, and then all at once the door opened wide and light flooded in. A group of four orcs entered, dragging Glart between them. His arms were draped about the shoulders of two of them, but his feet were trailing, his head was lolling, and his eyes were closed.

One of the orcs tossed Glart's small backpack to Macoby and let his wooden staff clatter to the ground. She caught the pack and dragged his bedroll out just as the others let go of him and he fell to the floor in a heap.

''Fraid your mate can't take his booze,' laughed a second orc. 'Mind you, he didn't do too bad for a 'uman.'

They turned and slouched out, slamming and bolting the door behind them. Macoby felt in her pack for her tinder-box, then struck a flame and lit the tiny stub of candle. Carefully placing it on the chair, she turned to drag Glart onto his bedroll, but to her surprise he was sitting up.

'Are you all right?' she asked him.

A slow smile spread across his face. It was like the tide gradually coming in on a wide, flat beach.

'Yeah,' he said, grinning at her. The grin seemed to get stuck, and Macoby waited for something to follow it. Nothing did.

'So what happened?' she prompted.

'Er. Well, we drank a lot and they asked me questions. I've found out quite a bit . . . It's very dark in here.'

'Your eyes have closed.'

'Ah.' Glart managed to get one of his eyes a quarter open. The other one appeared to have shut up shop for the night. 'I think maybe I'd better get a bit of sleep before we make a move. 'Nite.'

He lay down on the bedroll like a tree lying down after someone has sliced through its trunk with an axe, and within seconds he was snoring gently, dead to the world. Macoby looked across to where the ghost was hovering quietly in the shadows at the back of the cave.

'Darian, keep a watch at the end of the passage. Wake us if anyone is coming, okay?'

The ghost drifted obediently away through the door, and Macoby laid herself down once again and closed her eyes.

I doubt I'll get a wink of sleep with all this noise going on, she thought as the intensity of Glart's snoring increased, but, within seconds, she too was dead to the world.

When Macoby next awoke, she realised that she must have slept through the night. The room was lit by a strange, white phosphorescence that was emanating from the tip of Glart's wooden staff, which was leaning against the chair. Glart himself was sitting cross-legged on the floor, holding a whispered conversation with Darian's ghost.

'Hi,' he said as she sat up. 'Sleep well?'

'I must have done. What time is it?' All of a sudden she could feel a rising panic. How long had she been asleep?

Leaping up, she began feverishly rolling up the bedroll.

'Come on!' she snapped over her shoulder. 'We've got to get out of here!'

'Hey, there's no rush,' Glart told her. 'From what I gathered last night, the orc guards will be bringing us some breakfast. We'd better wait until they've gone before we do our vanishing act, or they'll raise the alarm.'

Seeing the sense of this, Macoby forced herself to be calm, and sat down facing Glart. His habital grin was in place, and she couldn't believe that he was looking so fresh and healthy. If there was any justice in the world, he should have had a crippling hangover. The only hint of his activities were the whites of his eyes, which looked like a street-map of a crowded city with the major roads marked out in red.

'Well, come on then. What did you find out last night? That is, if you can still remember last night.'

'Oh, I can remember. But I'll tell you later. I think I can hear someone coming.'

True enough, Macoby could hear the muffled snarls and faint footsteps of approaching orcs. There was the sound of the bolts being drawn back, and then the door opened and four suspicious, spear-carrying orcs peered in. One of them placed a tray on the floor.

''Ere's yer breakfast,' it muttered before backing out, and once again the door was slammed and bolted.

Getting up, Macoby wandered across to the tray and looked doubt-fully at its contents. There was a mouldy loaf of bread, a couple of cooked snakes, something green and hairy that might once have been cheese, four large jugs of wine and a bottle of brandy.

'Funny,' she said, grimacing. 'I seem to have lost my appetite.'

She walked back and sat down again opposite Glart.

'Okay,' she continued. 'What did you find out?'

'Well, for starters, the orc invasion wasn't part of any long-term plan of campaign that they've drawn up. Most of them thought it was the idea of their general, or as they call him, their party-leader, Kala-azar. Apparently he spent a couple of nights in the tavern, talking about the great party-leaders of the past, such as Gaz the Tall, and basically getting all the other orcs worked up into a fever. Then one night he told them that anything Gaz the Tall could do, he could do, and were they with him? And they were.'

'So it was all this Kala-azar's idea?'

'Apparently not. One or two of the orcs say they've heard that a human put him up to it. But after the battle, Mayor Bogbreath found out. Kala-azar has suffered the orcish equivalent of being cashiered . . . I won't tell you about that, as it's not very pleasant, but it does share some similarities with having your brass buttons snipped off.'

'Yeuch!'

'And now, apparently, Bogbreath is working with the human and his agents. And poor old Kala-azar has been demoted to the most menial position in the whole city.'

'Poor?' The vicious bastard caused the invasion of our country! So what is this menial position?'

'Keeper of the *Kazhavogs*.'

'Poor guy.' Macoby shook her head in sympathy. She had heard of *Kazhavogs*, the vast, foul-smelling, foul-tempered lizards that orc rulers sometimes kept as pets.

Glart stowed his few possessions quickly into his backpack, then hitched it over his shoulders.

'You ready?' he asked.

'Yeah. What's the plan?'

'I think we'll find out all we need if we can just talk to Kala-azar himself. So that's what we'll do. The amulet can get us out of this cave with a *Transference* spell.'

'We need to be careful. Those guards might be in sight of the other side.'

163

'Don't worry. I picked out a perfect place to go to when they were taking me down to their tavern last night. If you'll lend me the ring for a moment . . .'

Macoby slipped it off her finger again and passed it to him, then grasped his hand.

'You ready, Darian?' she asked.

The ghost roused himself from another of the inward-looking near-trances into which he was slipping more and more frequently.

'Yes,' he answered.

There was the usual blinding flash as the amulet did its business, and suddenly they were standing in a rough-hewn alcove beside a pile of wooden beer barrels. Unfortunately, they were standing behind a large orc, which was busily involved in knocking a rubber bung into one of the barrels.

Macoby opened her mouth to gasp, but before she even had time to think, Glart had stepped forward and belted the orc hard across the back of its head with his staff. There was a wonderfully loud *crack*, and the orc collapsed as though someone had dropped a house on top of it, and lay there unconscious.

'Oh, great!' said Macoby. 'As soon as someone finds him they'll let loose the alarm!'

'No, don't worry. He didn't see us, and the orc guards haven't seen us pass them. We're all right.'

'But someone will find him lying there, out cold!'

'Yeah, but they won't connect it to us. I noticed last night that there are unconscious orcs lying round everywhere. Apparently there's nothing an orc enjoys more than creeping up behind another orc and laying him out with a shovel or a baseball bat round the back of the head. They think it's funny.'

They paused as Darian's ghost came drifting sadly out of the rock wall beside them. He was looking so mournful that Macoby had the urge to hug him. However, hugging someone who has as much substance as a cloud isn't too easy, and she ended up making a vague patting motion beside his misty shoulder.

'Darian, this will all be over soon, I promise you. We'll find a way of releasing you from that *Soul Shackle* spell, won't we, Glart?'

'Of course we will.' Glart smiled reassuringly at the ghost, then peered out from the alcove to look up and down the passageway.

'It looks all clear, but we'd better not take any chances,' he whispered. 'I'm going to cast an *Aura of Familiarity*. Then if any orcs see us wandering along in the distance, they should take us for other orcs. Darian, if you just scout about twenty paces in front of us, that should give us enough warning to avoid any large groups. Okay, let's move. We've a general to visit.'

'Just one thing, before we go,' Macoby said. 'How exactly are we going to find him?'

'Easy.' Glart grinned. 'We follow our noses.'

Of course, it was obvious, really. Macoby knew that she should have thought of it herself. They had been going for maybe fifteen minutes, skulking along pasages and peering carefully round corners, when they came to a crossroads and Glart paused, sniffing the air.

'Smell it?' he said.

Macoby sniffed and caught a great waft of the foul, malodorous stench that was eddying from the left-hand passage.

'By the gods!' she gasped. 'What *is* that?'

'*Kazhavogs*, at a guess. I don't think they're going to be too difficult to find, do you? Come on.'

They turned down the passage and paced on, with Darian's ghost drifting ahead of them. Occasionally they saw a stray orc in the distance, trotting down one of the many side-passages, and once they had to hide when the ghost came whooshing back to warn them. They dodged down a small dark corridor and watched from safety as a group of twenty yelling, snarling orcs went past at the gallop, engaged in some violent game, before creeping back out again. And all the time, the smell was becoming more and more over-powering.

Eventually Macoby thought she could stand it no longer. She was holding a thick wodge of bunched-up cloth over her nose, but the dense, faecal stench was seeping through and was making her heave. She stopped and gestured desperately to Glart, and he nodded his understanding.

'Okay,' he muttered. 'I guess we can find our way there now without using our noses any more. I'll try a spell . . .'

He paused, thinking, and then muttered some words, and to Macoby's relief, the stench vanished completely. But then she realised that so had every other smell, as well. It was as if her nose had been switched off at the mains.

They carried on, following the curving stone passage as it slanted gradually downwards. There were far less side-passages here, and at each one they stood and listened. They could hear cries of the *Kazhavogs* now, a distant sibilant hissing sound that set the hair standing up on the backs of their necks at the same time as it guided them onwards.

Eventually the passage levelled out and curved to the right, opening out onto a wide cavern. They stopped, peering nervously around the corner, and Macoby was relieved to see that they had obviously reached their destination. This was the *Kazhavogs*' lair, all right.

The cavern was circular, and about forty yards in diameter. Equally spaced around the walls were a series of large arched doorways. Seven of them were sealed by barred metal gates, and behind two of them they could see the massive, pendulous bodies of a couple of the giant lizards, asleep in their cages. But the eighth gate, the nearest one on the left, was open, and coming from within the cage was a dispirited, tuneless whistle.

'Journey's end,' whispered Glart. 'Come on, let's go and talk to our demoted general.'

'What makes you think he'll tell us anything?' asked Macoby.

'Well, there's my irresistible charm and my open, friendly nature. And then there's this.'

Glart held something up in his hand, and Macoby saw that he had brought with him the bottle of brandy from their breakfast tray.

'You know what they say,' he continued. 'An orc would sell his mother for a bottle of brandy. Darian, you're on watch again. Stay here and let us know if anyone is coming.'

Glart and Macoby slipped out from their hiding place and crept across the floor to the open gate. Very carefully, they peered around the edge of the doorway into the room, and at the sight that met their eyes, Macoby was nearly sick.

The room was literally knee-deep in lizard shit. The slimy, oozing mass covered most of the floor and glinted wetly in the reflected torchlight. And in the centre of the room, up to his thighs in the stuff, was an orc armed with a small shovel. He was using this to

166

scoop up samples of dung which he would inspect closely before slinging them over his shoulder to join an ever-growing mound against one wall.

Taking a deep breath, Glart stepped carefully onto a comparatively dung-free piece of the floor in the gateway.

'General Kala-azar. Good morning,' he said, and the orc turned round and stared at them.

'What do you want?' it asked, suspiciously.

'Just to ask you a few questions,' said Glart. 'And then as a token of our friendship and gratitude, we'd like to leave you with a small present.'

He held up the bottle of brandy and the orc stared at it hungrily. Then, dropping its shovel, it paddled towards them with its eyes fixed on the bottle, drawn like an iron filing to a magnet.

'Ask away,' it said.

'You are General Kala-azar?'

'I'm Kala-azar, yes. I was a general, but now I'm Keeper of the *Kazhavogs*.'

'And you led your army on the raid into Kuhbador?'

'Sure did.'

'We gather that this wasn't your idea.'

'Nope. Ah-ha!' The orc dragged its eyes reluctantly away from the bottle to stare at Glart, and he could see the sly intelligence shining out of them. 'You want to know about the human and his great plan, right?'

Glart nodded.

'Well, he sent his messengers to me a couple of weeks ago. They said that their master, Myal of Minas Lantan, had a secret proposition for me . . .'

Macoby felt a chill sweep through her and shivered. So it *was* definitely Myal who had planned all this. And this was the man whom her father would have her marry!

'I was to get our troops to invade Kuhbador and sack the town of Lampa Sanda,' the orc went on. 'Then march on into Kuhbador. A human army would be raised to meet us in battle, but Myal would ensure that false information was fed back about the size of our orc forces, and the human army wouldn't be big enough to damage us. After we'd accomplished our aim, we were to retreat.'

167

The orc's eyes flicked back to the bottle and it licked its lips with a blood-red tongue.

'And what was your aim?'

'We were to kill or capture one of the humans in the army. Myal's men told us exactly where he'd be and even gave us a little picture of him. And then we were to take an amulet off his body and give it to Myal.'

There was a a silence filled only by the hissing breath of the sleeping creatures in the other cages.

'Marden!' breathed Macoby.

'Yes. That was his name,' the orc told her. Then it shook its head. 'But everything went wrong. Our troops fought better than the humans had expected, and we were winning the battle easily. When I gave the order to retreat they nearly turned on me. And then Myal found that this Marden had no amulet on him. He was furious, and he accused me of stealing it.'

Its voice faded away and it sniffed sadly, wiping its nose on the back of one scaly hand.

'Then Mayor Bogbreath found out what had been going on. He and Myal made a pact, and I was demoted to this.'

It gestured to the shit-filled room behind it.

'This is my army now,' it told them. 'An army of crap.'

'What exactly are you doing here?' asked Glart.

'Ah, now, you might well ask. After the battle we brought a couple of human prisoners home. They died in a rather sad accident during a drinking game, and Bogbreath had their bodies fed to his pet *Kazhavogs*. Then one of his guards said that one of the prisoners had been wearing an amulet. Bogbreath thinks it might be the amulet that Myal wants, and so I've been told to dig through all the shit until I find it.'

Glart screwed his face up in distaste at this appalling punishment, and held out the bottle. The orc took it gratefully and opened it.

'What an awful job,' said Macoby, sympathetically.

'Oh, it's not all that demanding,' replied the orc. 'I'm just going through the motions, really.'

It lifted the bottle to its mouth and began to drink thirstily. Macoby grasped Glart's arm and shook it.

168

'Glart! I think the spell is fading and I'm starting to get my sense of smell back! We've found out what we wanted to know, so let's get out of here quickly!'

'Okay. You go. I've just got one more question to ask, and then I'll be with you.'

Nodding, Macoby turned and scurried thankfully out of the room. The *Kazhavogs* all still seemed to be asleep, and she tiptoed across the cavern to where Darian's ghost was hovering patiently by the passageway. Seconds later Glart joined them, with a thoughtful expression on his face.

'Right,' he said. 'Do you want to try and find any other orcs from the battle?'

'No. It's time to leave this hell-hole.'

'Back to the city, then?'

Macoby shook her head. She felt that she needed time and space to think, to digest what she had learned and work out what to do about it.

'Tomorrow will be soon enough,' she said. 'Tonight, I want to sleep under the stars one more time. There's a place I know in the north of Kuhbador, by the Great River Leno. We used to go there when I was a child, to escape the midsummer heat, and we would have picnics beside the river. That's where I want to sleep tonight . . .'

Once again, the ring transported them effortlessly. They found themselves standing on a track by a broad, slow-moving river in bright, midday sunshine. This part of Kuhbador was soft, undulating grassland given over mainly to farming, with a few larger hills covered in vineyards, and after the claustrophobic foulness of the orc city it felt like the most beautiful place that they had ever been.

For a few hours they strolled, enjoying the peace and quiet, and talking. They found a small village, and after Glart had performed a few minor spells for a farmer, a couple of shopkeepers and a baker, they had enough food and wine to last them for two days, let alone a single meal.

In the late afternoon they found an ideal place to camp. It was a grassy bank surrounded on three sides by a copse of alder and beech trees that rustled in the light breeze. On the fourth side, the bank fell away to the rush-lined edge of the river, and they could see right across its width to the distant hills of the north.

For a while Macoby and Glart sat and ate, washing the cheese, bread and fruit down with white wine, while Darian's ghost hovered nearby, lost in his own thoughts. Then they fell to discussing what should be done next day.

'You need to keep well hidden in Koumas,' Glart urged her. 'I don't think you should go anywhere where you might be recognised. I have two friends in the student quarter, an elf and a cave-troll. You'd be safe with them until all this is sorted out.'

'I need to see Sarakkan and make sure that he's okay,' Macoby replied, and Glart tried to ignore the useless feelings of jealousy stirred up by the wistful way she said Sarakkan's name.

'What's he like, this Sarakkan of yours?' he asked.

'Oh, he's fun to be with . . . dependable . . . and he's handsome. Very handsome. And he's always laughing. You'd like him.'

Privately, Glart doubted that very much, but he said nothing, letting Macoby talk on, and listening as she talked of Sarakkan, of her father and of what he would do to Myal when all this plotting was exposed. After a while she stopped and looked sideways at him.

'I'm a bit hot,' she said hesitantly. 'I think I might go for a swim.'

'That seems like a good idea,' Glart enthused, and started to get up. Macoby narrowed her eyes and stared at him. Taking the hint, he sat back down again.

'You go and swim,' he told her. 'I'll stay here.'

Macoby looked relieved and jumped up.

'No peeking,' she told him, 'or I'll get the ring to turn you into something really nasty.'

She vanished into the trees, and Glart turned to Darian's ghost, who was hovering a few feet away underneath a beech tree with an awe-struck expression on his face, as though he had just undergone some profoundly moving experience.

'Hey, guess what,' he said to Glart, in a voice that sounded positively sprightly compared to the previous couple of days.

'You've remembered everything that Marden told you,' Glart replied.

The ghost looked stunned.

'How on earth did you know that?' he gasped.

'Because that's the only thing you've thought about for two days.'

Darian's ghost thought this over for a moment. He could see the logic behind it. He nodded, and then told Glart what his message from Marden had been. Glart nodded calmly.

'Yeah, I know. Well done for remembering at last, but let's not bother Macoby with it tonight. We're going to sort the scheming bastard out tomorrow, so we'll tell her then. Okay?'

'Well . . . okay, I suppose.' The ghost peered round, bemused. 'Where's she gone?' it asked.

'Swimming. And no, you can't go and watch. We're staying right here.'

And with that, Glart picked up the wine-sack and had another drink, desperately trying not to think about the naked girl who would be splashing about in the river just twenty yards away through the trees. But, somehow, he just couldn't seem to help it.

The man stared at the ugly, obscene pendant that the messenger had brought him and cursed. This wasn't the amulet! Swearing out loud, he hurled it hard against the wall and it shattered into fragments.

'Get back to Bogbreath,' he shouted at the quailing messenger, 'and tell him that he has found the wrong amulet. And tell him also that he had better not double-cross me! Macoby is to be back in Koumas tomorrow, as I told him, or I will not rest until I have his ugly head stuck on the end of a spear outside the city gates.'

The messenger fled, and the man stared down at a fragment of the pendant that lay at his feet. It was the broken-off penis, erect, bulbous and bodiless, and somehow it seemed like an awfully bad omen. He cursed and kicked it away, and it disappeared under the bed.

Damn the woman! It was vital that she be back in Koumas tomorrow, for that was the day that Myal had vowed to return for an answer to his proposal. But would the orcs bring her back, as they had promised? And how much had they let her find out? Surely not enough to hurt his plans.

He shook his head, determined to stop worrying. The orcs would return Macoby, and she would agree to marry him, for the pressure

171

on her would be too great to resist. Tomorrow it would all work out as he had planned. It had to, or else a lifetime of planning would all be wasted.

But this waiting was a pain! It was only early afternoon, yet already he was itching for action. The next twenty-four hours were going to crawl by . . .

Irritably, he grabbed the bell-pull by the wall and yanked it, intending to order a bottle of something alcoholic to be brought to him. But when, a minute later, there was a gentle tap at his door, he opened it to find not the expected servant, but another messenger . . .

CHAPTER SIXTEEN

Inspector Heighway had spent most of the day trying to keep out of the way of Superintendent Weird. It hadn't been easy, for the superintendent had spent most of the day checking up on Heighway to make sure that he was doing as he had been told. And so, to protect his own back, Heighway had been forced into setting in motion the machinery that would result in the framing and arrest of Sarakkan for the murder of Colonel De Wenchas.

Sergeant Raasay had, as usual, been happy just to follow orders blindly, but DC Kratavan had been quite indignant when told that they were being reined in.

'But why are we leaving Myal alone?' he'd demanded. 'We know he did it!'

'Politics, Kratavan. The chief would rather arrest an innocent man than upset the powers that be. And if we go against the chief, we'll end up on foot patrol, working permanent nights.'

Kratavan had nodded unhappily but had accepted the realities of the situation. Heighway had left him trying to cope with the mountain of paperwork that his last-minute change in their investigations entailed and had slipped out of the office unnoticed. He'd then been forced to spend five minutes hiding in a broom-closet off the entrance foyer in order to avoid being buttonholed by the superintendent, but at last he'd managed to slip out of the station unseen.

Now he was sitting in a tavern in the old town, waiting for Sarakkan to turn up and wondering what the hell he was going to say to him. It was going to be a difficult conversation. Oh, hi there. Sorry about this, but I'm supposed to arrest you for something you didn't do, and you'll probably be executed as a result, but hey! never mind, eh, I'll buy you a drink to make up for it . . .

He scowled into his beer. Normally, there was very little in life that wasn't greatly improved by a pint of Manticore, but sadly, the dark brown ale didn't seem to be helping the current situation one little bit. Mind you, there was no use in brooding. Heighway knew exactly what he had to do.

The door opened and Sarakkan walked into the tavern. He looked round, and seeing Heighway, half-lifted a hand in greeting before walking across to the bar. He looked tense and drawn, and Heighway wondered if he had some premonition of what was going to happen.

A minute later, Sarakkan was carrying across a beer of his own and another one for Heighway. Setting them carefully down on the table, he sat down in the chair opposite.

'I got your message, inspector,' he said. 'But I'm pretty busy, so I can only spare a little time. What exactly is this minor problem with which I could help you?'

'Quite simply,' said Heighway, 'it's about arresting you for the murder of Colonel De Wenchas.'

Sarakkan's face went ashen and he stared at the inspector, completely aghast. His mouth moved, but no coherent sounds came out. He looked so stunned that, for the first time that day, Heighway almost laughed.

'I'm sorry,' he continued, somehow keeping a straight face. 'We know full well that Myal did it, but my superintendent won't allow me to arrest him in case it causes an incident. He's picked on you as the ideal subject for fitting up instead. I'm supposed to arrest you tomorrow. But I promise you this. I will not be forced into framing an innocent man!'

He thumped the table with his fist and some of Sarakkan's beer overflowed from his untouched glass. The wretched man looked down at it and then picked up the glass and drank half of it in one go.

'With your help,' continued the inspector, 'I'd like to arrange a surprise for my superintendent. As you no doubt know, Myal is riding back into Koumas tomorrow, looking for an answer to his proposal of marriage to the Lady Macoby. Now, I'd guess that I'm right in thinking you wouldn't mind seeing that proposal turned down.'

'*Klatting* right I wouldn't mind!'

'Then I'd like you to help me. I've already got someone in the press printing a story about Myal to sow doubt in everyone's minds. But, even so, arresting him in front of a crowd of adulatory people could be a tough job for one man. I could do with a few soldiers to back me up . . .'

'How many do you need?'

'Ten should do. Myal should only have three or four of his personal guard with him. There's quite a few others already here, under cover, but thanks to an informant, I'll be able to round them up in the morning.'

Sarakkan nodded thoughtfully.

'Ten men it is, then.'

For a few minutes they sat discussing the details of how the men should be armed and briefed, and then Sarakkan made his excuses and left. He still looked shaken, and was frowning fiercely.

Heighway finished his second pint and debated whether to have a third, then decided against it. Picking his empty glass up, he carried it across to the bar before leaving (he'd always had a theory that bar-staff liked people who did this, and that if bar-staff liked you, you were more likely to get the occasional free pint). Then, leaving the tavern, he sauntered off towards North Gate.

It was late in the afternoon now, and preparations were under way for the arrival of Myal next day. Although it was supposed to be a low-key visit, the populace seemed to be turning it into a public occasion. People were stringing up flags, bunting and banners of welcome, and street vendors and stall holders were already picking out their sites and sorting out their wares ready for the next day's expected crowds.

As he walked, Heighway began to feel a little apprehensive. It was clear that Myal's agents had been doing a good job, for everyone he passed was talking about the guy in glowing terms and expressing their delight at the forthcoming wedding. No-one seemed to have any doubt that Macoby would accept the proposal, and the inspector was rapidly coming to the conclusion that, no matter what the truth about him was, arresting Myal was going to prove about as popular a move with the general public as slapping a tax on shagging.

Reaching North Gate, he turned and began to stroll along the route that Myal would take next day. After only five minutes, he found what he was looking for. It was a place where the street bent sharply

175

left before the road to the palace climbed away to the right. A place where, for a few seconds, Myal would be out of sight of the vast majority of the public. A place where he might stand a chance of arresting the guy without getting lynched by the mob.

The decision made, Heighway set off for home. He'd done all he could do for the day. Now, he had to wait for tomorrow and hope that everything went as planned.

He stopped off at the vintner's on the way and bought himself a bottle of good red wine, planning to cook himself a nice piece of steak for dinner, but when he got home he found that he was too preoccupied to feel like cooking. He pottered restlessly around his tiny flat for a while, trying to find something to do in order to take his mind off the events of the next day.

Of course! The crossword! He dug out that day's edition of the *Koumas Gazette*, dragging his slaloming mind away from thinking about the article that Colin the Sinister was planning for the morrow, and turned to the crossword page. And that's when he remembered that he'd lent the paper to Sergeant Raasay at lunchtime, and that Raasay had got very interested in crosswords lately . . .

The sergeant had made a good attempt at finishing it. In fact, there were only three clues that he hadn't answered. But there weren't any clues at all that he'd answered correctly. For one across, *animal in hutch or seedy cage (5)*, he'd put 'rabet' instead of 'horse'. He'd actually been on the right track for 2 down – *load of old cobblers! (7)* – but as he'd had a b as first letter instead of an r, he'd put 'bolloxs' instead of 'rubbish'. And after that he'd got worse.

Heighway screwed up the paper sadly, then unscrewed it and turned to the listings page. Maybe there was some entertainment on somewhere that he could watch or enjoy. A decent play perhaps, or an art exhibition, or . . . yes! There it was! Tonight, at the Koumas Opera House, Lucella DaGross would be performing a selection of operatic arias. He could go and lose himself in the wonders of her voice!

There was only one drawback to this plan. Heighway had always been of the opinion that opera singers kicked up such an infernal racket with all that hellish caterwauling that he'd rather listen to two tom-cats fighting in an oil-drum.

He screwed up the paper again and lobbed it at the bin. It missed, landing on the draining board instead and knocking over a plate, which in turn knocked his only remaining wine glass into the sink. Heighway swore. Standing up, he walked across and looked down at the sad, shattered remnants. Bugger! He supposed he could drink the wine out of one of his large beer tankards but, somehow, it wouldn't be the same. No, there was only one thing for it. With a feeling of inevitability, the inspector reluctantly jettisoned all ideas of a quiet night in and decided to go down to the pub for a few beers instead.

An hour later, after two and a half pints of Manticore, Heighway was feeling a whole lot better. He had convinced himself that the next day was going to mark a turning point in his career. He was just wondering how long it would be before he was offered the job of superintendent when someone pulled out the chair opposite him at the little corner table and he looked up from his beer to find that it was DC Kratavan.

'I thought I'd find you here,' the detective constable said, sitting down.

'Kratavan! What brings you here? No, don't tell me . . .' The inspector studied his subordinate, taking in the worried expression and the hands that had picked up a beer-mat and were already unconsciously shredding it.

'The superintendent has been poking his nose in all day, right?' he continued. 'He's been trying to find out if I'm planning on arresting Myal despite everything he's said, and he's been dropping warnings to you about what will happen if we don't haul off some innocent suspect instead. You're quite rightly worried about your job, and you think I might be planning on causing trouble. So you've come to see what I'm up to.'

Kratavan nodded wryly.

'I know it doesn't seem right, sir,' he said, 'but if arresting Myal could cause a war between our cities as he says, then . . .'

'Don't worry, constable.' Heighway held up a hand to stem the flow of explanation. 'When you come to work tomorrow, you'll find a warrant for the arrest of a man called Sarakkan for the murders. But we're not letting Myal get clean away!'

He hammered his index finger onto the table to emphasise the point.

'Thanks to our little informant, we know that a group of Myal's undercover men are meeting tomorrow morning in the *Black Wand*. I want you to go with Hogman and his toughest constables, and round them up. At least we can let Myal know that we're on to him.'

Kratavan nodded, satisfied. He looked a lot happier now.

'And is there anything else you want me to do, sir?'

'Just the one thing, Kratavan. But it's very important. I want you to get me something.'

'What, sir?'

Heighway drained his glass and held it out.

'A pint of Manticore.'

When he eventually got to bed, the inspector found sleep difficult to come by, despite the soporific effects of several pints of beer. For a while he tossed and turned, his mind full of relentless images of himself being lynched by an irate mob, but just as he was becoming convinced that he would never get to sleep, he woke up and realised that it was morning.

Leaping out of bed, he resisted the urges to go dashing out. It was early, not yet seven o'clock, and he had plenty of time in hand. He washed and shaved, made coffee and even ate a piece of toast before leaving the flat.

But once out on the street, a sense of excitement overtook him, and he ran down to the news vendor's stand to buy the morning edition of the *Koumas Gazette*. Handing over his coppers, he turned to the crime pages with fumbling fingers, and as he read, exhilaration filled him. Yes! This would do for the conniving, treacherous sod!

Colin the Sinister had produced a remarkable piece of journalism. Under the banner headline, *The Riddle of Deferred Myal*, he had pointed out that, although Myal's proposal of marriage had been made quite a while previously, the Lady Macoby was taking an unconscionably long time in replying. Why should she defer her answer for so long? Surely she must have a very good reason . . .

He then went on to raise the possibility that maybe she knew something about Myal that was not general knowledge, and from there, the article became a maze of innuendo, a subtle series of hints that suggested (without stating anything libellous) that Myal was not such a nice guy after all. Anyone reading it would be left in no doubt that there was something distinctly shady about him. In a single page, he was transformed from a battlefield hero to a highly dubious, possibly dangerous, man. It was a masterpiece of character destruction.

All of a sudden, Heighway knew with an inner certainty that everything was going to go like a dream, and with a quietly confident smile on his face, he set out for the police station. The city was just coming alive, but it was a gloomy, overcast morning, and the banners and flags that had seemed so jaunty the previous evening now looked limp and unhappy beneath the heavy grey clouds. And then, as if to emphasise that this was not to be a day of joyous celebration, it began to rain.

Heighway ran the last few yards to the door of the station, then turned from its shelter to look back at the street. The rain had turned into a downpour, coming down like stair-rods, as his dad had used to say. Already, the pavement was awash, and there wasn't a living soul to be seen. The inspector grinned. If only this kept up, he and Myal would be the only people to witness the arrest!

He ran up the stairs to the main office. As he had hoped, the building was virtually deserted. Only Sergeant Raasay was in, and he was fast asleep at his desk with his head resting on his folded arms. He had at last realised that if he ate in the police canteen and didn't go home at nights, he didn't get food poisoning. It was a fairly basic piece of deduction, but for Raasay it was positively inspired.

Heighway tiptoed across to Kratavan's desk and laid on it a page of written orders and a warrant of arrest for Sarakkan. It was vital that everyone should think that he was going ahead with the superintendent's orders. Then he crept out again and skipped up the stairs to Weird's office. It was unlocked, thank the gods, and he eased the door open and strode across to the desk.

Pulling open the bottom drawer, he reached in and took out a sheet of paper. It was an official arrest warrant, already signed and sealed by the superintendent despite the fact that no name had been filled in (strictly against regulations, but the chief liked to have a few handy, just to save time). Heighway picked up one of the chief's quill pens, dipped it in the distinctive purple ink that his boss always used, and filled in the missing name. *Myal of Minas Lantan.*

There! It was done! Blotting it, he shut the drawer, then tiptoed out of the office and ran down the stairs. It was still pouring with rain and so he shoved the newly-signed warrant inside his cloak before pulling his hood over his head and setting off along the street. Now all he had to do was keep out of the superintendent's way for a few hours, until it was time to make his arrest.

With hope in his heart and a whole flock of butterflies in his stomach, Inspector Heighway set off along the rain-soaked street in search of a tavern that served early-morning breakfasts and decent beer.

For the first time since they had met, Glart and Macoby were having a major disagreement. They had woken up to find that the cloudless, warm night had given way to a sullen, overcast, chilly morning. The dew had soaked through Macoby's bedroll and she was cold, hungry and shivering. All of a sudden she had realised that she had just about had enough!

For three days now she had been pursued, harried and chased around Midworld, and all because of this vicious, power-mad sod Myal. Well, she wasn't going to run any more. *He* could start worrying about *her* from now on! Today was the day that he was supposed to be returning to Koumas, and Macoby had decided that she would use the amulet to go straight back to the palace, get Sarakkan and his men behind her, and have Myal arrested the moment he showed his face. Simple!

But Glart had advocated a more cautious approach. He thought that they should go to Koumas and see exactly what was happening before they made any moves, and he recommended staying out of sight. He'd told her that he had two friends who lived in the student quarter, and that they should head there.

For a while they argued, and after a fair bit of should, shouldn't, will, won't-ing, Glart remembered that he was dealing with the daughter of the Regent of Koumas, a girl who was used to getting her own way. And so he stopped arguing, grabbed hold of her hand, which once again sent a tingle right up his backbone, looked her straight in the eyes, and asked her to trust him just this one more time.

Unwillingly, Macoby did so. After extracting a promise from Glart that they would confront Myal that day, she agreed to slip quietly

180

into Koumas. After a little discussion, she was able to produce a memory of a quiet street in the student quarter which was good enough for the amulet to use. And so, after quickly warning Darian's ghost that they were off again, the two of them held hands, and the ring took them back to the city.

When DC Kratavan found the written orders and the arrest warrant for Sarakkan on his desk, he was a deeply relieved man. He had hardly slept that night, for he had a lingering suspicion that the inspector might still be planning to arrest Myal, and he was worried about the outcome of such a move.

He hadn't told Heighway, but the superintendent had gone on quite a bit about all the unpleasant things that would happen to the inspector if he was to do anything so stupid. The least unpleasant of these, but the most worrying for Kratavan, was instant demotion to the rank of constable. That in itself wasn't bad for Kratavan, as he would get promoted to detective sergeant. No, the worrying thing was that Raasay would be promoted to inspector, and Kratavan had no desire to be working under a man who couldn't even pronounce the word 'investigation', let alone conduct one.

And so it was with relief that he read his orders for the day. He was to go to the *Black Wand* tavern with Raasay, Hogman and several of his burliest constables and arrest a man called Gutslash and his companions, who would be meeting there at ten o'clock. After interrogation, they were to be safely locked away in secure cells. In the afternoon, at four o'clock, he was to proceed to the palace and arrest Sarakkan for the murder of Colonel De Wenchas. And it was only when he read the short rider after this sentence that Kratavan suddenly regained all his doubts about Heighway's intentions . . .

Sarakkan also had doubts about Heighway's intentions, but not too many. He was fairly certain that the inspector could be taken at face value, and that when he had asked Sarakkan to arrange a back-up of soldiers to help him in the arrest, he had no ulterior motive.

He scanned the faces of the ten loyal, devoted guards, who had been with him for years. They were all crammed together in a small guardroom on the floor below his quarters in the palace.

'Today, if everything goes as planned,' he told them, 'you will witness a certain well-known and loved royal personage arriving for what they think will be a hurriedly-arranged but joyful marriage.' He paused and smiled. 'They are, as you know, walking into a trap. Your job is to make sure that they don't escape, and that no-one else interferes. The public are to be kept well clear until the whole thing is over. I do *not* want the target escaping. You know what to do. Get to it, and I'll see you later.'

The soldiers all saluted and shuffled out. Sarakkan watched them trooping down the stairs before turning and running up the flight that led to his quarters. He let himself into his room, then sat down on the bed and steeled himself to be patient. Everything was in place. There was nothing he could do now but wait, and trust that his judgement was right.

It was a scene of complete devastation. Bodies lay sprawled on the floor and across the three moth-eaten, beer-stained couches which, together with two rickety tables, were the only items of furniture in the room. Debris covered every inch of the tables and all of the floor-space that wasn't occupied by bodies. Dirty plates, empty bottles, ash-trays containing miniature mountains of cigarettes ends, filthy glasses and half-eaten food provided a carpet of waste. The morning after a student party is never a happy sight.

One of the bodies stirred. It was a male body, a philosophy sophomore called Schléagol, and he was suffering. There was a pounding in his head, an insistent hammering that wouldn't go away, and it was making him feel ill.

He sat up and eased his eyes open. There was an insistent hammering, all right, but it wasn't in his head, it was on the front door of the flat just a few feet away from him. The ill feeling was actually separate from the hammering and was probably caused by the three bottles of wine he'd drunk the previous evening, but it wasn't being made any better by the racket on the door.

'Go away,' he shouted, weakly.

The hammering stopped for a moment, then began again with a vengeance.

'*Klat* off!' he yelled. 'Go on, sling your hook!'

This seemed to do the trick, for the hammering stopped again. Schléagol was just congratulating himself on a job well done when something started to come through the door. It came through very slowly and it didn't bother opening the door to do so, either, and as Schléagol gawped at this ghostly apparition, the hairs on the back of his neck stood up and he began to tremble.

He scrambled backwards, his hands and feet slithering on the drink-soaked and food-smeared carpet, until his back was against the wall and he could retreat no farther. The apparition watched him with interest and then, to his horror, drifted after him. He shut his eyes and buried his face in his hands, willing it to go away, but it hovered above him, and then its spectral mouth opened and it spoke.

'Sorry to bother you,' it said, 'but have you seen a chap called Ugman anywhere?'

'Schléagol opened his eyes and stared at it, almost hypnotised with fear. Extending a trembling finger, he pointed towards a vast figure that was curled up on one of the couches with its arms wrapped round a beer-barrel as though it was hugging a long-lost lover.

'Thank you,' said Darian's ghost. He turned away to drift towards the person Glart had sent him inside to find, but then paused. He had only this morning discovered that people could actually see him if he wanted them to, and he found the average reaction fascinating. He leaned back towards Schléagol.

'Boo!' he said.

Schléagol screamed and tried to back through the wall, his face a mask of fear. Darian's ghost grinned. He was definitely getting the hang of this haunting business, and for the first time since he had died, he was starting to realise that there might possibly be an enjoyable side to it all.

'Boo!' he said again, and this time he raised his arms and shook them.

Schléagol was beyond screaming. He was so frightened that most of his upper body parts had stopped working. Luckily, his legs still functioned. Unluckily, so did his bladder. Scrambling damply to his feet, he positively raced for the front door. Yanking it open, he rushed out, bounced off a young monk in blue robes and ran off down the road in the pouring rain.

Glart watched, bemused, and then turned to Macoby, who was standing beside him.

'What's got into him?' he asked, and she shrugged.

They stepped through the door and peered round the room, lowering their hoods. Although it was a fairly dull, gloomy day outside, it was so dark in here that, at first, their eyes could hardly make anything out. Their noses, however, were almost overwhelmed by the smell of stale beer, tobacco smoke and sweat that was overlaid with just a hint of vomit. But then, as their sight adjusted, they began to take in the scene of devastation around them.

'By the gods!' muttered Macoby. 'That must have been some party!'

'Not really,' said a voice from a nearby couch. 'Just a fairly normal Friday night.'

Peering through the gloom, they could just make out a vast, bulky figure hauling itself up into a half-sitting position on the couch and carefully positioning a beer-barrel on the cushion beside it. Glart realised that it was Ugman.

'Hey, Glart!' said the cave-troll. 'You're late! The party ended four hours ago!'

'No,' replied Glart. 'We're just very early for tonight's party.'

Ugman chuckled, then lifted the beer-barrel and drank from it. He wiped his mouth with the back of one enormous hand, then belched. It sounded like a dragon roaring deep underground.

'Sorry 'bout that,' he said to Macoby. 'The problem is, I've got the manners of a cave-troll. This your ghost, is it?'

Macoby was staring about her with an air of disbelief. She had heard that the desperately poor were sometimes forced to live in absolute squalor, but this was the first time she had realised that some people lived like that because they happen to enjoy it. Shaking her head, she marched across to the window and hauled back the curtains.

Daylight flooded into the room like a laser beam, bringing a chorus of groans and protests from the scattered bodies. In the dull, grey light the room looked, if anything, worse. The walls were bare and peeling, and the only thing decorating them was old food. Macoby didn't dare look down. She had a horrible feeling that the soft, green carpet underfoot was actually mould.

'This is your idea of a safe place to stay?' she asked Glart, increduously.

'Trust me. You'll be as safe as houses, as long as you don't eat anything prepared in the kitchen. I mean, who would think of looking for you here?'

Macoby had to concede that Glart had a point. Myal wouldn't credit that she might hide in some place like this, mainly because he thought that she was sane. She gave a shrug of acceptance, and Glart grinned and sat down on the arm of the couch next to the yawning cave-troll.

'Listen, Ugman,' he said, 'is there somewhere we can talk in private?'

Ugman looked from Macoby to the ghost and back again.

'Yeah,' he said, 'that's cool. Come with me.'

Hauling himself upright, he picked his way through the debris, stepping over bodies until he reached a door on the other side of the room. Glart and Macoby followed him through the door, leaving Darian's ghost drifting about and amusing himself by scaring the gradually awakening revellers.

Ugman led them up a flight of wooden stairs so warped that some of them were nearly vertical. At the top, three doors opened off a landing so minute that the cave-troll looked as though he was wearing it. He pushed open the middle door, and they followed him into a bedroom that was, if anything, more of a mess than the room downstairs. It seemed to consist of a sea of discarded clothing that lapped about the edges of a large, wooden-framed bed. Across this bed was draped a quilt, and beneath this quilt, something was snoring.

Ugman waded through the seething mass of clothes to the window and dislodged the piece of cardboard that was acting as a blind. Once again, grubby grey light flooded into a grubby, grey room.

'Wake up, Legless,' boomed the cave-troll. 'We've got company.'

He grabbed hold of the filthy, stained duvet (which, for Macoby, proved just how brave he was) and pulled it down, revealing a pair of feet nestling on the pillows. The snoring stopped.

'Boogaroff,' muttered a voice from the middle of the bed, and a tousled head emerged reluctantly to stare at them, blinking in the light.

'This,' said Ugman to Macoby, 'is my friend and flat-mate Legless. Unlike most other elves, he's not at his best in the mornings. Or the evenings, come to that.'

'Hey, Glart!' mumbled Legless, who was beginning to get his bearings. 'Nice to see you. Who's the babe?'

'Babe?' muttered Macoby. '*Babe*?'

'Forgive him,' said Ugman, hurriedly. 'He may be a slob, but he's a kind-hearted, reliable slob. So, what can we do for you?'

'We need somewhere to stay for a while,' said Glart. 'Somebody very unpleasant is after, um . . .'

'Lona,' prompted Macoby.

'. . . Lona. It should all get sorted out today, but it would be a great help if you would look after her for a few hours, while I check out the lie of the land and see what's happening.'

Ugman nodded.

'No problem,' he said. 'You can have the spare room. Stay for an hour or a week, whatever you need. Right, Legless?'

'Zzzzzzzzz . . .' said the elf, who had dozed off again.

Ugman turned and led them out. He opened another door, and with a sinking feeling Macoby peered into this next room. She had braced herself for something that was even worse than the two rooms she had so far seen but, to her surprise, it was neat, tidy, and nicely decorated. There was a bed covered with a clean quilt, a couple of chairs, and a window framed by curtains that matched the quilt. There were some small pictures of country scenes on the walls. There were even some flowers in a vase.

'It's not really to my taste,' said Ugman, 'but I know you humans like this sort of thing.'

'It's fine,' said Macoby, and winced inwardly at the surprise that was evident in her voice.

'No, it's really nice,' she added, sincerely. 'Thank you.'

'You're welcome, Lona.' Ugman grinned. 'I'll go and clear out all the surplus bodies from downstairs. Let me know if you need anything.'

He went out, closing the door behind him, and Macoby sat down on the bed. She was beginning to feel restless. Last night she had decided to come back and face Myal down, and yet here she was, hiding again, skulking in someone's spare bedroom, whilst he rode openly into the city, probably to a hero's welcome. The urge to get out there and *do* something was almost overwhelming.

Glart saw the frown on her face and knelt in front of her.

'Look,' he said. 'It's far safer if I spy out the land before you show your face on the streets. We really need to know what's happening. Give me a couple of hours, and then you can go back to the palace, okay?'

Macoby nodded reluctantly. Glart grabbed her hand and squeezed it. The action was meant to be reassuring, but, once more, the touch of his skin against hers felt incredibly intimate and he quickly took his hand away.

'Can I have another quick look at the amulet?' he asked her, flushing.

'Hmm? Oh . . . yes.' Macoby dragged the lion's head ring off her finger and held it out to him. He took it and began to examine it, and she stood up, preoccupied, unable to shake off the restless feeling.

Crossing to the window, she peered out. Down below, Ugman was getting rid of the last party guests. He was doing it by carrying them out by the scruff of the neck two at a time, one in each huge, ham-like hand, and dumping them in a puddle in the middle of the road. Already, there was a pile of four semi-unconscious bodies, and as she watched, he deposited another couple on the pile.

Behind her, she heard Glart muttering something.

'What did you say?' she asked him.

'Eh? Oh, nothing.'

He handed her back the ring, and she slipped it onto her finger.

'Listen,' he told her, a frown on his face. 'That thing really is powerful. Please don't use it, and be very careful what you say while you're wearing it, okay?'

Macoby nodded reluctantly. She didn't like being told what to do, but in the short time that she'd known him, she had come to accept that Glart really seemed to know what he was doing.

'I won't be long,' he continued. 'Ugman will look after you. You couldn't be safer. See you later.'

And with that he was gone.

Macoby looked out of the window again. A few seconds later, she saw Glart emerge from the front door below and scurry off down the street, head bowed against the rain. She watched him go, all of a sudden feeling alone and vulnerable. Then she began to think of Sarakkan. She really missed him, and she hoped he was all right. She wondered what he was doing at that moment. She could really do

187

with seeing him and telling him what they had found out about Myal.

She looked down at the lion's head ring. She had only just promised Glart that she wouldn't use the amulet, but she felt confident about using it for *Transference* spells, as for the past few days she had been zipping hither and thither without any trouble at all. And she really needed to see Sarakkan . . .

And so she shut her eyes. And wished.

'Gutslash?' said the barman. 'Yes, I know him. He drinks in here regular. But he ain't been in today.'

Kratavan nodded, resignedly. He, Raasay, Hogman and eight other burly plain-clothes policemen had been sitting round a table in the corner since the tavern opened, waiting to arrest Gutslash and his cronies the moment they showed up. But, so far, the only customers had been an elderly priest and a couple of old ladies. Sergeant Raasay had wanted to arrest them on the grounds that they might be Gutslash in disguise, but Kratavan had managed to persuade him not to.

He looked across to the clock that ticked arthritically on the wall behind the bar. They should have been here an hour ago. Maybe they had been delayed, but Kratavan didn't think so. His instincts told him that this stake-out was a waste of time.

Had the prisoner lied? Again, Kratavan didn't think so. He shared the inspector's belief that Boron had told them everything he knew. It followed, then, that either Gutslash had changed his plans, or else Boron had been fed with false information. But there was a third, and more worrying, possibility. Maybe the inspector knew that this was a false lead, and he just wanted everyone out of the way this morning.

For a few more minutes, Kratavan sat sipping at his beer and following this train of thought. He didn't like where it led him one little bit. If the inspector wanted them out of the way, it could only be because he was planning some sort of stunt which his colleagues would prevent, if they knew about it. Such as arresting Myal . . .

Kratavan stood up.

'Sarge, there's something I've got to do for the inspector,' he told Raasay. 'I'll be back a bit later. He said for you to wait here for another hour and then head back to the station if I'm not back. Okay?'

Raasay grinned and gave him a thumbs-up sign, and Kratavan strode out of the tavern into the rain.

Ugman looked round at the room and grunted with satisfaction. Now that there weren't any crashed-out bodies draped about the place, it looked a lot tidier. True, there were still dirty plates, empty bottles and other rubbish all over the floor, but that was normal for this room. As far as Ugman was concerned, they lent the place a homely, lived-in appearance.

He turned to Darian's ghost, who had been watching him removing the bodies, and he was just about to ask him where he had met Glart when suddenly the ghost shot violently sideways, as though yanked on a string.

'Oh, *klat!*' he cried, 'she's off again!' And then his voice was cut off as he disappeared through the wall.

Ugman stared after him. What the hell had caused that? She's off again? That could only refer to Lona, but she was upstairs – wasn't she?

Worried, he lumbered across the room and up the stairs. The door of the spare bedroom was closed, and Ugman knocked on it. Getting no reply, he opened it and stared in. Nothing. Lona had vanished.

Ugman turned round and opened the door across the landing to check his own bedroom. It was just possible that she had decided to explore and had fainted at the sight or the smell of the place. But the room was unoccupied – or, at least, unoccupied by anything with less than four legs. Scratching his head, he closed the door and then wandered into his elven friend's room. Lona wasn't there either.

'Legless,' he said, 'we've got a problem.'

'Zzzzzzzzzz . . .'

'Our guest has disappeared.'

'Zzzzzzzzzz . . .'

Ugman sighed. Reaching out one vast hand, he took hold of the bottom of the bed and lifted it quickly upwards until it was vertical. Legless slid gently out from under the duvet like a sword from a sheath and rolled across the floor. It seemed to do the trick, for he shook his head and then peered blearily at Ugman.

189

'Wha's up?' he asked.

'Our guest, Lona. Remember? The babe?'

'Oh, aye.'

'She's vanished. The last thing Glart said before he went out was, *don't leave her side*. She's in some sort of trouble, and so we'd better go and look for her.'

And so they did.

Inspector Heighway had been waiting a good half-hour for Sarakkan's soldiers before he began to accept the fact that they weren't going to show up. At first, he refused to believe this and told himself that they had only been delayed and that they'd be there any minute. But gradually, the realisation crept over him, and he began to wonder what the hell he was going to do.

He could always give up on the idea of arresting Myal, of course. But Heighway was a determined, almost stubborn, man. The guy was guilty and he, Inspector Heighway, was going to run him in. Even if, as seemed likely, he got lynched by the populace for doing so.

Apprehensively, he made his way through the rain-sodden streets, and as he did so, his spirits began to lift again. The foul weather had kept a lot of people at home, and the streets weren't lined so much as populated by small clusters of bystanders. And from what Heighway could hear as he scurried past, quite a few of these bystanders had changed their minds about the proposed marriage. Some, in fact, were openly hostile to the idea. Colin the Sinister's article was doing its job.

Heighway came to the place that he'd picked out for the arrest, and was delighted to see that there were only five or six people standing there. He was just beginning to think that this would be a doddle when he remembered that he was dealing with the son of the ruler of Minas Lantan, and that royalty doesn't ride into cities with just a horse for company. Myal would have several servants and attendants, and at least four of his personal guard with him. They weren't going to stand back and allow their lord and master to be run in by the fuzz without some sort of protest, and that protest was likely to involve large, sharp swords.

Heighway was just wondering whether it would be wiser to try an arrest at the royal palace, when he might be able to tackle Myal on his own, when a familiar voice spoke up behind him.

'I thought I'd find you somewhere round here, sir.'

He swung round to find Kratavan standing there, his hair plastered down by the rain and a look of outright suspicion on his face.

'Oh! Er, hello, Kratavan. I was just, er . . . just going to, er . . .'

'. . . arrest Myal, sir?'

Heighway gazed sheepishly at his subordinate. All at once he realised that this arrest was becoming less and less feasible by the minute. Without Sarakkan's soldiers, he was stuck.

'No, I don't think I'm going to arrest him, Kratavan. Not right now, anyway.'

'Perhaps we'd better be getting back to the station, sir. We've got someone else to arrest this afternoon.'

Heighway sighed. It looked as though he had no choice.

'Yes, you're right, Kratavan. Okay, let's go.'

'And so, as the first faint cheers rang out down by North Gate, the two policemen turned and began to splash away through the puddles, leaving Myal to make his uninterrupted way to the royal palace.

Macoby crept up the dimly-lit stairs again and knocked gently on the door at the top. It opened almost immediately, and Sarakkan stared out at her. Before she could move he had grabbed her in his arms and was hugging her, but then with a muttered exclamation of annoyance at his own stupidity he stepped back, dragging her with him into his room and shutting the door behind them.

'You mustn't be seen here!' he told her. 'Myal rides back today for an answer to his proposal of marriage. And your father is determined that you shall agree to it!'

Macoby stared at him, horrified, as he told her of the messenger from Minas Lantan who had brought the official protest about Myal's treatment at the hands of a Koumas police officer, and of her father's determination to cement relations between the two cities by marrying her to Myal.

'I won't do it!' she told him, when he had finished. 'He can't make me! Sarakkan, I'll flee the city rather than marry Myal!'

He grinned and hugged her again.

'And I'll come with you!' he vowed. 'I dare not stay here much longer. It looks as though there's a plan to frame me for De Wenchas's murder.'

Quickly, he told her about Inspector Heighway, and she listened, open-mouthed.

'Oh, Sarakkan!' she whispered. 'What are we to do?'

He hugged her tightly, then held her by her shoulders and stared into her eyes.

'There is one thing we could do to stop all this,' he said, and she was startled at the intensity in his voice.

'What's that?' she asked.

He looked away, and she got the impression that he was embarrassed.

'Well . . . we could . . .' Sarakkan stumbled to a halt. He took a deep breath, as though nerving himself for some difficult task, then met her gaze again.

'Marry me!' he burst out, and the words began to flow as though a dam had broken. 'If we were married, then you wouldn't be able to marry Myal, and your father couldn't make you! And no-one would dare to frame me for a crime I didn't do!'

Macoby was shaken by the passion in his voice and stunned by the suggestion. Marry him? Yes, she loved him, but . . .

'Macoby, this isn't some desperate plan I've thrown together!' He was staring into her eyes, his fingers digging into her upper arms. 'I've loved you for years! I have wanted to marry you since we were children!'

She nodded. Somehow, she had always known. And she could do a lot worse than marry Sarakkan. Suddenly, a thrill ran through her. Yes! Why not?

'But surely you need licences, and banns to be read out and things like that,' she said. 'These things take time, and we only have hours!'

He released her, and his eyes slid away towards the ground. Once again, he looked desperately embarrassed.

'I've wanted to ask you for months,' he confessed, slowly. 'I had thought of suggesting that we elope. I even sorted out all the arrangements in the hope of persuading you, but I didn't have the nerve to ask. But we could be wed in half an hour, if you will it. I have the licence still . . .'

Macoby looked at him in amazement, then threw her arms around him and squeezed him tight.

'Then, yes!' she told him, happily. 'Let us get married, and then let's see how Myal likes that!'

Sarakkan stared at her, almost dumbstruck.

'You will?' he asked her, disbelievingly.

She nodded.

'Just tell me when and where,' she said.

'In half an hour, at the Registry Chapel in Fetter Street.'

'I'll be there!'

She turned and ran to the door.

'Wait,' he cried.

'There's something I must do first,' she told him. 'I'll meet you there!'

'Macoby! I need to . . .'

But she had slammed the door and was gone, scampering down the stairs and ignoring his despairing cry. She was a woman in a hurry now, for she needed to tell Glart what was happening and then get to the Registry Chapel. She didn't see Darian's ghost hovering beside the wall, nor did she know that he had been listening to her conversation with Sarakkan through the door. And if she had known, she wouldn't have cared.

The ghost, however, was perturbed. There were things here that he needed to discuss with Glart. That is, if he could find him. Unfortunately, he was still tied to the amulet and was forced to go where Macoby went. He gritted his insubstantial teeth. Any second now she'd use the amulet and he'd be dragged after her again . . . and then she did, and he was.

Inside his room, Sarakkan swore quietly but intensely to himself. There had been one other thing, one vital question that he had meant to ask her, but she had gone before he could do so. Ah, well. He'd have to ask her at the Registry Chapel.

By the time they reached the police station, Inspector Heighway was feeling considerably better. He realised that he had been relying too heavily on Sarakkan's soldiers, and that when they had failed to turn up he had panicked. He shouldn't have told the guy that they were planning to arrest him, that's where he had gone wrong. It had obviously worried him, and he must have decided to lie low for a while.

But now, Heighway had several plans buzzing around in his brain, although he had been careful not to let Kratavan know. He might have lost out this morning, but he was still an inspector, with all the resources of the constabulary at his beck and call. All he had to do was keep out of the way of the superintendent, and then, after lunch, Myal could expect a nasty shock at the palace.

Heighway pushed open the main doors of the station and walked up the steps, with Kratavan following dutifully behind him. He was so lost in his plans that he didn't even see Superintendent Weird until he literally bumped into him.

'Ah, Heighway,' said Weird. 'I've been looking everywhere for you. I want to see you in my office now.'

'But I'm just on my way to . . .'

'Now!' said the superintendent, in the sort of voice that brooked no argument.

'Yes, sir,' said Heighway, dejectedly, and followed his boss towards the main stairs. He had a horrible feeling that he wasn't going to enjoy the conversation one little bit.

Macoby materialised in the downstairs room of Ugman's flat amidst a whirl of litter and dust. She looked round expectantly but, to her surprise, there was no-one else there. Muttering to herself, she crossed to the door and marched upstairs.

Seconds later, Darian's ghost whizzed through the wall into the room and jerked to a halt. He was feeling decidedly queasy, but he had no time to worry about that. Somehow, he had to let Glart know what was happening, but he knew he didn't have much time. As he looked round at the plates, bottles and piles of cigarette ash, an idea slid into his mind. He didn't know if he could do it, but it was worth a try. He marshalled all his ghostly energy and began to concentrate.

Upstairs, Macoby had looked into all three rooms, but there was no-one at home, although something underneath Ugman's bed was scrabbling about and squeaking. For a few moments, she dithered over what to do, but not for long. She dare not be late at the registry, for marrying Sarakkan was easily the best way out of this mess. She would have liked to let Glart know what was happening, but there simply wasn't time. She'd have to go, and tell him all about it later.

194

For a moment, an image of his lopsided grin sprang up in her mind and she wondered guiltily what he'd say when he found out that she had got married, just like that. He'd formed quite an attachment to her in the past few days and, she had to admit, she'd become very fond of him. But then she quickly dismissed these thoughts from her mind. This was the best way, for sure. In fact, it was the only way.

Ruthlessly suppressing these first, faint feelings of doubt, Macoby turned and scurried down the stairs. Despite tradition, she didn't want to be late for her wedding.

Darian's ghost had nearly finished when Macoby strode through the room and out of the door. Luckily, she was so intent on where she was going that she didn't look round and see what he was up to. As the door closed behind her, he redoubled his efforts. He knew that, any second now, he'd be yanked after her. Concentrating as hard as he could, he came to the last . . .

Klat! Cursing with annoyance, Darian's ghost was pulled after his captor and out through the front door.

Glart was having a very frustrating time. Although he had told Macoby that he just wanted to scout round, in actual fact he had gone out with some vague idea of possibly sorting out this whole business without her. He was convinced that to let Macoby confront a man who had been trying to kill her and get possession of the amulet would be extremely foolhardy. Unfortunately, he didn't think that he would be able to hold her back much longer.

He got as far as the gates of the royal palace, but the whole place was heavily guarded. And then he began to get a feeling that all was not right with Macoby. This rapidly changed into a nagging, gnawing certainty that she was up to something. Cursing himself for leaving her alone, Glart began to hurry back to the student quarter.

He was scurrying up the street towards the flat when someone called his name and, turning, he saw Ugman and Legless hastening after him. To his perturbation, there was no sign of Macoby.

'I thought I asked you to . . .'

'She vanished,' Ugman cut in. 'Just disappeared into thin air.'

'*Klat!* She's used the amulet again.'

'What amulet?'

'Never mind. It's powerful magic – she could be anywhere! And after she promised me she wouldn't use it!'

He strode backwards and forwards, disconsolate, trying to work out where he might have gone. Sarakkan! It must be! She must have decided to visit him!

'Look,' said Legless, slowly. 'If this amulet can take her somewhere by magic, then it can bring her back. And if she promised you that she wasn't going to use it, she'll probably try to be back in the flat before you know she's gone, right?'

Glart stared at the elf in wonder. Of course! He was dead right! Macoby was bound to come back and tell him what had happened. Unless . . . no, best not to think about that possibility unless he had to.

'Back to the flat, then,' he cried, before scampering off through the rain with the others chasing after him. They raced up the street, splashing through the puddles, their feet slithering on the treacherous wet flagstones. Glart reached the front door just in front of the others. He flung it open and dashed in, about to go leaping up the stairs, yelling her name, but at the sight in front of him he screeched to a halt.

Someone had written a message on the wall by smearing cigarette ash across it very shakily. It read:

MACOBY MARRYING SARAKKAN REGISTRY CHAPEL MIDDA

'What the hell?' muttered Ugman.

'Oh, no!' breathed Glart. It felt as though someone had thumped him hard in the stomach with a lump of lead.

'What do you suppose the Registry Chapel Midda is?' asked Legless.

'It must mean midday,' said Glart. '*Klat!* We've only got ten minutes! Ugman, where's this Registry Chapel?'

'It'll be quicker if I show you,' said the cave-troll. 'Come on, follow me!'

He turned and lumbered out of the door, and Glart followed him. Legless paused only to grab a long, inch-thick stick that was propped up by the door and then he followed the others, and the three of them were racing down the street as though their very lives were at stake.

*

196

Superintendent Weird sat down behind the desk and rested his hands palm-down on top of it. He looked up at Heighway and frowned. The inspector looked round for a chair to sit in, but realised that there wasn't one. He was going to have to stand. That didn't bode well at all.

'Inspector,' growled the superintendent, 'where have you been all morning?'

'Oh, out and about. Checking on a few last details about the . . . about the Sarakkan arrest, sir.'

'Is that his arrest warrant poking out of your inside pocket?'

'Er . . .' Heighway looked down at the incriminating document. 'Yes, sir.'

'Let me see.' The superintendent held out his hand.

'It's all in order, sir, if that's what you're worried about. I've made . . .'

'Give it here!'

Heighway knew when he was beaten. With a sinking heart he pulled out the warrant and handed it across the desk. Weird unfolded it and studied it.

'So why does it say Myal on it in your handwriting, eh, inspector?'

'Erm, well, I was meaning to change . . .'

'You were going to arrest Myal, weren't you? Despite my explicit orders, you were planning on plunging our city into a confrontation with Minas Lantan.'

Pride made Heighway thrust out his chest and try to explain.

'With respect, sir, I'm a police officer, and . . .'

'Respect my arse. You're a prat, Heighway, that's what you are. And as of this moment, you are not a police inspector, you are a police *constable*. You are hereby demoted to patrolman on traffic duty. Now get out of my sight.'

Heighway turned and stumbled across the room to the door. As he pulled it open, the superintendent spoke again.

'Oh, and Heighway?'

The ex-inspector turned back, half-hoping that Weird was going to tell him that it was all a joke.

'If I should find,' continued Weird, 'that you have handed out parking tickets to any horses from Minas Lantan, *especially* those belonging to Myal's party, I will cut your head off myself with a very large sword. Do I make myself clear?'

'Yes, sir.'

'Now *klat* off. And if you see Raasay, tell him to pop up and see me. I want to tell him that he's been promoted to inspector.'

Macoby trotted down the street, relishing the feel of the rain on her cheeks. It had eased off now to a soft, gentle shower, and there were few people about to recognise her, so she had pulled back her hood to let the cooling dampness coat her face.

She felt relaxed and calm. At last she was doing something, taking some positive step to end the nightmare, instead of letting herself be harried and chivvied about the place like a frightened rabbit. Marriage might seem like a drastic step, but she and Sarakkan had been growing closer for months, and she couldn't think why she hadn't come up with the idea herself.

She came to the entrance to the Registry Chapel and paused. The chapel itself was set back from the road and was surrounded by slightly overgrown gardens which were sealed off from the outside world by high stone walls. A small gatehouse guarded the entrance to these gardens, but it was unmanned, and Macoby guessed that the gatekeeper must have slipped out to join the crowds watching Myal ride into Koumas.

She walked through the gate and down the path. The rain had given everything a fresh, clean smell, and moisture glistened on the leaves of plants and shrubs. Ancient weathered tombstones poked drunkenly through the grass on either side of the path, and ivy swarmed up the statues of angels and warriors that guarded the graves closest to the chapel. There wasn't a soul to be seen, and Macoby wondered whether Sarakkan was here yet, or whether she would have to wait.

She came to the arched doorway of the chapel and paused. For some reason, she had a strange feeling that she was being watched. Then she saw Darian's ghost hanging back by the gatehouse almost guiltily, as though he didn't want her to see him. Smiling, she hauled open the massive oak door of the chapel and walked through into the darkness inside.

As the door closed behind Macoby, Gutslash eased himself upright from his crouched hiding-place behind a large shrub.

'Okay, lads,' he said to the other nine men who had also emerged from their various places of concealment, 'her royal *klatting* highness is in place. You all heard Sarakkan's orders this morning. We're to stop any members of the public barging in. And remember, we're supposed to be Myal's guards again, so wear your helmets, right?'

He shoved his helm with its recently-added red cockade onto his head and then, pausing only to give his sword a last wipe on the clothes of the gatekeeper's corpse, he stomped across the grass to the chapel doorway, and the others followed him. The trap had closed behind the blissfully unaware Macoby.

Sarakkan watched from the shadows as Macoby walked hesitantly up the aisle. She was here! At last, after all these years of planning! But there was no sign of the amulet, nothing hanging around her neck! Sarakkan scowled. Well, if she had left it somewhere, he would just have to charm her some more until she told him where it was.

Meanwhile, there was no reason why the wedding shouldn't go ahead as he had planned. The registrar was waiting, trussed up like a capon in his office, and he was so scared that he would do anything that Sarakkan told him.

Hastily arranging his features into a loving smile, Sarakkan stepped out from behind a stone pillar.

'Macoby!' he said. 'I thought you weren't coming!'

She ran to him and flung herself into his arms, and they hugged. Then she stepped back and looked round doubtfully.

'Is there no-one else here?' she asked him.

'The registrar is in his office, sorting out the papers,' he told her, smiling reassuringly. 'I'll go and let him know that we're both here.'

'Don't we need witnesses or anything?'

'Apparently not. And I haven't dared to tell anyone what we're doing. I don't know who to trust any more. Apart from you, that is.'

She smiled at him, pleased at this statement of faith, and he paused, trying to work out how to phrase the next question without raising her suspicions. He decided to try his solemn, I've-been-doing-a-lot-of-thinking approach.

'Listen my love,' he said. 'You remember I told you that Marden took a dagger from that grave-robber shortly before he died?'

'Yes. The one you found in Myal's room.'

'That's right. Well, he also took some sort of pendant from the man, and . . .'

'The amulet!' burst out Macoby.

Sarakkan looked at her, carefully keeping his expression a mixture of polite interest and bewilderment.

'Amulet?' he repeated.

Macoby nodded eagerly.

'Yes. It's very powerful. Marden passed it on to me to look after.'

'Have you still got it?'

'Yes. It can change shape, and we . . . I . . . thought it would be safer like this.'

She lifted her hand and Sarakkan saw the lion's head ring on her finger. Excitement coursed through his veins, but not by the slightest change of expression did he give any sign that he knew anything of this jewel.

'Fascinating,' he said. 'Can I have a closer look at it?'

And he held out his hand.

Macoby took an involuntary half-pace backwards. Her whole instinct was to follow Glart's advice and not allow anyone else to touch the amulet. But then she looked at the gentle, vaguely-interested smile on Sarakkan's face and knew that she should trust him. After all, she was about to marry him, and if she couldn't put her trust in him, she was in real trouble anyway.

'Yes, of course,' she said, and pulling the ring off her finger she handed it to him.

Sarakkan stared at the artefact lying in the palm of his hand, and a fierce exultation filled him. He could feel the power in it reaching out to him and he knew that, in tandem with his own natural aptitude for magic, this would give him greater power than any magician alive. At last! He had it!

Macoby stared at his face. She could tell that something was wrong. There was a strange light in his eyes, a glow almost of avarice as he gazed at the ring in his palm. She followed his gaze and gasped as she saw that the amulet had changed from a ring into a pendant once more. But this time it had taken the shape of a grinning devil's head, an evil, frightening visage that made her stomach churn.

'Can I have it back now,' she asked, mentally cursing, for her voice had quavered like that of a scared little schoolgirl. She held out her hand, but Sarakkan stepped back from her and slipped the amulet around his neck. And then he laughed, a horrible, cold laugh of triumph that made her shiver.

'Sarakkan, don't mess about!' she said. 'You're scaring me!'

But even as she spoke the words, she realised that she had made a horrible, fatal mistake. The amulet wasn't affecting him, it was the other way around. It was his personality that was being mirrored in the amulet's new, disturbing shape.

'Dear, sweet, trusting little Macoby.' Sarakkan made the adjectives sound like insults. 'You still don't understand, do you?'

But she did, at last. All of a sudden, everything was starting to piece itself together, and she realised just how completely she had been duped by this man.

'Marden came to you with the amulet, didn't he?' she said, slowly, 'when he thought it might be magical. Of course! Who else would he ask for advice but his closest friend?'

'And he knew my secret, that I dabbled in magic myself, so he thought it would be of interest to me. Interest! I could feel its immense power the very instant he showed it to me, but I must have been too eager. Something of my thoughts must have showed, for Marden refused to let me touch the amulet, and grew suddenly wary. And then he hid it from me, and ceased trusting me.'

Sarakkan turned away and began to pace angrily up and down. Macoby watched him, wanting to turn and run, but somehow unable to do so.

'But it was too late for him. My plans were too far advanced. He could not prevent the trap from closing about him. The orcs invaded, as I had arranged, and he was killed.'

'*You* arranged his death? Are you working for Myal?'

Sarakkan laughed and turned to face her, shaking his head.

'Oh, Macoby,' he told her. 'I'm disappointed in you. Don't you see, this is nothing to do with that prim, upright idiot! This is all my own work.'

She began to back slowly away from him, but he followed her, step by step, the foul, grinning devil-face bouncing gently against his chest.

'But why? What do you want?'

'You, Macoby!' he laughed. '*You* are at the centre of all this. With your brother dead, you will one day be the ruler of Koumas. And if you were to marry Myal, the two of you would rule Minas Lantan as well. But if Myal was then found to be the one responsible for the murder of your brother, he would be deposed, and you would rule alone. And you would need a shoulder to cry on, a close friend to turn to, a man who would be friend, lover, and eventually husband . . .'

'You!'

'That was my original plan. That was what I have been working towards almost since we were children, since your father laughed when I said I wanted to marry you, and told me that someone of my parentage could never marry a royal princess. But the amulet changed everything. With that in my possession, the whole plan could be speeded up, for none could stand against me. Myal was now only needed as a goad, a figure of fear to drive you into my arms.'

'Did you kill Colonel De Wenchas?'

'Of course. I told you that he criticised Myal. I had to kill him before you could find out that he'd said no such thing. And it helped to scare you, to drive you here today.'

'But the orcs said they'd been dealing with Myal!'

'I'm afraid I wasn't exactly honest with them. But they had to believe that they were dealing with a man of power, and so I told them I was Myal, and dressed my men in a few stolen uniforms.'

Macoby was having trouble in accepting the sheer scale of Sarakkan's treachery. Even now, she kept thinking that there must be some mistake.

'Were those your men who tried to take me from the tavern?'

'Of course. Twice they nearly had you.' Sarakkan frowned at her, his face suddenly turning ugly, and for a moment she thought he was going to hit her.

'That was when it started going wrong,' he growled. 'You suddenly disappeared, and I couldn't work out what had got into you. Some hint from Marden, I suppose. I nearly panicked.'

He shook his head and smiled ruefully, and for a moment she could see a hint of the man she had loved.

'I *did* panic yesterday,' he went on. 'That *klatting* policemen sent a messenger asking me to go and meet him. I did, and the first thing he said was that they were going to arrest me for De Wenchas's murder. I thought I'd had it, but it was all a mistake. Like everyone else, he thinks Myal is guilty.'

'And he isn't.'

'Well, he's guilty of possessing a gigantic ego and no sense of humour, but that's all. But we're wasting time here . . .'

He smiled coldly at her and held out his hand.

'There's a registrar waiting to marry us,' he continued, 'and if we leave him much longer he may well suffocate. Or die of fear. So why don't we . . .'

'I won't marry you!'

'I'm afraid you will, my sweet. You won't be able to stop yourself. *Come here!*'

Suddenly, there was a hard edge to his voice, a commanding timbre that seemed to brook no resistance. Macoby stopped retreating. Desperately, she willed her body to obey her, but it seemed to have a mind of its own. Slowly, step by step, she moved forward, and Sarakkan reached out, took her hand, and drew her unwillingly to his side.

Darian's ghost didn't know what to do to help Macoby. He had thought of trying to attract the attention of some passers-by, but there were a couple of small drawbacks to this idea. Firstly, there were no passers-by, and secondly, if there had have been, and they had tried to stage a rescue, the ten large, ugly soldiers guarding the door of the chapel would probably have cut them into little tiny pieces and used them as confetti.

Maybe he ought to do something himself, but what? He couldn't think of a thing. He was eddying about near the gatehouse like a small, turbulent, indecisive cloud, when all at once, Glart, Ugman and Legless came charging through and down the path to the chapel. The ghost yelled out a warning about the soldiers lying in wait and Glart skidded to a halt, but Ugman and Legless ignored him and just kept running.

Gutslash and his men drew their swords, grinning at the stupidity of this attack, for the cave-troll had no weapon and the elf carried only a long stick. But then Ugman burst into their midst and they stopped grinning, for it was like being hit by a planet. They had expected him to be strong, but he was fast and he was clever, too.

Beside him stood Legless, wielding his quarterstaff, and it was plain to Glart and to the ghost that he was an expert with this weapon.

Two soldiers went down with skulls cracked by the elf's quarter-staff, two more with skulls cracked after being slammed together by Ugman. Two others suffered ruptured diaphragms after powerful stomach-punches from the cave-troll's huge fists that nearly drove their hearts up into their skulls. One broke his back after being thrown against a wall, one broke his neck after being thrown against a tree, and one broke his back and his neck when Ugman threw him at Gutslash, who was making a run for it. He missed, but Gutslash tripped over whilst trying to dodge, and Legless rendered him unconscious by whacking him behind the ear with the end of his staff.

Glart stared at the devastation, awestruck. He'd never seen such a one-sided contest. The fight had lasted about ten seconds, and a bunch of violent, hard-bitten thugs had been spread across the landscape like so much butter. But then he realised that Darian's ghost was half-through the chapel door and was urging him to hurry up. Yelling to Ugman and Legless to stay outside in case any more of Sarakkan's men turned up, he ran to the door, hauled it open, and slipped inside.

The chapel was dark and silent as Glart paced slowly forward between the ranks of wooden pews, desperately trying to prevent his footfalls making any sound on the marble-flagged floor. The row of thick stone columns that supported the roof stretched away in front of him towards the flickering pool of candle-light that marked the altar.

At first he thought that he was too late, and that Sarakkan and Macoby must have left through some other door, but then he saw them. Macoby was kneeling on the steps at the right-hand side of the altar. Beside her stood a tall, grinning man who was holding a dagger to the neck of the third figure in the tableau, a small, fat, elderly monk who was presumably the registrar, and who was standing in front of them, visibly shaking. He was gabbling something, and Glart recognised it as a part of the marriage ceremony.

Realising that he was only just in time, Glart strode forwards into the light.

'Stop this farce!' he ordered, and all three faces whipped round to stare at him.

'Glart!' whispered Macoby. Sarakkan looked from her to the intruder and back again, and a sardonic smile spread across his face.

'So Macoby had a companion on her recent adventures,' he drawled, and the menace in his voice was almost visible. 'How pleasant for her. It was nice of you to come to her wedding, but I'm afraid you weren't invited.'

'Glart, go!' Macoby was almost weeping. 'He's got the amulet! You can't do anything! Please, go!'

'Sarakkan, you have one chance,' said Glart, firmly. 'I have come from the Monastery of Magical Research to take Adomo's amulet back to where it will be safe. Give it to me.'

'So it belonged to Adomo, eh?' laughed Sarakkan, fingering the devil's head at his chest. 'No wonder it has so much power. This gets better and better!'

'One chance,' repeated Glart. 'Don't dabble in things you don't understand. I was trained for this task.'

Sarakkan's eyes blazed, and he began to pace slowly towards the young monk.

'You really think I would meekly hand over such power to a jumped-up, wet-behind-the-ears novice like you?' he spat out. 'Oh, yes, I recognise that blue habit of yours. And I recognise the silver hood-pin that shows you to be a mere novitiate. You've stumbled into something far above your head. Leave, child, before I blast you into fragments!'

'Run, Glart!' Macoby cried, desperately.

'Well, don't say I didn't warn you,' said Glart, trying desperately to keep the fear out of his voice. 'Let's see how you fare against a *Lightning Ball* spell . . .'

He knew that, with the amulet, Sarakkan had enough power to blast the whole chapel into pieces, let alone him. His only hope was that Sarakkan might not have quite as much magical ability as he thought he had. He raised his hand to point at Sarakkan, but it was trembling like a leaf in a gale. There was a pause, but nothing happened. It was as if Glart had forgotten the words of the spell.

Sarakkan threw back his head and laughed delightedly.

'Oh, dear!' he said. 'Poor Macoby! Is this all you could find to defend you?'

Then he raised his own hand casually to point it at Glart, just as Darian's ghost drifted out from the shadows.

'Sarakkan,' said the ghost. 'Marden bade me give you this message before you died. I am to tell you that this was his revenge.'

For several seconds, Sarakkan stared at this apparition, his face working as he tried to work out what this meant. Then he snarled a curse, stabbed his finger at Glart, and spat out the words of the spell.

A brilliant yellow ball of energy fizzed out from the tip of his finger and shot round in a tight circle to slam into his back. Sarakkan gave a brief, agonized scream as he literally exploded, the sound reverberating around the stone walls of the chapel. And then there was a silence that was broken only by the clang of the amulet hitting the floor and the pattering sound of thousands of tiny pieces of flesh raining down onto floor, altar, pews and people.

Macoby stared at the spot where Sarakkan had been standing, trying to work out what had happened. Then she looked at Glart, who had gone very pale. She looked at the registrar, who appeared to have fainted. And then she staggered to her feet, ran to Glart, and threw herself into his arms.

'That was you, wasn't it?' she asked him. 'You caused that!'

Glart nodded slowly, wiping a few stray pieces of Sarakkan off his face.

'I fixed the amulet, when you gave it to me in the bedroom at Ugman's. I put a *Backfire* spell on it, so that if anyone used it to cast a spell on someone else, that spell would hit them instead. It was a risk, because Sarakkan might have detected it. But then, I didn't know you were going to run off and give him the amulet, it was just a precaution.'

Macoby buried her head into his shoulder in embarrassment, then looked up.

'You knew it was him!'

Glart nodded tiredly. Taking her hand, he led her to the altar steps and sat down.

'Yes.'

'How?'

'A number of things gave me doubts, but I knew for sure when we talked to that orc, Kala-azar. My last question, the one you didn't hear, was "What did this Myal look like?" He said that he had brown

206

hair and smiled a lot. That isn't Myal, but it fitted your description of Sarakkan. And then, last night, Darian's ghost finally remembered what Marden had told him.'

'But why didn't you tell me?'

'You wouldn't have believed it. Sarakkan put a *Charm* spell on you. That's why you were falling for him, and that's why you kept going back to see him.'

Macoby thought about this. Now that the spell was broken, she could remember how she had always found Sarakkan a little creepy and had shunned him until the past few months.

'He wasn't a bad magician,' Glart told her.

'But not as good as you!'

Macoby put her arms around him and hugged him again, then stood up and walked across to where the amulet was lying on the ground. It had reverted to the shape it was when she had first seen it, the ugly, grinning orc-face.

'We still haven't solved the problem of what to do with this,' she said.

'I think you'd better keep it for a while. But don't go giving it away to any smooth-talking wide-boys.'

Macoby smiled ruefully. Slipping it over her head, she dropped it down inside her jerkin. She could feel the cool metal nestling between her breasts.

'Hey! Home again!' it muttered. 'That's better! That last guy was really uncomfortable. All that chest hair!'

'Shut up!' she told it, then she looked round. 'I need to thank the ghost,' she added. 'Where's he gone?'

But although they searched the chapel, the ghost was nowhere to be seen. It was as if he had vanished from the face of the earth. Which was, in fact, exactly what he had done.

The moment that the lightning ball had struck Sarakkan, Darian's ghost had felt as though some huge weight had been lifted from his shoulders. The chains which had been holding him to the amulet had vanished, and something was drawing him upwards. He shot up through the roof of the chapel like a rocket. All at once, the real world was like a dream that was fading fast. He was being called.

Suddenly he was aware of a glow ahead of him, a brilliant yellow light that filled him with wonder. Instinctively, he knew that it was Valhalla. As he got closer he could see that it was a vast place surrounded by walls of cloud. At the front were a pair of massive iron gates, and beyond them he could see all his fallen comrades waiting for him. There was Toran Blackshield, and beside him was Ankas the Stout. They were laughing and drinking, and had their arms about a couple of tall, statuesque, blonde Valkyrie.

As he neared them, the gates swung open, and his comrades turned towards him and beckoned him to join them. And so it was that, somewhat belatedly, Darian's spirit made it to Paradise.

EPILOGUE

Macoby rode through the cheering crowds on horseback, waving and smiling to acknowledge their approbation. Beside her rode the unsmiling figure of Myal, and behind them came a whole phalanx of guards and dignitaries. It was an official procession to bid Myal farewell, for he was riding back to Minas Lantan, his proposal of marriage politely but firmly rejected.

He had been disappointed, but Macoby had told him that, although it was a great honour that he was doing her, she was not yet ready for marriage. Her father, the Regent, had then issued an official statement apologising for the embarrassment caused to Myal during his last visit, and re-emphasising the friendship and the close ties between their two cities.

Myal had been further mollified by the banquet they had thrown in his honour, and by the reception they were receiving today as they rode through the packed streets towards North Gate. A small blight had been cast upon the proceedings when a clearly insane police constable on traffic duty had leapt out from the crowd and grabbed Myal by the leg, shouting that he was Inspector Heighway and he was arresting Myal for the murder of Colonel De Wenchas, but the man had been jumped on and wrestled to the ground by a dozen burly guardsmen and had been hurried away.

Macoby squinted sideways at Myal. How on earth had she ever thought him capable of all the scheming and planning that Sarakkan had carried out? The man might be good on the battlefield, but there was an honour, a decency and above all, a downright lack of intelligence, that made him incapable of such deeds.

She smiled to herself. It was good to be back at the palace, good to be out here in the sunshine, wearing fine clothes and jewelry, and riding through an adoring crowd, but the past few days had

awakened in her a sense of adventure. She wished that she was . . .
no! She caught herself in time. She didn't wish! She *hoped* she might
soon *possibly* be back travelling through the wilds with Glart and
sleeping out rough under the stars. Although her father and his
courtiers might have a thing or two to say about that.

But then she thought of the amulet that nestled against her skin.
Of course, if they objected, she could always make that wish . . .

Ex-inspector Heighway sat in the stocks and winced as another
overripe tomato caught him on the side of the head. He had been
sitting there for six hours now, and had another three hours to go
before someone would come along and undo the wooden bar that
imprisoned his ankles, releasing him. He was covered in bits of rotting
food, and was filthy, starving, and bursting to go to the loo. In fact,
he felt completely miserable.

The only thing that was keeping his spirits up was the fact that he
had so nearly been right. Sergeant Kratavan and Inspector Raasay
had popped by to see him a couple of hours before, and they had told
him how impressed they had been with his reasoning. Sarakkan had
laid a very clever trail that had been far too complicated for most
people to follow, and only Heighway had been clever enough to
follow all the red herrings that led to Myal. In fact, he'd heard that
the Lady Macoby herself had also suspected Myal, and that she'd
realised it was Sarakkan only when he tried to murder her.

Heighway sighed as he saw yet another old lady tottering purposefully towards him. What was it about these decrepit old biddies that
made them so eager to enjoy the misfortune of others? Fully ninety
per cent of the people who had hurled rotting food at him that day
had been sweet-looking, white-haired old dears.

He shuddered inwardly as he saw that this one was carrying what
looked like a home-made pasty. *Oh, no!* he thought to himself. *Surely
I'm not going to get a red-hot pie in the face?*

But then he realised that this particular old lady was smiling at him
with concern.

'You poor man!' she said. 'I'm sure you must be starving! I've
brought this along for you. I made it myself – I hope you enjoy it.'

Heighway took the pasty gratefully and thanked her, and she

hobbled away. He sniffed at it gently, trying to remember where he had seen her before, for her face was familiar. The pasty smelled wonderfully appetizing and his stomach gurgled hungrily, and so, raising it to his mouth, Heighway bit into it and began to chew.

Hmm, he thought, looking down at the pasty. *Vermicelli pie. Unusual.* It was only when some of the threadworms began to wriggle and writhe that he realised the old lady was Raasay's gran, but by then it was too late. He had swallowed the first mouthful . . .

Glart sat on the bed in the small, sparse room that had been allocated to him. It was probably the smallest room in the palace, but by monkish standards it was quite luxurious, and he was just wondering if he could find an excuse to stay for a week or two when the door opened and Macoby came in.

'Hi,' she said. 'Busy?'

Glart leapt to his feet. Dressed up to the nines as she was now, she fully looked the part of a royal princess instead of the scruffy, dirt-streaked traveller whom he had come to know. All of a sudden, he felt awkward and shy.

She sat down and patted the bed beside her, indicating that he should sit down too, and he did so.

'I've been thinking about this thing,' she said, pulling the amulet from its usual resting-place. 'I think you should take it back to your monastery. It would be safe there.'

Glart's heart sank. This sounded awfully like orders to be on his way.

'I guess so,' he said. 'Mind you, I'm a bit worried about carrying it. I almost feel that you've become its official guardian.'

Macoby smiled.

'That's odd,' she said. 'I feel the same. Maybe I'd better travel with you when you go.'

'What, with all those guards and maids that have been fussing round you for the past twenty-four hours?'

'Oh, no. They'd be no fun. No, I want to travel like we did when we went to Great Retching. Sleeping under the stars, getting food in return for a bit of your magic. That sort of thing.'

Glart suddenly realised that his leg was touching hers.

'I don't want to get back to the monastery too quickly,' he said. 'Once I'm there, I might never be allowed out again. I thought I'd travel in a bit of a circuitous route. Just to see a bit of the world . . .'

He paused and stared into her eyes. For some reason he was finding it difficult to breathe.

'Could take weeks . . .' he added casually.

'Or months . . .' she said, just as casually.

'Yeah. Or months.'

Once again, for the umpteenth time, Glart was seized by the overwhelming urge to grab Macoby and snog her within an inch of her life. Only this time, he didn't resist the urge.

And nor did she.

APPENDIX

Unfamiliar words or concepts that are not covered below may be found in the appendices of the *Ronan* books.

BROTHERS OF MORTALITY – A fraternity of nomadic monks who spend their lives travelling, usually cruising the open roads in groups on sleek, powerful horses. Also known as the Angels of Heaven or the Hoss Bros, the basic tenets of their order are founded upon the Third Epistle of Saint Stavro the Strict, in which he declared as a heresy the current vogue for reincarnation and stated plainly that man has but one life. These tenets are listed in the Three Commandments of the Brothers of Mortality, thus:

1. Remember that you have but one shot at this life, so make the most of it.
2. Try everything once. If it doesn't kill you, try it again. If it turns out to be fun, try it a few more times, just for the hell of it.
3. Enjoy.

Unsurprising, the Brothers of Mortality have come out top in the 'most popular religious order' category of every magazine poll for the past ten years. However, be warned. They have a huge number of people trying to join their sect, and are the only religious order with a six-year waiting list.

CARBON DATING – Brother Carbon, a monk at the Monastery of Magical Research, was gifted with a form of second sight that enabled him to tell with remarkable accuracy the age of any item or artefact. This made him very popular with archaeologists and other scientists, but very unpopular with their wives. It was a sad loss to science when Brother Carbon died after an unfortunate incident at the (supposed) thirty-ninth birthday party of the Dean's wife, when he

213

was stabbed several times with a kebab-skewer after revealing that she was in fact forty-seven.

CHEWING-WEED – A form of tobacco that is meant to be chewed instead of smoked. It was developed in Orcville, a city in the northern mountains that has one of the worst climates in the whole of Midworld. It rains persistently, and it is almost impossible to stop things from becoming damp. Chewing-weed is thought to have been invented when some addicted smokers found that their cigarettes were too wet to light and were reduced to eating the things in order to get some nicotine into their system.

KAZHAVOGS – Domesticated reptiles that are extremely unpopular with humans as pets because they are enormous, foul-smelling, flatulent creatures that deposit vast quantities of dung everywhere and are liable to rip off your guests' heads at a moments notice. They are, however, extremely popular with orcs as pets, for exactly the same reasons.

KLAT – The orcish for a very rude word. No, not that one, the other one.

SISTERS OF PERPETUAL AROUSAL – An order of nuns dedicated to combining orthodox religion with the pleasures of the flesh, they were the first order to introduce the micro-habit and the see-through wimple, and are credited with the invention of blessed implants. They are also the only nuns who shave their hair into a tonsure. Interestingly, it is not the hair on their head that is so shaved . . .